Comeback

A black comedy

To Linda,
my professional
proof reader.
Enjoy.
Ken x

Ken Jones

Published in 2012 by FeedARead.com Publishing –
Arts Council funded

A CIP catalogue record for this title is available from the
British Library

Acknowledgements

The writing of this book would not have been possible without the support and patient encouragement of my wife Joan. Thanks are also due to numerous friends who read early chapters and gave positive feedback, without which I seriously doubt the work would ever have been completed. Special thanks to Grant who supplied some of the worst jokes for the character Freddie to perform on stage. Characters and plot lines have changed, sometimes on a daily basis, to try and make the story work. Some characters have been reluctantly cut; placed in a dry place to return centre stage in future publications, while others have forced their way onto the pages as if they had a will of their own. Although this is a work of fiction, there maybe similarities with people I know; this is purely coincidental. Some scenes are reconstructions of actual events, but I can assure you that nobody was actually killed during the research.

Chapter 1

It was always the same dream, a persistent scene replaying in his brain. The bill arrived on a tray of mints. He kissed his wife Mary and encouraged her to wait for the taxi while he paid the bill. It had been such a wonderful evening, the best anniversary meal ever. She looked beautiful as she smiled her agreement, her dark hair shimmering in the subtle restaurant lighting. She was half way out of the door as the card machine arrived. Thirty seconds, that's all it took to enter his PIN number and carefully slide the receipt into his wallet. He noticed that the expected rain had arrived as the maitre d' held his coat open at the door like a butler, brushing the collar down and then handing him the umbrella.

"Hope to see you again soon, sir," congeniality oozed from the maitre d'. Ben nodded his confirmation and stepped into the dark street, flipping the umbrella into its extended canopy. The streets were wet, the restaurant neon lights reflecting red and green in a kaleidoscopic haze. No sign of the taxi or of Mary. He glanced to his left; and then to his right, concern turning to fear as he focused on a black car with what appeared to be a body trapped under the driver's side front wheel arch. He recognised the red coat; he always teased Mary about her garish taste in clothes even though her style was impeccable. The coat concealed a body, arms and legs contorted at unnatural angles. Mary's matching red shoes were unmistakable. The car was twenty yards away. Ben couldn't take his eyes off the shoes. The driver's arm was resting on the lowered window to give him a better view. The electronic window started to rise, the driver had seen enough. The arm disappeared and the window nestled home. Ben began to run as the car sped off into the night, lights off to conceal the registration plate. He stopped at the body, sweeping Mary in his arms; looking for any sign of life. There was none. He stayed there, weeping openly, until the ambulance arrived. The umbrella, spinning like a top where he had dropped it, was his only witness.

Sunday was beginning to be another bad day. He was still in bed at twelve. Ben just couldn't get himself going. He lay there remembering lazy Sunday mornings spent under the duvet with Mary. He drifted off again recalling the laughter, the leisurely ritual of the Sunday papers, the morning coffee, and the sex. The longing was gut wrenching. He rolled over and buried his head into the pillow, partly to protect his eyes from the sunlight that was slanting into the bedroom above the curtains, and partly to stay in the dream and remember. Remember the time when he had a life, a partner, a son at home, and a future. He started to bang his head repeatedly into the pillow.

"Come on, come on, get up," he shouted. He calmed down, rolled over and decided to have ten more minutes. Ten more minutes for him to wonder about the tattoo on the driver's arm. "Come on, think."

The street had been dark, the rain persistent. Mary's body had been a huge distraction. That was an understatement. He had only seconds before the tattoo disappeared behind the electronic window. What was it? There was definitely an animal, that was certain; and a building with a pointed roof. Maybe it was a farmhouse or a church. Ben was only guessing and he knew it. He was no nearer a clear picture. It had all happened so quickly. One minute you are the happiest man in the world and within seconds your world has turned upside down. It just wasn't enough, a fact that the Police had reminded him of repeatedly.

He dragged himself into the bathroom and studied his face in the mirror. His curly dark hair was too long, wild and unruly. Simon, his best friend, had described him as 'The best White Afro in England', and it was difficult to argue against. Lately his face had been consumed by a large unruly mass of facial hair, giving him the appearance of an extra from 'Jesus Christ Superstar.' He cupped his hands under the cold tap and gave his face a quick rub down. I need to get out on my bike. I need a bit of fresh air to clear my head.

She was walking her dog in the local park when Ben first noticed her. He couldn't determine her body shape because of the enormous coat that was wrapped around her to protect against a stiff onshore wind that was whipping up sand from the beach. The low coastal hills offered little protection as the wind grit blasted her from the side. The dog, some kind of long haired Spaniel, was taking the lead, dragging his owner along the path. It was wide eyed with excitement, its tongue fully exposed, as it strained on the leash. It obviously didn't get out much and was making the most of its partial freedom. The smell of fireworks was still in the air from last night, a night that most animals dread, resulting in the dog being nervous.

Ben hated dogs. He hated all pets. He could never understand all the time, energy and devotion that were bestowed upon them throughout the world. The Spaniel was approaching him and it was clear, in close up, that the dog was wet through. Its coat was encrusted with damp matted sand. The hair around its rear was particularly long and bedraggled being stained, like a smokers fingers, from years of use. Somebody has got the pleasure of washing and drying it, he thought, with all the fur shaking, splashing and carpet rubbing that are inevitable with such an operation. He just didn't get it. Where was the attraction? It was just unnecessary work. As she passed the bench he noticed that even though she was preoccupied with trying to maintain control of the dog with one hand and keeping her collar up for protection against the wind with the other, she had a quick look at him, a smile crinkling up her eyes.

Ben was still miles away, deep in thought. Nobody could replace Mary, but maybe Simon was right, maybe he should move on. It had been a whole year since the accident. There was no timetable; no acceptable period of grief, but maybe he had rushed into things with Jane. Simon had advised him to take things slowly; maybe meeting an unstable 'Cougar' was not the best course of action at the time. Ben recalled his last conversation with Jane.

"You are a great guy. You make a success of being busy. You are into poker, cycling, and your son. I always seem to be at the bottom of your list of priorities."

"That's because you are." He had said it before he thought it. It was out in a millisecond, but he genuinely regretted the comment the moment it passed his lips. The look of pain and loss on her face was truly distressing. The last time he had seen such anguish was on his own face reflecting from the shop window as Mary died in his arms. She really thinks a lot of me, even loves me. Oh God.

"Things don't change overnight. I need time to adjust my timetable. I enjoy our time together and want to spend more time, quality time with you." He thought, at the time, he had added this quickly enough to appear seamless with his original statement, but it was too little too late. She was crying; sobbing her heart out. He gave her a big hug and comforted her with genuine words of kindness. But that's all they were, kindness. She wasn't Mary. Nobody could replace his wife. But Mary herself had always said.

"I want you to be happy. If I ever go you should find somebody else. I don't want you to be alone for the rest of your life." Just thinking of Mary caused Ben's eyes to fill up. His brown eyed girl was gone – forever.

"Don't you start. It's bad enough that I am blubbering like a fool," Jane said. She thought he was crying for her, and in a strange way he was because he didn't want to hurt her.

"I think you should go."

"Maybe if I hadn't asked for your door key, if I'd taken it slower." Jane chastised herself out loud. His face had a distant look; he was in another place. It was over. Tears continued to cascade down her cheeks. She let them fall unashamedly until they hung from the point of her chin. Only then did she drag her sleeve across to dry them like a child.

"I suppose this is it then. It's the big goodbye." She looked into his eyes, still sniffling, but he looked away, unwilling to meet her searching gaze. He was gone and she knew it.

"Your key." she said as she threw it against his chest. He showed no reaction as it bounced off onto the floor. He was not good at this breaking up malarkey.

"You should go."

Ben shook himself back to the present. A year is surely long enough; the dog lover seemed really nice. Was she checking me out or was she laughing at me? This is all so confusing. The moment passed as quickly as it had arrived. The dog was gaining speed down the path, pulling its owner until they disappeared around a bend in the sand hills. Was she laughing or smiling?

9

Ben was obsessing. He liked eyes, especially brown eyes. Her eyes were dark vibrant brown, but on the down side she had a dog; a shitty arsed dog. Maybe she is a regular in the park; a creature of habit and routine that gets dragged around the pathway every Sunday afternoon. I'll have to see if her body is as good as her eyes. I wonder if her voice is as appealing as her face. Slow down boy, remember the dog.

She had been laughing, but not in a nasty vindictive manner, more with a caring amused attitude. He did look odd. Mid forties, with longish curly hair tied back in a ponytail. Normally older men with pony tails are in an advanced state of balding, holding on to their youth with a symbol of rebelliousness and attitude that sang out 'hippy' thirty years ago, but today looked pathetic. He had a full bushy head of wild curls bursting out of his florescent orange head band. Normally this would have been sufficient for him to be noticed. However, he had compounded his appearance with a garish combination of Lycra cycle wear that would not have been out of place in a Picasso. Yellow and lime green dominated within a kaleidoscopic mixture of colour that looked totally out of place on a dull cloudy November day. He had completed his look with bicycle clips around the ankles. Gok Wan would have had a field day with him.

Although he had laugh lines around his eyes that gave an indication of his age, Bobbie couldn't really tell how attractive he was because of his enormous bushy beard.

She noticed all this in a millisecond as she nonchalantly passed the bench he was resting on. She had also noticed his piercing blue eyes. She had been glad that Spangle had been so frisky on his walkies, whisking her away before the encounter could develop any further. He had been disarming with his startling appearance but Bobbie had the gut instinct to believe, that given the right clothes and a makeover, he would brush up rather nicely. She would have to keep an eye out for him in the future. It shouldn't be too difficult. You could spot him three miles away.

The rain had eased, enabling Ben to remain on the bench in a reflective mood. Will I ever really be happy again? Life isn't so great after all that has happened? He had felt guilty about it when early retirement was first awarded. All the interviews with his doctor, the shrink, the Local Authority, they had not been easy. Depression isn't an easy condition to fake. Who would have expected that an English teacher, a man that had devoted his life to the classics and modern literature could let himself go so easily? His appearance and behaviour had gradually deteriorated until he was dishevelled, grumpy, rude, absentminded, distant, depressed and totally lacking in confidence or personal pride. His classes had become increasingly disruptive and unruly, unheard of in top set English classes. On his last working day he had not spoken to anybody, staff or pupil, he had a thick bushy beard with matching matted hair. His clothes, which he had picked up at charity shops, were ill fitting and dirty. All this behaviour,

11

however worrying, would not have been enough to convince the review board without his final masterstroke. During 4G's Thursday morning class he exposed his penis and urinated over Russell Gorman's desk, splashing copious amounts over the shocked pupil's shirtfront. Crucially he defended his behaviour and wanted to continue at school, insisting there was nothing wrong with him. He was displaying classic denial symptoms. It was his last day at school. The only down side was Tommy being taken into Care.

The first thing Bobbie did when she returned to her flat above the Florists was to run a bath for Spangle. He loved being fussed over. Not the full 'candles and mood music' ambiance she afforded herself, just a gentle scrub down in warm water followed by a towelling down which left his coat gleaming. She left the taps on while she checked her phone messages, hoping she had had some response to her dating agency profile. She keyed in the code to open her account, still thinking about the mysterious stranger in the park. He was lovely in a hairy biker sort of way. She conceded to herself that most hairy bikers have a Harley Davidson not a BMX. Maybe I should cancel this dating agency search and track him down. Bobbie's mind was racing.

"You have four messages," the machine informed her. Shit, I have invested so much time agonising over the perfect choice of words to make myself sound interesting and fun; available but not desperate. Now I've met someone normal; well nearly normal; in the park, in the flesh. It is such bad timing. Still four messages after all her hard literary work, they had to be heard just out of politeness, it's rude not to.

Message one. "Hi, loved your message. You sound sooooo interesting."

Bobbie hit the delete button without a second thought. The use of the word 'interesting' instead of 'attractive' or 'sexy' was not a good sign. What a nerd, and that loud extended 'sooooo' that sounded so annoying. Did he really expect a call back?

Message two. "Hello. Hi. Yo. I'm ..."

Delete. Am I getting too picky here, Bobbie thought? But come on, any message starting with 'Hello' is way too formal, and he recognised that by quickly following up with a 'Hi'. Which is OK I suppose, but the 'Yo' took him too far down the 'Boys in the Hood' route. For Christ's sake, he was probably forty years old and still living with his mother.

Message three. There was a four seconds pause before she heard some deep heavy breathing. There was a further two seconds of silence before a low monotone cut in.

"What are you wearing?"

Delete. "There was always one." Bobbie sighed in disappointment. Is there any point to any of this? What a sad motley collection of losers. No personality or future amongst any of othem.

Last one. Message four. "Hi, I hope you've had a good day and are having a well deserved glass of wine

13

while you check your messages." Bobbie's finger felt for the delete button.

"Don't hang up on me yet." How did he know? Bobbie was curious.

"I deleted all my responses too; all way too weird, but I have read eight messages on the classified and you sound the most attractive. I was dubious about this whole cold case dating process, but once you've started you have to see it through, right? I'm normal, busy, friendly and solvent. I'm interested in hooking up for a chat to see if we hit it off." Why am I still listening to this? Bobbie questioned herself.

"So if you think that it's a runner give me a call back." Mmm. Probably married. Bobbie was looking for problems. She didn't delete. She called back and got a mobile number. I can text; no first hand contact, but I won't get a read on his personality without a conversation, and I need a photo before deciding.....whoa slow down. Spangle was barking excitedly in the bathroom. Bobbie finished entering the number into her contacts as she walked into the bathroom to discover the bath overflowing.

"Why does it always happen to me? I'm so forgetful." Bobbie turned the taps off and tossed towels onto the floor to begin mop up operations.

Chapter 2

The room smelt of disinfectant as though someone's presence had been clinically removed. The bed was firm; the other furniture was functional. The walls were white, institutional white. He had been there three hours in his sanitised country retreat. Rolling green hills with an occasional tree peppering the skyline were all that greeted his gaze as he scanned the view from his window. He had not understood why he had been put into Care. 'Parental issues' was the official line from Social Services, but his Dad was OK, a little vacant for sure, but OK. He tried to open the window but was met by a restraining bar which limited it's movement to three inches, just enough for him to squeeze his frail body out onto the outside ledge. The view of the building from the outside was not dissimilar to Hogwarts. It was dark and threatening. The drop to the gravelled driveway was eighty feet, four storeys, potentially fatal.

"Case number two is the Thomas boy. Mother killed in a hit and run. Father assessed as incapable of providing a safe habitat. Roger, how is he doing at school?" The LAC chairman enquired of the Head of

Welfare at the school.

"His grades have suffered, but not dramatically, he was top set and flying high in the sciences. But they are down. As for Tommy himself, he has become withdrawn and distanced himself from his friends." Roger tapped the papers he was reading on the table to straighten the edges. He was finished. The chairman looked around the room. The heavily populated bookshelves provided a sombre academic backdrop, an appropriate setting for serious issues. His eyes fell upon Joan, the attractive representative from Social Services. He smiled a professional smile before enquiring.

"What support is in place for young Tommy?'

The slight drizzle made the handholds on the drainpipe treacherous, but Tommy still managed to descend as far as the barbed wire cluster situated ten feet below his room.

"So much for an unsecured unit," he cursed. He felt like screaming in frustration but knew that it would alert the staff, so painstakingly he climbed back up, considerably slower than his descent in the drizzle, until he was back on his window ledge. What now? He thought. Give up and get to bed or try again? The only way was up the drainpipe onto the roof. It was worth a shot. The only tricky spot was at the top when he had to get up and over the guttering, which was half full of leaves and moss, onto a steeply sloping wet roof. Without the luxury of the co-axial wire that led to the centrally mounted TV aerial, he would have been stranded on the guttering. However this safety rope gave him all the encouragement he needed to climb to the apex of the building, like a tug-of-war contestant, and consider his options. There were not many open to him; back down the drainpipe to his room, or off the roof to freedom. The problem, as he saw it, was that there was no way off the roof unless he could ride the phone line that stretched down to a distribution pole sixty feet away at an approximate angle of twenty five degrees.

Tommy withdrew into his Maths world. A world he was comfortable in, being a bona fide 'Gifted and Talented' Maths geek; bordering on genius. He began his mental calculations. He included the distance to pole, the angle from the roof, his body weight. He believed that given the correct support he could slide down to the telegraph pole without building up too much speed as to make it a dangerous manoeuvre.

"Listen to yourself you maniac," but what alternative did he have?

"He is already receiving 'Bereavement Counselling', responding quite well. The real issue in this case is the family home. We recommend that until it is stabilised he should remain in Care." Joan finished her assessment with a sad glance from her stunning brown eyes.

Tommy removed his trousers; his belt had been

confiscated by the staff, and twisted them to create some form of rope. He then traversed the wire with them one end in each hand; tested them for strength with a quick knee bend, and was off into the night like an army cadet at Boot Camp. The air whistled through his hair and into his face making his eyes water. His biceps were bursting with the effort but fortunately the pole zoomed into focus quicker than he had expected. He braced himself with legs forward expecting his knees to act as shock absorbers. He realised that his calculations were incorrect when his knees absorbed the shock by bending past his face until his backside hit the pole with a thud. His head jack-knifed forward between his knees, into the pole. He held on to his trousers after he heard the seams giving way. In a semi concussed daze he climbed down the pole using the metal climbing footholds until he was on solid ground. He discarded the lower potion in his left hand; and put his trousers back on. They resembled homemade cut offs; shredded just above the knee, where the wire had worn them. Another ten yards and they would have failed in flight. 'Strength of materials' not in the calculations, I must be slipping, he thought as he made his way down the access road into the night.

"In summary, let the minute's show that we, as a committee, recommend that Tommy Thomas should remain in care here at Haverford House until his domestic situation stabilises. Next Meeting scheduled for the fifteenth." The LAC chairman concluded. Joan thought that sometimes LAC stood for LACK of care rather than 'Looking after Children.'

It was a typical country road. The poor lighting, little traffic and plenty of bends suited him perfectly in his quest to travel back home unnoticed and unchallenged. He continued to count his footsteps as he walked. 35, 36,37. He often did this. He put it down to being a maths geek but maybe he didn't do it before his mother had died. He couldn't remember. His thoughts drifted to plans on how to get home. Never mind get home, how did I end up in that dump in the first place? He was getting angry. Why had my Dad allowed them to put me away? Why hadn't he kept it together for the sake of the family? 62,63,64. He had been dodging cars as their headlights announced their arrival in the distance, but had been so engrossed in his thoughts, or his counting, that a car cruised past him whilst he was in mid stride before he had time to hide. It slowed and then stopped. What do I do? He was starting to panic. 92,93,94. The electric window descended revealing a fresh faced smiling man in his late thirties.

"Need a lift? It's too cold to be walking this road on a night like this. Come on, get in." He smiled an oily smile. His Dad had always told him to be wary of strange men, cars and sweeties. However, it was cold and he was getting tired. What harm can it do?

"OK," he heard himself say as he opened the passenger door and slid into the warm stylish interior.

"Hi, I'm Derek. So, where are you off to on a night

like this?" The driver asked as he lowered the radio volume on his steering wheel. Queen faded into the background just as they defied the laws of gravity.

"I'm doing my Duke of Edinburgh Award, walking section, endurance test. I'm cheating, accepting your kind offer, but it was so cold I couldn't resist the temptation". Tommy couldn't believe how quickly the lie had passed his lips. Was it plausible? The driver seemed to take it at face value as he continued the conversation.

"Oh, I think we've all cheated on something at some time in our lives, I mean, I lied on a job application once, about qualifications. Who hasn't? It's also perfectly acceptable, in my book, to invent an exotic job just to impress a prospective conquest." This last statement was accompanied by a knowing smile and a nervous glance in the mirror. Small droplets of perspiration were beginning to form on his temples.

"So where does the endurance walk end, where is your bed for the night?" This guy was beginning to ask too many pushy, awkward questions. Tommy's eyes danced for an answer. He nervously rubbed his bare thighs, realising that the cut off point on his jeans was just a little too high. He must look like George Michael in a Wham video.

"I have a spare room, it's basic but a bed's a bed, right?" Tommy remained silent, shocked into silence.

"Look you seem like a nice kid, but your story doesn't add up. You have no rucksack with emergency provisions. Your cut-off denims shorts are too impractical for a cold night, and the bump on your head is the size of Ireland. I reckon you are on the run." Tommy didn't answer, how could he? This guy had looked into his soul and read him one hundred per cent. The radio was the only sound in the vehicle. 'Queen' were quietly burning through the sky and Tommy was reddening from the radiation.

"Look, I've seen my share of troubles; so if you need a bed for the night to freshen up and start again tomorrow, I only live ten miles from here." This little speech was accompanied by his best sympathetic puppy eyed expression. Unfortunately Tommy took too long to respond and the knowing smile grew wider. Tommy wasn't very streetwise but even his homophobic radar was giving out warning signals, and the Queen CD was still ominously playing. Despite his reservations he heard himself agreeing.

"Thanks, that's very kind of you." There was no escape from the speeding car but Tommy promised himself he would make a sharp exit at the first available opportunity. The next few minutes were spent watching the dark shadowy countryside as it sped past his passenger window. Conversation dried up rather quickly so he let the music relax him. Stealer's Wheel didn't know why they came here tonight and Tommy was wondering the same thing. He just hoped he could get away in one piece. Suddenly the car pulled up in a lay-by.

"I need the toilet. Coming? " Derek nodded to the

dimly lit building that was obviously the local meeting place for like-minded souls.

"Don't need one." Tommy answered too quickly and way too aggressively. Derek shrugged and ambled off, disappearing into the bog. Should I make a run for it now or get nearer civilisation? Tommy mulled over his options. It was really cold, miles from anywhere; he would make a move once they arrived at Derek's place.

"I needed that." Derek was back in record time. No way had he had time to have a slash in that time, confirming Tommy's suspicions regarding his intentions. Derek had the car up to speed and cruising in no time. The rest of the journey was spent in oppressive silence. Tommy didn't know what to say and Derek was too embarrassed about his clumsy manoeuvre at the toilets to engage in any casual chit chat. They listened to Simon and Garfunkel muse about the flash of neon lights. The car turned left into a residential area just as they passed a sign welcoming them to 'New Hutton'. Respectable dwellings with neat gardens filled Tommy's window as Derek slowed for a speed bump. The car stopped in what must be Derek's drive.

"Here we are, home sweet home. This is Chez Derek. Follow me." He was out of the car and opening the front door in one fluid movement. Time to think, run now or eat first. Would he ever get out of the house again if he entered? Hunger overcame doubt as Tommy followed Derek into the bungalow.

"Make yourself comfortable," enthused Derek

sweeping a welcoming open arm towards the sofa.

"Sky plus" he said, tossing the remote in an easy arc. Tommy caught it and sat in one smooth motion and was surfing the channels as Derek left the room.

"I'll cook something quick, be back soon."

Tommy settled for 'CSI' but wasn't really watching. He drifted off into deep thought. I'm out of here as soon as I'm fed. Got to get home to Dad, but what will he do? Send me back into care? Why did he let that happen in the first place? I know life hasn't been easy since Mum went and maybe it affected Dad more than me, well a lot more obviously. It's hard to forget seeing him sobbing late into the night with a vodka bottle when he thought I was asleep. Wanting to hug him but not knowing what to say to your own Dad in such a situation; when he was supposed to be the strong one. He was the strong one when he was with me; but to catch him off guard, alone and desolate, was difficult to witness. He is all I have. We will work something out once I'm home. Family is family, right?

"Beans on toast; a veritable feast." Derek was back carrying a steaming tray. Worryingly he had changed his clothes. He now wore a silk dressing gown. Tommy hoped there was more clothing underneath but somehow knew there wouldn't be. 'CSI' was finishing.

"Who ...are... you ..." accompanied the credits. Tommy recognised the irony of the moment but was too nervous of the situation to make a comment.

"Eat up while it's hot." Derek fussed as he placed the

23

tray on Tommy's lap, his hands lingering too long around Tommy's bare thighs. The smell of his Cologne was strong as their heads momentarily came together.

"I'll get your bed made up." Derek was gone again. Tommy wolfed down the food in double quick time and opened the window. Ground floor; No problem, much easier that the Care Home. He picked up the cover blanket off the sofa, remembering how cold the night was, and vaulted to freedom. The blanket took most of the impact with the rose bush, limiting the scratches to his lower legs. He was up and running into the night with the blanket billowing from his shoulders like a Batman Convention delegate. Once he was on the main road he slowed down. 124, 125, 126. He continued to watch for traffic in the distance. Mustn't get careless again, he promised himself.

The rest of the night was spent dodging traffic until, overcome with fatigue, he accepted a ride from a lorry driver who seemed rather more genuine than Derek. Tommy tried to stay awake but the heater was too comfortable, making it very difficult. The friendly driver only spoke when it was necessary; Tommy stayed awake all the way down the motorway in the stifling heat, too frightened to relax after his episode with Derek.

"You have to get out here, son." The driver was shaking Tommy's shoulder, thinking he had dozed off. "You are not allowed into the Container Terminal."

Tommy said his thanks and goodbyes. As the lorry turned in through the gates, it revealed a forlorn figure on the pavement, shrouded in a pink blanket. Tommy wandered the streets of Liverpool, using the prominent landmark of the Liver Building to navigate to the ferry terminal. Once I'm on the ferry, I'm as good as home. A cruise ship was docked at the terminal. Tommy was transfixed by the size of it. It was huge. So many decks, so much activity with the food deliveries being lined up by the side. The ship's name was displayed proudly down the side of the ship; 'Armistice of the Waves' in vivid giant red letters. Tommy stared in amazement; he went for a closer look, mingling with the fork lift trucks that were moving pallets of fruit and vegetables. He had a sudden overwhelming urge to sleep. He found a small recess between the bananas which was comfortable if he pulled his knees up; out of sight. He listened to the workers chattering away in a foreign language, fascinated. He was fast asleep within seconds.

Chapter 3

It had been eight hours since they had been bundled into the van. Eight hours without food or light. Katrina was tired and hungry, but she never let go of her sister's hand. Anna lay exhausted and asleep by her side. The other girls, she thought they were Romanians from their speech, now lay asleep and motionless on the other side of the van. All the girls were bound and gagged. How could we have been so stupid as to believe their story? Katrina chastised herself. There was a clammy airless feel to the van; she was beginning to worry about ventilation. She had heard of cases where illegal immigrants had suffocated from lack of fresh air. It was so hot and stifling in here. Why had she allowed this to happen?

Back then, in Nitra, watching the waters of the River Zobor gently flow past the imposing castle, she had waited with her beautiful younger sister Anna. A future as a nanny in the UK awaited them both. They had replied to the advert in the local press. They had sailed through the interview and were waiting for the courier, passports in hand. It had happened so quickly. They were expecting to meet the friendly respectable woman that they had conversed with on the phone. She had arranged the meeting point; the travel arrangements were all complete. As they waited in the sunshine; excitedly discussing the journey, making plans for their future, the back doors of a passing white van suddenly burst opened. They were both bundled in. It was the last they had seen of Slovakia. Suddenly she was jolted out of her reminiscence as the van came to a shuddering halt. Male voices were excitedly discussing things outside the doors; which burst opened again, flashing lights examining the girls. Could they not open it quietly? She was the only one awake. She watched in seething hatred as each girl was given an injection.

"Pomoct mi." She whispered. She was soon comatose with all the others, ready for the Channel ferry crossing.

-.-

DI Page was pacing the office. His case load was growing. He had the on-going case of the Russian gangster, Roman Chavic. He wanted him more than anything; for all sorts, but he was short on evidence. The hit and run from last year had gone cold, he may have to file that away as long term. His priority at the moment was the 'dogging' site near the beach. There had been too many complaints from the public; it was time for action.

"Barnes, get me the file on the car registrations," he snapped.

Sergeant Barnes scurried over with a manila file wondering why his boss could not have the decency to include his 'sergeant' prefix.

"Here you are sir." Barnes was eager for promotion, prepared to do whatever it took to climb the ladder. The office was a hive of activity with a constant stream of officers wandering in and out. Animated conversations were taking place all over the open plan area, only being interrupted by the constant chiming of desk phones. DI Page undid the button on his designer jacket to allow it to drape perfectly, exposing his elegant cargo pants. His snakeskin boots were prominently on show as he put his feet up on his desk. He never wore anything else on his feet; never. The lord of the manor was studying the file.

"All six of these cars were clocked entering the lane. We can do house calls and caution them regarding their future behaviour." Page was tapping the papers with his left hand for emphasis.

"Technically, they have not committed an offence sir; unless driving is now illegal," offered PC McNally the young female rookie. She wasn't interested in promotion, plain speaking was her speciality.

"Evidence is the key. Barnes, take McNally under cover, on surveillance. Park up at the site and film some footage of what is going on down there." DI Page was pleased with his plan.

"Yes sir," Barnes was pleased to be involved.

"What do you expect us to do in a parked car? Do you expect us to put on a show at a known 'dogging' site to attract a crowd? There is no way that is happening, sir."

PC McNally was defiant, her chin tilted upwards in a confrontational stance.

"Once you are parked," DI Page was talking slowly, as if to a child, "take a walk with the hidden camera in your bag. What is wrong with a couple walking for God's sake? It is the most natural thing in the world. Ok, that's it. We have a plan." He closed the file, threw it on the desk and reached for his coat on the door hook. This was the universally understood signal to call it a day. Business was closed.

"Goodnight sir," offered Barnes. DI Page did not reply as he closed the door.

Page parked his BMW in the Morrison's car park as near to the main entrance as possible before entering and cruising the aisles with his trolley. He was pleased with his reflection in the stainless steel cheese counter. His genuine snakeskin boots were his pride and joy, light brown with yellow flecks. They clicked loudly; announcing his presence, if he flicked his ankles in a certain way. He dithered in the wine aisle before selecting an expensive Chardonnay. She will like this, it is her favourite. All I need now is the food. He dawdled over a gingerbread man in a clear wrapper, snapped it's head off and replaced it on the shelf. In the next aisle he pushed his pen into a bag of sugar and enjoyed watching it cascade onto the shelf. Little things, but they made him feel better. He eventually arrived at the checkout; after much agonising, with a trolley containing best beef, a selection of healthy vegetables, some tofu, a sherry trifle and, of course, the bottle of

Chardonnay. A disinterested checkout with a goatee beeped his way through the tiresome process allowing Page to load his car and drive home. He struggled to insert his front door key. He tried to get all of the carrier bags on one hand, but they were hurting his fingers so he was forced to put them down on the driveway so that he could open the door. He was welcomed by light cascading out from the hallway, just as he had left it this morning.

"Hello, I'm home. I have some wonderful food, and your favourite wine," Page shouted in a pleasant sing song voice. He was greeted by silence. No reply was forthcoming. No television or radio disturbed the stillness. Page stepped out to retrieve the shopping, closed the door behind him and tried again.

"Hello, are you there Mother." He dumped the bags on the kitchen floor, unopened, and bounded up the stairs. She was half asleep in bed, where she had been all day.

"What time do you call this?" His mother was not a happy bunny.

"I tried the new Morrison's; the one on the seafront, just to see what it was like. It took longer, the aisles being set up differently than Tesco's," he apologised.

"Just get my tea done; bring my magazine, and my glasses."

"Yes mother," He was looking at the floor. Another long night of caring was all he had to look forward to. In the kitchen his mobile phone beeped to signal an incoming message. He stepped out into the garden before checking the screen.

'Liked your message. Coffee @ Starbucks on corner of Morrison's 1300 Friday?'

He hadn't expected this. He hadn't thought it through. If you leave messages on dating agencies, you are going to get replies, Sherlock. He was starting to feel nervous about the whole situation.

-.-

The van finally stopped. The journey north had been uneventful. Katrina hardly remembered anything due to the drugs. Her sister Anna remained still beside her. They were both disturbed from their stupor by the doors opening suddenly; the girls were dragged out by men shouting aggressively. They were slapped around the face repeatedly until they walked without support. They were subservient slaves shuffling to an unknown future; huddled together for comfort.

"Get over there," one of the hyperactive men was shouting, pointing at the wall. Katrina, knowing some English, dragged Anna over, backs against the wall to protect her from the beatings. The other girls were not so quick in their understanding, receiving more attention from the sadistic mob, before eventually following the sisters. Once they were all together, a motley crew of tired hungry dominated girls, the door opened. A tall handsome man entered. His blond hair was neatly cropped revealing chiselled facial features. He ahs high cheek bones, a deep tan, a cruel smile. He oozed vindictiveness as he paraded down the line, checking out his girls.

"Take off their clothes. Let's see the merchandise." It wasn't a request, it was an order. Although they tried to resist, the girls were stripped and dragged away. Two men attended to each girl. Roman Chavic always insisted that his new girls were test ridden to break them in. He always had first pick, the prettiest one. All of the girls were attractive, but one stood out from the crowd, one was stunning. He chose Anna. Katrina suffered her ordeal in silence; thinking only of her young sister, of what Chavic was making her do. He seemed capable of anything. With hatred in her heart Katrina vowed that she would find a way out of this hell and make him pay.

-.-

Friday had come around quickly. The rain was heavy, torrential, as it battered the pavement. Most people were cowering in shop doorways, idly watching the raindrops bounce off the pavement. The few that had listened to the weather forecast, and taken an umbrella, were most unpopular. They looked smug as they casually strolled along with their lethal weapon, putting the scurrying crowds at risk of losing an eye on the spokes.

Bobbie sat in a window seat sipping her coffee at the local Starbucks. She was watching the soaking street activities with the detached amusement that only comes with the comfort of an indoor dry front row window seat. The bars across the street, on the other side of the roundabout, were showing their age in the cold light of day. Why did she always have to eat when she was nervous? She asked herself, as she played with the lemon and poppy seed muffin that lay half eaten on her plate.

She hadn't deliberately dressed up for the first date. Was it a date or just a coffee? She wasn't sure. However she now hated herself for wearing her best daytime black business outfit with a hint of bosom on show. Did she look too keen? She checked herself out in the window reflection, not bad for forty. All that expensive eye cream had been worth the trouble. Her face was her best feature, so she had been told on numerous occasions. She checked her watch again. How long do you wait for a date before it becomes obvious that you have been stood up? Why did I send that damn text message? She was beginning to regret it. Luckily the rain was a distraction and she was largely un-noticed at the window.

He burst in, umbrella flapping violently, shaking gallons over an empty corner table. A bit selfish, thought Bobbie, but his clothes were immaculate. She knew it was him from the way he nervously glanced around the coffeehouse checking out the three females that were drinking alone. Their eyes met and he recognised her enquiring gaze.

"Sorry I'm late, the rain was horrendous. Been dodging puddles all the way from the car park. Don't want to ruin these boots, snakeskin." he said with a proud half smile that screwed up his face in a most peculiar manner. Oh God, she wasn't sure. Normally first impressions are made within the first thirty seconds, but she wasn't sure. He was attractive, but obviously annoying and maybe a bit arrogant. Good looking, cruel facial features, high cheekbones, blue eyes, full lips, slight scar on his left cheek. He seemed the type that probably pulled the legs off of spiders as a kid. I have met them too often; I always go for the wrong ones. This thought process flashed through her brain during the polite hello and handshake. She took the opportunity, while he was hanging up his coat, to checks out his ass. His trousers were not too tight, but tight enough to reveal a well-toned butt. It resembled a nerdy overgrown sixth formers fighting to get out of its grey flannel uniform. What is it about trousers? In her world tight trousers indicated a nerdy character. Loose, in a hanging off the hips teenager manner, indicates someone hiding a XXL physique. He walked to the counter, buttock cheeks rotating, confident about his appearance. He was fastidious about his clothes, he had ironed creases in his shirt, and his socks were at the same height, folded down symmetrically.

When the coffee finally arrived he enquired about food, and bought her a sandwich. Conversation covered the usual stuff, introductions, jobs, interests. She still wasn't sure. Apart from his annoying arrogant manner, he was a cop, that didn't bode well. The bill came.

"I'll get that," said Peter, as he drops his American Express card next to the mints on the saucer. Was he trying to impress her with the card? The bill was less than twenty pounds; did he not carry any cash?

"No, I pay my own way," she said with a smile, hoping he wouldn't make a fuss. You never can tell what some men expect once they have bought you a drink never mind a sandwich. Life was much simpler and less problematic, stalker wise, if you paid your whack. She was opening her purse. He agreed far too quickly; the mingebag.

She was desperate for a number two. If she didn't get to the ladies room soon she thought it was inevitable that she would fill her knickers, ending the date on a rather low note.

"Do excuse me, I need the ladies. I won't be long." She was already standing. He nodded his approval with an understanding half smile. She was out of there like a shot. Trap two was empty. She closed the door, removed the necessary items of clothing in record time and deposited a shit load of shit, loudly.

"I hope that isn't going to stink the room out?" enquired the anonymous voice from the next booth.

"Sorry, it's an emergency. I've been holding it in for thirty minutes." She finished, wiped, dressed and flushed. No, not embarrassed flushed, but toilet flushed. Nothing happened. Her jobbies remained motionless in the pan. She flushed again out of panic but this time she heard the mechanical thud of the handle as she cranked, indicating a malfunction. Another wave of bowel cramps hit her. She had no alternative but to add to the problem with another deposit. Spladoosh. Another layer appeared on top of the toilet paper as if she was making her own special recipe lasagne. For a second she thought the extra weight would help it around the U bend, but it only compounded the problem, half filling the pan. She had no alternative but to walk away, after all it was not really her problem. Health and Safety issues in the food industry must be commonplace. She composed herself; took a deep breath, not too deep under the circumstances, and breezed out. It was only then that see saw the 'Out of Order' sign on the door. Why does it always happen to me? Head down, she exited as quickly as she could, ignoring the comments from the two girls touching up their make-up in the mirror.

"Can't you read." And seconds later as she was almost out.

"Ugh, you dirty bitch!"

She returned to the table, but he was already collecting his umbrella from the stand.

"We must do this again," said Peter as he nervously released the restraining strap on his umbrella.

"We must," she agreed, but she wasn't sure. She was already looking forward to the next blind date. The two girls from the toilets returned to their table, looking daggers. He must think that they are jealous of her date, him being so gorgeous and all.

Chapter 4

Ben woke with a spring in his step. He jumped quickly out of bed and drew back the curtains. Pale winter light invaded his world. He closed his eyes and turned his head away wincing. He was excited and a bit apprehensive about the meal at Simon and Brie's; a blind date with a friend of Brie's. He shuffled into the bathroom and began the dismantling of his beard. A pile of matted hair slowly filled the basin as he went to work with the scissors. Once the beard was reduced to manageable proportions he cleaned up the sink and lathered up ready for the razor. He hadn't shaved for a while and was nervous of cutting himself. He didn't want to turn up on a blind date looking all nerdy with blood stained tissues dotting his face. The new razor did its job without incident leaving Ben with a smooth silky finish. He stepped into the shower and shampooed his freshly cut hair. Visions of the black car on that fateful rainy night invaded his mind as he closed his eyes for protection from the lather. The electric window rising. The shaven head viewed from behind. No facial features visible. Neon lights from the restaurant were reflected on the wet road, red and green. The tattooed forearm disappearing as the window finished its climb.

What was it? He was certain it was an animal for sure, with buildings behind. What was the pointed roof? He towelled his hair vigorously as he wandered around the house with another towel tied around his waist He needed a coffee. He passes the open study door. Mary's easel was still in place with a blank canvas, just as she had left it. He still didn't have the heart to clear her stuff away. All the paintbrushes were stored in jam jars. The tubes of paint were scattered on the table. He had kept her portfolio of paintings in the large zip up folder. He realised that they all had to be cleared but he just couldn't do it. Not yet. He half expected her to produce one last piece of work, the brushes moving magically in her invisible hands, but that was irrational indulgent sentimentality. He forced such thoughts from his mind. He liked the feel of the brushes against his fingers as he gently stroked his hand over their tips. The act somehow brought him closer to Mary. He went in to have another brushstroke before walking around to Simon's.

He always felt at home at Simon's. The sofa was deep; the music was always playing that soft West Coast rock that soothed his soul. A beer was always in his hand. Life was good and he drifted into thoughts of the 'Shaggability Factor.' He believed that you don't necessarily have to be drop dead gorgeous to be shaggable.   There just needs to be some kind of attraction. This could take the form of a killer smile, a tilt of the head, good flirtatious conversation, tasteful clothes, soft hair, a nice perfume, the way you walk, a personality. OK, he would shag anything that moved at the moment. He was, as they say, carrying a full sack.

"Want another?" It was Simon's wife Brie nodding at his empty bottle.

"Sure, it's going down well."

"You seem deep in thought today, what's on your mind," she asked as she passed him a Bud and curled up on the other end of the sofa. Her head was at a certain angle, her Next catalogue colour co-ordinated outfit tastefully blending in with the Giraffe motif of the settee. She had always been a bit off the wall with regards to furniture and interior design. Everything had to be unusual, but tidy; very tidy. She was known amongst friend as Mrs Bouquet, after the control freak from the TV Sitcom.

"Just taking in the music and chilling." Ben answered. Mrs Bouquet and the 'Shaggabilty Factor' did not belong in the same sentence. She was dressed nicely for sure; was not unattractive; but sexy? No way.

"You haven't taken off your shoes, you must show some respect for the carpet," said Brie. In a world that favoured solid wood flooring or plain beige simplistic carpeting, Brie (she insisted on being called Brie for short, like the cheese; even though her name was Bryony) had opted for a swirling multi-coloured retro seventies monstrosity that she ordered from Turkey. It was so heavily patterned that a herd of elephants could camp on it for a month; with all the ensuing deposits and scuffing of feet, and still not affect the overall feeling of head-spinning nausea that the carpet caused. His clean slip-ons would have no detrimental effect at all.

"No problem," he smiled as he kicked them off.

"In the shoe box please." She did the nod of the head again towards the hall. If she ever did have a 'Shaggability Factor' rating it was rapidly plummeting towards zero.

"Look who has just blown into town." It was Simon as he descended the stairs doing his John Wayne impersonation. He loved cowboy films; he had a boxed set of DVD's.

"If you call me stranger again, I'll swing for you" Ben said as he closed the lid on the shoebox.

"The hell you will," Simon replied with an exaggerated swagger.

"No, no, no. The shoes must be in size order from right to left." Suddenly John Wayne had left the building and the new Simon was back in residence. Simon had been a carefree fun loving soul; everything a best mate should be. Then he met Brie and started to change quickly so that now he fussed around tidying up around visitors. He had forgotten how to relax and enjoy himself. Or was he so afraid of annoying Mrs Bouquet that he was now thinking 'What would she want in this situation?' He was displaying classical signs of brainwashing. He would have been a push over for the Moonies.

"Are they classified by colour as well?" Ben asked with good natured sarcasm.

"Black then brown." Simon wasn't joking. They both wandered into the lounge with a drink in their hand. Deep burgundy and terracotta walls predominated with cream cloth drapes covering the conservatory windows. They could have been models in a 'Dulux brochure.'

"Fancy a game of golf next week?" Simon asked.

"You know I don't play golf."

"How about Tennis?"

"That is even worse. What is this all about?"

"I just fancied doing something physical to get the old endorphins pumping."

"For God's sake Simon, I was an English teacher before I retired, not a sports jock."

"I've been thinking of maybe writing a book." Simon suddenly launched into an unexpected rant. "Anyone can write a book. I mean some of the stuff I've read in my time has been painful. You get seduced by the cover; nice colours; a catchy quote; a few recommendations received from literary critics. 'Unputdownable,' 'I was up all night reading this masterpiece,'" Simon's arms were flying around in dramatic emphasis. He was enjoying himself.

"'Best book I've read this year,' 'If you only ever read one book in your life..' Yeah right. I always promise myself, when reading, that I will persevere with any book for one hundred pages to give it a

41

chance, but you know when it's not floating your boat. It's always names with me. I hate foreign names especially Russian ones which are invariably too long. Names like Mashtikavich. I never try and pronoun it in my mind; he's just the M guy. Similarly Anytolyofski is the A guy. The British are just as bad; pompous Colonel Mustard types like Hetherington, Templeton, or any double-barrelled dick."

"Calm down, what has brought all this on. I haven't seen you this animated since the film 'Stagecoach' was released." Ben teased, but he was genuinely pleased to see some of the old fire in Simon.

"I have started to write again." Simon was holding a folder. "I would appreciate it if you could have a quick look at my first draft, only the first chapter really. I would value your opinion, a professional critique," Simon was thrusting the folder forward, urging Ben to take it. Ben shook his head.

"I haven't done this for a while. I don't think I'm in the right frame of mind."

"Please, for an old friend. I am serious about this. You can be honest with me." Ben flicked the pages to estimate the length of the tome.

"I can't do this now, it's too long."

"Just a browse; do a quick précis. Please?" Simon was whining like a schoolboy.

"Okay, okay." Ben took the manuscript and began to read. He sat at the table illuminated in a spotlight. He read quickly, flipping the pages over onto the table as he finished them. He was making notes in the margin, in red pen of course. Simon smiled as he watched Ben work, but when Ben looked up at him, in a moment of reflection, Simon's face changed to one of nervous concern.

"What do you think? Is it alright?" Simon was searching Ben's face for any sign of approval. Ben put the pen down and began to talk in an animated, professional manner.

"OK, let's start with the positives. The opening scene in the orphanage is promising; you set the mood very well. The description of the father using 'indeterminate and determined' in the same sentence is good. 'All knowing but unseeing' is also effective. This alien in Victorian London could work." Ben paused and sneaked a quick look at Simon whose smile changed to nervous anticipation.

"Now let us look at the negatives. Why do you have to include a cowboy? It just doesn't fit. There is too much going on, plot wise. If you insist on the cowboy, drop the alien. A cowboy in Victorian London could work; 'Crocodile Dundee' has explored the country hick in the big city scenario before. It is nothing new, but it could work. I prefer the alien storyline myself.

'So you like it, then?"

'It needs work, that's for sure. The whole carrot and banana thing is a bit weird, but you can do anything in a science fiction piece of work. Definitely drop the cowboy."

"The hell I will." Simon was strutting around in an exaggerated swagger, rolling his shoulders in time with his hips. He thought it was a perfect imitation of John Wayne; not realising that in reality he resembled a ballroom dancer performing a Paso Doble. The scene was interrupted by the doorbell chiming 'The yellow rose of Texas.'

"I'll get it," shouted Brie from the hall.

"Sorry I'm late, had a late funeral order, wreaths are so fiddly…"

"Hi Bobbie, do come in. You have brought wine. How thoughtful of you. You shouldn't have. Take your shoes off please," Brie gushed as she performed a theatrical air kiss on both sides of the visitor's face." The act was accompanied by the now obligatory sound.

"Mmwha, Mmwha."

Brie had pulled out all of the stops. She was using the best china; the wedding present that only appears on special occasions, and white napkins in silver rings. The table looked impressive; it would not have looked out of place in a five star restaurant. Music was playing in background, one of those contemporary girls at the piano types. Ben didn't know her name, she was singing of hopes and dreams in a breathy vulnerable adolescent style. Ben had also made an effort. He had cut his hair, still thick and curly but his ears were now visible and more importantly he was clean shaved, with a smooth boyish face. He had also made some sort of effort with his clothes. He hadn't bought anything sharp and trendy, but in his defence, he was wearing the grey slacks and white shirt that he had always worn when the OFSTED Inspection took place at school. Not the trendiest look; but neat and tidy. He resembled an overgrown schoolboy. Brie was smiling with her head tilted to the left. He does look better. This could be the beginning of his recovery.

"Let's get the introductions out of the way before we sit down," Simon was taking control for once. "This gorgeous creature..." he began.

"..Is a friend of mine who owns a florist shop in Hoylake." Brie completed the sentence. "She is just your type, Ben" she continued to the embarrassment of both guests.

"My type was Mary," Ben said out loud. He thought that he had only thought it, but the words actually came out of his mouth.

"Not the best of starts," said Bobbie smiling generously.

"I know it is terribly sad, but Mary has been gone a year now. She would have wanted you to move on eventually," Brie was in matron mode.

"This is Bobbie," Simon said brightly, trying to retrieve the situation. Ben recognised her from the park. She looked much more attractive without the dog and the large coat.

"Let me get you a drink. Wine?" Simon continued.

"Yes please," replied Bobbie.

"We have Red and white?"

"White would be lovely."

"Let me take your coat." Underneath the coat Bobbie was wearing a red dress just above the knee, with delightful jewellery. She looked stunning.

"And this is Ben," Brie finished the introductions. The meal passed without too much incident, apart from Bobbie knocking over a glass of red wine, turning the crisp white tablecloth into a war zone.

"I'm so sorry. This always happens to me."

"Don't worry Bobbie, it's only red wine. Not a problem," soothed Simon. Brie's face was not in agreement. She hated any blemish to her perfect world. Later Simon told a cowboy story, a rerun of an old John Wayne film, prompting Ben to enquire about the plot of 'Brokeback Mountain'.

"Are all cowboys like that? You know, sharing a tent."

Simon took the hint and changed the subject, asking Bobbie about her florist shop.

"Christmas is my busiest times, apart from Mother's Day, and Valentine's Day." The night ended all too quickly.

"Nice to have met you," said Bobbie accompanied by a showbiz air kiss to the side of Ben's face. Simon was holding her coat open, the perfect host.

"Can I get a lift home?" asked Bobbie

"I don't have a car, I use a bike," said Ben.

"I can just see you on a Harley in a pack of Hell's angel," teased Bobbie.

"It's a pushbike," clarified Ben. It was only then that the dawn of recognition appeared on Bobbie's face. He had undergone quite a metamorphosis. Without the cycling clothes and beard he looked rather striking.

"It is nice to meet you again," Bobbie smiled. "I didn't recognise you without the Bin Laden look."

"I was wondering when you would recognise me. We could share a cab," offered Ben.

"That would be nice," said Bobbie. When it arrived, they both walked to the waiting taxi in animated conversation. Brie and Simon exchanged knowing glances. Ben lived around the corner; but was prepared to escort Bobbie home. Result. Brie had the tablecloth in the washing machine before the taxi had left the street.

"How did the book reading go?" asked Brie as she loaded the dishwasher.

"It did the trick. It seemed to snap him out of his lethargy." They seemed comfortable together as they set about tidying the kitchen.

"It must be awful for you; having to write badly just to stimulate him."

"A man's gotta do what a man's gotta do," Simon drawled.

They climbed the stairs together and checked on their daughter, Holly. She was asleep in her bed. Her seven year old face looking peaceful and serene. Nobody would know there was anything wrong if it wasn't for her bald head. They spent a long time at her bedside in silent vigil.

Chapter 5

After five hours of fitful sleep Tommy woke to his new surroundings. A brightly lit food storage area with clinical white walls came into focus. He broke the plastic seal on a bunch of bananas and devoured two while he decided on his next move. He remembered that he was on the cruise ship. He just needed to dodge a few staff and walk the gangplank. Then he would be home free. He struggled to his feet and swayed unsteadily. 'You need more sleep; travelling takes it out of you.' He could hear his Dad's voice in his head. He continued to sway all the way to the door and realised, when his hand was on the handle, that it was the ship that was swaying and not him. The ship was moving. Tommy's thought process now went into fast forward. A moving ship meant the ship had left Liverpool. How long have I been asleep? How far has the ship gone? Where is it going? How am I going to get off? Tommy opened the door and stepped into the corridor, which appeared similar to the storage room he had just left. Brightly lit white walls were everywhere. He took a left and hurried to the elevator, thirty yards in quick time. He was on Level Two; he pressed the button and was surprised when the doors slid opened immediately. He randomly pressed six and was relieved when the doors closed. A mixed feeling of dread and excitement raced though his body as he started the ascent up the lift shaft. It stopped on Deck Four and two couples got in wearing florescent orange lifejackets. The men were fastening their belts, while one of the women was inspecting the whistle attached near her shoulder. Oh my God, I've only been on here for what seems like five minutes and the ship is sinking, thought Tommy. They all got off at Deck Six and Tommy followed them as they milled with the growing crowd. Everyone was chatting excitedly, but more importantly, everyone was wearing a lifejacket. An official looking oriental girl with a 'Kade' nametag challenged him very politely.

"Please be wearing your lifejacket, it is in your cabin. What cabin are you in?"

Tommy's face was a picture. Panic mixed with guilt. He didn't have a cabin but the ship was sinking. Which was worse? His mouth was open but no words were coming out. Eventually he nodded an implied understanding and scurried off down the stairs. Deck Five was pretty much the same scene as six. There were lots of people chatting; lots of lifejackets being worn, and staff everywhere directing operations. Tommy walked down a corridor, against the flow of humanity, with his head down. Most of the cabins had their doors chocked open with a wedge of wood. Lots of recently delivered suitcases were standing outside cabins in the corridor. Tommy stepped into an empty cabin and shut the door behind him. He frantically began searching for lifejackets and soon found them in the wardrobe. He reached up to grab one off the top shelf when he heard the toilet flush and the bathroom door handle snap open.

"Looking for something, son?" enquired a male voice. Tommy slowly turned around wearing an open mouthed expression. He was just about to start into his best Hugh Grant apologetic routine, when he noticed that the man was smiling. He had a shocking red curly mop of hair. Medium height, casually dressed with clear green eyes. Tommy realised that he couldn't possibly outrun this guy, but he needed to go before the ship sinks.

"I could do with a lifejacket myself .You can show me where the muster station is," said the green eyed monster with a slow smirk.

"Sure," replied Tommy. "We can get to the lifeboats together". Tommy was playing along.

"And when the safety drill is over you can tell me why you are in my room."

"The safety drill?" Tommy's high-pitched voice was a bit hysterical. Feelings of surprise and relief coursed through his body. He started to laugh nervously; the stranger joined in laughing with him, a surprisingly immature giggly laugh.

"You thought the ship was sinking didn't you?"

"No," protested Tommy with his best indignant expression; lifting his chin in defiance. The giggles were infectious.

"My name's Freddie," he spluttered through his giggles. He held out his hand in welcome. Tommy shook it nervously and replied.

"Tommy, Tommy Thomas." Freddie's giggles grew in intensity.

"That's a funny name, kid. It could be a stage name."

"Freddie what?" asked Tommy; still laughing.

"Freddie Fungus."

"That's funny too," said Tommy.

"Most people don't like it, but it grows on them." They were both holding their stomachs as they giggled.

"You're really funny, Freddie."

'I hope so, kid. Come on; let's get the drill out of the way"

The lifejacket drill was performed underneath the lifeboats on Deck Seven. Tommy noticed that all of the lifejackets had codes on them that must indicate cabin numbers. The young girl; 'Kade' from her name tag, was supervising their area. She was doing a head count; ticking off cabins on her clipboard. She was giving Tommy a hard stare. He decided to make a sharp exit once her back was turned. He was quickly down the nearest stairway and onto a magnificent street that had been built right through the centre of the ship. Tommy was open mouthed in awe. It seemed to go on forever, disappearing into the distance. Both sides were populated with various shop and bars, giving it the appearance of a bustling high street. At both ends glass elevators glided silently up to the highest points, giving passengers an unparalleled view of the crowds milling around the street. Tommy sat down at a coffee shop, just to take in the scene.

"Hello there." It was an old man with an arm crutch who had sat at the same table; out of breathe. "Do you want a drink, son."

Tommy was beginning to wonder if he had a sign on his head attracting older men. The episode with the driver yesterday had unsettled him; that had been a close shave. Then there was Freddie; who seemed very friendly, but that was my fault, I suppose, as I had wandered into his cabin unannounced. And now there was this guy.

Numerous family groups wandered past, getting their bearings. The children were pointing out features in an excited manner. Tommy was struck by the seriousness of his situation, alone on a ship; no food or bed. He really had to get back to his Dad.

"Have a soft drink with me son, I don't bite." The old guy was still at his table. He looked harmless enough.

"OK," he heard himself say.

Once the drinks were delivered, the old guy, he had introduced himself as Ron, handed over a plastic card to pay. It wasn't a credit card; it had the ship logo on, some kind of ship pass. Ron was quickly into his life story. He was a permanent cruiser. He had sold his house when his wife died. Now he planned to jump from ship to ship until the money ran out.

"There's plenty of that; I've got lots of cruises to look forward to. Do you want a slice of pizza? It's free." Tommy was warming to him, when suddenly loud music started to cascade from the wall-mounted speakers. Costumed characters on stilts began walking past, in time to the music, right in front of their table.

"The welcome parade," smiled Ron, "They always do this. It's my favourite part of the day." The costumes and makeup were very impressive, lots of vivid colours. A clown in pink trousers tottered past, followed by a "Beau Peep' in an orange and yellow dress.

"Wow this is great," Tommy was getting in the mood. A huge red Afro was next; with piercing wild green eyes.

"There you are, Tommy; I've been looking all over for you." It was Freddie.

"Hi, I was talking to Ron. Ron, this is Freddie." Tommy was good with introductions.

"Yeah, yeah, it's nice to meet you." Freddie was impatient to get away. "Come on let's eat."

"I've just ordered a pizza."

"I mean proper food." Freddie was looking angry. Tommy decided to leave, as the prospect of rooming with Freddie was preferable to Ron, at the moment.

Over dinner Freddie began chastising him like a parent.

"Don't be talking to any strangers, you should know better than that."

"Ron's OK."

"Stick with me, kid. I know you have stowed away. What's the story?" Tommy felt that they had bonded during their fit of giggles. Freddie seemed to understand his dilemma, so Tommy let all of his concerns pour out over the buffet lunch. He left nothing out. He talked about his dead mother. How his Dad had lost the plot and allowed him to be put into care. All about his subsequent escape from the Care Home; and the road trip.

"I just want to go home," Tommy said between mouthfuls.

"You could borrow my cell phone; but there is no signal at sea, I have tried it. You could log on using my pass." Freddie took a sip of his cold drink from the tall glass.

"My Dad is computer illiterate. He doesn't have a computer; he wouldn't know Facebook or Twitter if he tripped over them."

"You could contact a friend; get a second hand message to him," Freddie said as he refused a top up from the hovering waiter.

"The police will be watching my account; be able to trace the IP address of the ship. They would be waiting for me when the ship docks."

"You are hardly 'Public enemy Number one.'"

"Top ten though." Tommy was starting to laugh again.

"Oh yeah, definitely top ten. You are a real danger to the public." They were both giggling.

"Look. You can stay in my cabin until we get back to Liverpool. This is only a four day cruise. Cork and Dublin then back. You will be home in no time. Come and see me perform tonight,"

"Perform?"

"Yeah, I'm the comedian in the 'Tropical Lounge.'"

Freddie bounded onto the stage and grabbed the mike. He started straight into his act without an introduction. The audience hadn't settled down; were still chattering.

"This guy's wife is in a coma. All the family are around the bed. Doctor tells him 'I have good news and bad news.'

Freddie scanned the crowd with a knowing look; a sweaty smirk lighting up his face. There are slight groans from the back. Freddie smiled and snorted a bit as he unsuccessfully tried to stifle a giggle. He continued, playing both characters in his story.

'What's the bad news, doctor?'

'Your wife's dead.'

'What's the good news then?'

"You are the new favourite to win this year's 'X Factor.'"

Nobody laughed except Tommy, who was sitting quietly at the back. Freddie continued on stage.

"What a crock of shit that X Factor is, right. I entered it myself, two years ago. I spent twelve hours waiting to be seen by some spotty production flunky and then didn't get through, but the woman in front of me did. Oh yeah, the ninety year old toothless granny got through. Then I overheard producers discussing a terminally ill contestant."

He was back into character again, using different voices for various production staff.

'We can use this.'

'We must have a human interest story.'

'Kept him in until he croaks; won't be a dry eye in the house during the final ten. Think of the ratings.'

'Just imagine the song choices. 'Died in your arms tonight' or 'Here in heaven,' the list is endless."

The crowd were starting to chat among themselves; a few were leaving, with audible derogatory comments. Fraser, the Cruise Director, was standing, arms folded at the back, assessing the whole scene. Freddie noticed all of this but continued with his prepared material, a real trooper.

"I hate Reality TV - why not a big brother for the over nineties – no evictions, you leave when you die. Imagine the annoying Geordie accent – 'This week's task, for a luxury budget, is to design a decoration for Agnes' coffin.'" Freddie did his best Geordie accent, which wasn't good. Tommy was enjoying himself. He loved the way the darkness of the room contrasted with the glare of the lighted stage. He thought Freddie was doing well, but he was in the minority. Freddie was back in the spotlight holding the mike.

"The Padre of Notre Dame was overwhelmed with grief when Quasimodo died. Who would ring the bells? He decided to hold open auditions, half of Paris turned up hoping to get the plum job of master bell ringer. One guy had no arms but performed brilliantly; butting the large bells with his head and nose to produce richly melodic sounds from the bells, a joy to the ear."

Freddie was miming his actions; thrusting his head violently from side to side.

"He lost his balance and fell to his death on the pavements below. The Padre rushed down the stairs; parted the shocked crowds to see if he could be of any assistance.

'Did you know him Father?' asked a local urchin.

'No, but his face rings a bell.'"

Freddie was laughing at his own joke; looking around the room for acknowledgement. A few drunks laughed, but most were appalled at the feeble joke. He hadn't finished; he was only half way through the story.

"The armless guy's brother arrived for an audition, determined to pay a lasting tribute.

'Have you ever rang any bells before?' asked the Padre.

58

'No, but if my brother can do it without arms, I'm sure I can do it.'

Freddie was doing both voices; playing the parts with a faint French accent.

'OK, you can have a go out of respect to your brother.' Well he didn't last long. He also fell from the treacherous bell tower; dying on the side of the Seine, where his brother had recently perished.

'Do you know him Father,' asked the same street kid.

'No but he is a dead ringer for his brother.'''

At the end of his act Freddie received polite applause. He stormed off to the back of the room as the canned music began.

"Can I have a word?" It was Fraser, the Cruise Director.

"Sure."

"How did you think that went, Freddie?" It was clear, from his facial expression, that Fraser wasn't impressed.

"They were quite a tough crowd. I was expecting an easier ride, you know, from a cruise ship."

"The trouble is, Freddie, your material isn't suitable for this audience. You need to tone it down, make it more family friendly, for the older crowd."

"But it is funny, right?" Freddie was searching Fraser's face for any signs of encouragement.

"Honestly? No, it isn't. Not here."

Freddie was beginning to lose his temper, the red mist was descending. He remembered the last time a boss had done this to him. He remembered that the house lights were on giving the club a garish appearance. The purple and orange walls which looked so cosy and appealing during a performance now looked shoddy and cheap. Freddie's set hadn't gone as well as he would have liked. The crowd had been small and unresponsive to his comedy style. He hated it when people didn't laugh, hecklers being particularly annoying. His temper always got the better of him resulting in him wanting to lash out and kill again. He just couldn't help himself when the red mist appeared. The impulse was far too great to ignore, it had to be fed. Charlie, the club owner, wandered over; a cigar in its usual position between his lips. He was very thin and frail; feminine without being too camp.

"Things are a bit tight these days Freddie, the credit crunch and all that," said Charlie. He had to use the credit crunch didn't he? He had to hide behind topical buzzwords, the prick.

"Hardly anybody is going out weeknights, darling. So we are pulling the plug on the Wednesday night set, see you Friday for the open mike night."

"Is that it? I'm down to just one night?" Freddie spat with as much venom as he could muster. He beginning to lose it big time.

"You will be the resident host, a five minute slot and then introduce the new hopefuls. The crowd love to get stuck into them."

"Five minutes in front of a baying mob?"

"You catch on real quick don't you Freddie boy?" Charlie smiled in a condescending manner. Freddie's temple was pulsing, his fists clenching, sweat was forming on his upper lip as his face reddened. Charlie was enjoying the moment; relishing the power play. Freddie could tell by looking at him.

"Cat got your tongue Freddie?" Freddie had to let it go. There were too many witnesses. The cleaner was mopping the stage pretending not to listen, but she was. The barman was stocking up the optics. He missed nothing. Most ominously, the bouncer had appeared at the door to witness the scene.

"OK, no problem Charlie." Freddie forced a smile.

"It is Mr Parker to you." Freddie walked out with a fixed smile firmly in place, but the smile was real. He was thinking nice comforting thoughts.

Charlie didn't make it to his Mercedes parked by the stage door. He was bundled into Freddie's van with the help of a baseball bat. When he regained consciousness, his hands were bound behind his back and Freddie was sat astride his shoulders. Freddie was enjoying the struggle as he pulled Charlie's tongue from his mouth; a strange gagging sound accompanied the performance. Freddie produced a knife and proceeded to slice off the tongue. A terrified guttural noise emitted from Charlie's mouth. He couldn't scream properly without a tongue. The pain was excruciating as he watched Freddie collect a wicket basket from the corner.

"Oh no, what have you got in there? Are they Pliers? Is it a drill?" Charlie's mumbled. That's what it sounded like to Freddie, it was difficult to understand him as his tongue stump wriggled around his mouth. Freddie brought the basket closer so that Charlie could see as he opened the side flap. Inside was a mangy stray cat. Freddie made a theatrical display of feeding the tongue to the hungry animal.

"Here you are baby, Daddy has your dinner, that's it; enjoy." Suddenly Freddie was in Charlie's face snarling.

"What's the matter Charlie, cat got your tongue?" Manic laughter filled the basement as Freddie threw his head back.

"Come on Charlie that's funny." Freddie recovered his composure and rolled Charlie into a shallow trench face up.

"What's the matter Charlie? Speak up; oh you can't, can you?" More hysterical laughter echoed around the cellar. Freddie was enjoying himself. He was in control, well out of control really, but he felt in total control. He quickly covered Charlie with soil, working the shovel with a rhythmical intensity until only Charlie's face was visible. His eyes were panic filled and his mouth was open in a pathetic pleading display. No words came, only an animalistic squeal as his bloody stump of a tongue wriggled pointlessly around his mouth. Freddie playfully tossed some soil into Charlie's mouth and enjoyed his futile attempt to splutter it out. His head was tightly packed in the soil not allowing any movement. Gravity played its inevitable part in the grotesque pantomime. Death didn't come quickly to Charlie but that's just how Freddie had planned it. Charlie choked to death on soil and the remains of his cat-chewed tongue.

"Are you listening to me? Freddie, are you listening?" Fraser was suddenly in Freddie's face. Front and centre.

"Sure thing, Fraser." Freddie was flustered as he was forcefully dragged back to the present.

"If you don't sort your act out, make it more appropriate for the audience, this will be your last cruise," Fraser nodded for emphasise, looking for agreement from Freddie.

"Got it?" Fraser was persistent.

"Got it," Freddie replied reluctantly. He was fuming; his eyes scanning the room checking that his dressing down was not too public.

"Come on Tommy, it's time for bed." They walked in silence down the corridor to the cabin. It took one hundred and forty two paces to return to the cabin as Tommy considered what he had just witnessed. There was no need for the way that guy had spoken to Freddie, it was harsh. When they were back in the cabin they rotated around the bathroom, getting a system worked out. Freddie gave Tommy some shorts to sleep in; they were soon tucked up in separate beds.

"Thanks for letting me stay here. I thought you were good on stage." Tommy was trying to be supportive.

"Thanks. Have a good sleep, kid. Tomorrow is another day."

"Goodnight Freddie."

"Goodnight kid." Tommy felt safe with Freddie.

Chapter 6

Thursday was always the worst day of the week. It was not because of the constant traffic of male libidos, or the imminent weekend rush. Katrina could deal with all of that; it was her worst day because of the appointment with Mr Badger. She didn't know if this was his real name, probably wasn't, it would only be prudent for him to have a pseudonym. He had an uncanny physical resemblance to the furry creature. The little man would always arrive, unwashed, at eleven o'clock on the dot and perform his ritual greeting.

"Good morning, such a nice day, don't you think?" He always asked good-naturedly. When he was alone with Katrina he became a different person. Mr Badger became a much more aggressive animal once the bedroom door was closed. He was a good customer, he always paid well. Frank, the proprietor, would not have a word said against him. Katrina complained often enough, but her words fell on deaf ears.

"He pays good money, darling. He can do whatever he wants to you, within reason."

He did do whatever he wanted. He wasn't a creature of habit; he would turn up every week with a different demand, as if he was working his way down his very own depraved wish list. He had performed every imaginable sexual act with Katrina, all performed in a snarling intimidating vindictive manner. She hated him, hated the place. Her room had become rather tatty and threadbare in appearance. She tried to keep it looking nice, for her own peace of mind, but the constant footfall of customers had worn the room down. It didn't help that Mr Badger insisted on using the curtains as a towel when he wiped parts of his anatomy down after use.

Her sister Anna was different. Anna was settling into their new life rather better, she had a steady client base and seemed to enjoy her work. She could have been 'Young Apprentice of the Year' if there had been a category for her work. She didn't go as far as to enjoy the work sexually, but she liked the power. Her clients were submissive, almost in awe of her beauty. She had become a classical dominatrix; patent leather thigh boots, whips, mask; the whole nine yards.

In comparison Katrina was a subservient sex slave. In the rare quiet moments Katrina watched everything like a hawk. She knew every nuance of the boudoir. She knew the times of the shift switch over on reception. She knew when Frank had a day off. Food deliveries always arrived on a Sunday, delivered in a big white van with the supermarket logo emblazoned down the side. When Roman visited to collect money, he always called Anna to his office.

Anna also watched when she was in Romans office, watched from under his desk. If she twisted her head while titillating with her tongue she could see the computer screen and the keyboard. She had memorised the password a long time ago.

-.-.-.-.-.-.-.-.-.-.-.-.-.-.-.-.-.-.-.-

Holly was unconscious, propped up by a pair of voluminous pillows. Her head was drooping to one side; her neck unable to support the weight. She looked so thin; her skin having a translucent membrane appearance, being stretched tightly across her protruding cheekbones. A ventilator mask covered her mouth and nose, elastic supports strapped behind her ears. The machine produced a slow rhythmical whooshing sound as it mechanically operated her lungs. Simon and Brie were seated on chairs either side of the bed, they did not notice the doctor enter the private side room, they were both miles away in their respective reflections; both remembering earlier days when Holly was a baby, her first days at school, happier times.

"Hello, Mr Brookes, can I have a word," the doctor interrupted their thoughts. The couple both looked at him without speaking, waiting for him to continue. He started talking about life expectancy, about Holly's ventilator, about the shortage of beds in the Hospice. Brie couldn't listen. She had noticed that the doctor was talking directly to Simon. Why do they always do that? It is so sexist and rude. They would discuss everything as a couple later, she knew that. I'll leave it to Simon, she decided as she took in the view offered by the large window. Beautiful manicured lawns surrounded by splendid flower beds displaying a vivid splash of contrasting colours. It was a truly magnificent horticultural creation. A huge oak tree dominated the grounds, decorated by white lights twinkling on the branches. It could be seen from miles away and had become an icon for the Hospice. It was said that every light represented a life, a patient at the Hospice, but Brie wasn't sure how true that was. She just hoped that Holly's light would continue to shine.

-.-

Roman was back from the brothel, sitting behind his desk studying some paperwork. He was proud of his club. 'Krème de la Krème' was his idea of a gentleman's club; not the biggest but he was proud that he owned every last brick, along with the four brothels he had set up in the terraced streets that ran down to the river. The club catered to the low end of the 'pole dancing, late drink and gambling' market. The name was his idea. He knew it was down market, so it was really a parody of the 'Prime of Miss Jean Brodie' quote, 'Creme de la Creme' with a Russian twist, using a K instead of a C. The name suggested a reference to the Kremlin, and had become known locally as 'The Krem'. He began reading the accounts. The paperwork didn't add up, he knew the figures down to the last penny; knew his organisation inside out. He was just making Frank wait, increasing the tension. Frank waited silently in his chair. He knew his place.

"Don't I pay you enough Frank?" Roman finally looked up from the papers revealing a cold detached stare that Frank couldn't match. He looked away, down to his left, gathering his thoughts.

"I wouldn't steal from you, boss, no way; I swear on my mother's life." Frank looked nervous, his fingers fiddling with his shirt which hung loose outside of his black trousers.

"Would you really swear on your mother's life?" asked Roman, his face a porcelain mask of malevolence. The door of the office opened allowing two smartly dressed, heavily muscled men to enter and stand menacingly against the back wall. They knew their role; they waited patiently for the cue from their paymaster. Roman Chavic was looking at the photograph on his desk. His parents looked happy; so proud standing outside of their home. That was before the soldiers had come and taken everything; taken the family home and his parent's lives. Roman had grown up quickly on the streets; had learnt how to survive. He ran with a crowd of similar street children, all desperate to get out of an impoverished homeless hell. Anton had offered him a way out, a way into organised crime, and into his bed. The things that he had done with Anton were out of necessity; Roman didn't consider himself 'gay', he had just done what had to be done to survive. Once he was old enough he had killed Anton at the first opportunity. He had sliced his throat while he lay sleeping beside him. He took enough money to flee to the UK and set himself up; as far away from the Ukraine as he could get.

"I would swear on my own life." Frank was fronting it out; but had chosen the wrong place, the wrong time and definitely the wrong man.

"Three thousand pounds has disappeared over the last four months Frank. I didn't take it, did you take it Sven?" Roman asked the tall blond figure standing by the exit door.

"No boss."

Roman nodded to Sven's sidekick without asking. He shook his head in reply.

"So that leaves you Frank." Roman's voice was becoming agitated. The accent, which he tried hard to conceal, was accentuated; betraying his roots.

"Nobody else had access to the money. When I left you in charge of the girls you had a duty to collect all the payments. This is a very clumsy attempt to hide the facts." Roman was tapping the papers with his hand. He appeared to be considering his options, but in truth, he always knew why this meeting was organised. He nodded to Sven. The two soldiers obediently stepped forward and seized Frank. They tied him to his chair and started a systematic beating. Roman watched in a detached manner.

"Where is my money Frank?" Roman kept asking the same question, but Frank had passed out within seconds of the beating starting; such was the intensity of the attack. Roman stood and walked over to the chair. Frank was slumped, head to one side in unconscious submission, a helpless captive.

"Nobody steals from me. It is sign of weakness to let this go unpunished," Roman said, as he casually withdrew a knife from his pocket. He would have preferred that Frank was conscious; to listen to the screams. He would have enjoyed watching him flinch with terror as the knife played around his face, caressing his cheekbones. He would have lingered longer; drawing blood to tease, but with Frank unconscious he did what he had planned in a nonchalant manner. Without preamble he stabbed the knife into Frank's left eye socket, twisting it until the eyeball was a white congealed mass. When he withdrew the knife the eyeball came with it. He could have been eating calamari at a restaurant if it wasn't for the colour of Frankie's pupil staring back at him. Roman left the knife on his desk, eye ball still attached, and wandered casually to the door. He turned to look at his henchmen; they nodded their understanding. They knew exactly what to do with the body. Roman was wondering how different life would have been if his parents were still alive. He walked out of the room nonchalantly straightening his collar; he had a vacancy to fill.

Chapter 7

Ben was standing in the hallway with his back to the wall, talking on the telephone.

"Hello. Yes, I was wondering if there has been any progress on the Mary Thomas case. Yes, I'll hold." The doorbell rang; he opened the door to reveal a smiling Bobbie dressed in casual jeans and a sensible sweater. Ben nodded his head forward and mouthed 'come in'; as he did the 'I'm on the phone' mime with his free hand, thumb and little finger protruding as he wiggled his hand. He didn't really have to do this as the phone was in his other hand, making it plainly obvious that he was, in fact, on the phone.

"Won't be long," he whispered to Bobbie, "I'm really looking forward to our day out on the bikes. I haven't been able to stop thinking about you. No. Not you." He was addressing the phone again.

"There is someone else here, I was talking to them. Sorry. OK, I will ring again next week." He hung up, disappointment showing on his face.

"Still no progress?" asked Bobbie.

"It's just as I told you in the taxi last night. All I get is 'We are pursuing inquiries', but I don't think the Police

are doing much. Just one more call and I'll be ready."
Ben started punching numbers into his cordless; the line
was connected immediately.

"Hello. Yes, it's Mr. Thomas here. Is there any update
on my son, Tommy, since he absconded from your
care?" Ben enjoyed suggesting that the Care Home was
responsible for Tommy being 'at large', so to speak.
Bobbie could hear an unintelligible electronic voice in
the earpiece of the phone.

"Well I think you are. Your security should be tighter.
Have you any idea where he is; Yes or No?"

He waited for an answer. "OK, thank you." Ben's
face indicated that it was a 'no.' "He can't just
disappear into thin air. He has to be somewhere." Ben
hung up.

"I'm sure it will all work out for the best," Bobbie
was trying to be positive, trying to be encouraging.

"Let's not let it spoil our day. I'll get the bikes ready."
Ben made a move towards the kitchen.

"Come on boy," Bobbie ushered Spangle in through
the open door. He was on a long extended lead.

'You didn't say the dog was coming."

"Spangle comes everywhere with me." Bobbie had
the adoring look on her face; the face that only dog
owners possess. The dog was straining on the extended
lead. He had that wild eyed look on his face that Ben
recognised from their first fleeting meeting in the park.
Ben was already opening the back door. He quickly dug

73

out the bikes from the garage. His own; much used and in mint condition, and the one that Mary refused to use. She always intended to ride but was always too busy with her painting. The chain was a bit rusty; in need of a spot of oil.

"Here is your chariot. We are good to go." He was holding the handlebars steady so she could straddle the seat safely.

"Is this bike..?" Bobbie paused in embarrassment.

"Yes, but don't worry. Mary would have wanted you to use it." Ben re-entered the house to set the alarm then appeared on the front.

"Over here," he waved her down the driveway that ran the whole way down the side of his semi detached. She was busy getting her feet on the pedals without letting go of Spangle's lead. The dog was getting exited, as he always did when it was time for his 'walkies.' He was circling around the bike; entangling the lead in the bike chain, causing an inevitable tumble. Bobbie came off the bike in a heap, landing heavily against next door's parked car. A scratch had appeared on the car, etched by one of the handlebars as it fell in a slow arc to the floor.

"Sorry about that. Heal Spangle."

Once Ben had left a note on the car's windscreen, they were off on the bikes. Spangle was enjoying the speed, fifteen yards behind. They chattered away just like they had the night before, oblivious to the overtaking traffic, until they were on the promenade overlooking the river. They stopped for a coffee at the park with the bandstand. It was an imposing site, the ornate cream dome of the bandstand in the foreground framed by the grandeur of the city's skyline across the river. A poetry recital was in full swing. A very demonstrative reading from a middle aged woman was in mid delivery. Her literary efforts were far outstripped by her physical exertions. Her arms swung wildly, book in hand, as she banged on poetically concerning the subject of aging. Ben was not impressed. The poem sent him off into his own thoughts. Middle aged, who would have thought it, but here we are, both the wrong side of forty. Suddenly he was feeling older. He remembered walking in West Kirby by the marina. He couldn't fathom the reason why he felt so low at the time, it being before recent tragic events. Then it hit him like a bolt of lightning. He was surrounded by old people taking their constitutional, I mean really old. He had wondered how quickly a life passes. One minute you are running through forests kicking leaves, a carefree child. The next, you are thinking about replacement hips and heart bypass surgery. The poem had finished. The polite applause from the sparse crowd jolted Ben out of his reverie.

"We should push on; the weather looks like it may be closing in."

'Fine by me, just let me get Spangle organised." Bobbie untied his lead from the railings. "Come on boy." Spangle didn't move from his position, sprawled out on the grass. Out of the three of them, he was the one who had enjoyed the poetry reading the most. He had nodded off. He only needed persuading with a gentle tug on the lead before they were all mobile again, speeding down the cycle path.

It seemed that the whole town were out enjoying the sea air. Numerous kites were billowing in the wind; young boys were playing football on the grassy dips that ran parallel to the pathway; the cycle path was littered with bikes of all descriptions. There were mountain bikes, racing bikes, tandems, children with stabilisers. It was so crowded that they decided to take a break and just observe the view as the pale winter sun cast its last rays upon the sea; giving a shimmer to the water. It started to rain slightly so they took shelter on a bench situated in the recess of the public toilets building. It was painted white, like a Greek holiday home. If they half closed their eyes they could have been in Santorini or Mykonos. Bobbie tied Spangle to the bench while Ben secured the bikes together with his lock. They both sat watching the sea change from a silver lake to a dull grey as the pale winter sun disappeared on the horizon. Lights were coming on all around them. Street lamps, house lights, even vehicle headlights were flashing on in the gloom. Ben took the opportunity to snuggle up close on the bench, putting a protective arm around Bobbie's shoulder.

"This is my favourite time of year. Just before Christmas; if you wrap up against the weather there is no better time to bike the coastal pathway," Ben enthused. Bobbie took the opportunity to get closer. She turned so that their faces were almost touching.

"This is very cosy," she said with an inviting smile. Ben needed no more encouragement; he slipped his free handed underneath her sweater, feeling bare skin on her ribcage. He could see the car headlights twinkling in her eyes.

"You are the best thing that has happened to me in a long time," he whispered as he kissed her tenderly on the lips.

"I've wanted to do this since the first time I saw you," replied Bobbie breathlessly between kisses. They were both getting excited; Bobbie's right hand was under Ben coat as their clinch developed into a full scale frantic embrace. The moment seemed magical to them both; their bodies silhouetted against the sky by the car headlights.

"OK, we've seen enough." It was PC Barnes suddenly appearing from nowhere, ID badge thrust forward, with McNally still filming the scene from a distance.

"Switch it off and read them their rights." Barnes was very dogmatic when he thought he was in charge.

"You do not have to say anything but it may harm your..."

Ben wasn't listening. He was in shock. What was going on? Why was the policeman cuffing him? Why were the parked cars, which had looked so pretty in the fading light, suddenly leaving the car park and driving off? Bobbie was also being cuffed by McNally as she finished her speech.

"Anything you do say may be…"

"What is going on?" Ben demanded with as much indignation as he could muster.

"This is a well known 'dogging' site. We have footage, video evidence, of your performance on the bench; enticing the parked voyeurs to join in. We had to stop you to protect public decency; there are children in the area." Barnes lectured in a disapproving tone. McNally was looking down at the screen on the camcorder as she replayed the footage. She seemed comfortable with the controls.

"All there; in full colour close up." She was proud of her work; she could have been Steven Spielberg on location.

"This is ridiculous; the only dogging going around here is over there," Ben nodded towards Spangle, who was barking madly, trying to protect his owner. Not much of a watchdog, thought Ben. Not much use at all.

"Watch your head as you get into the car," Barnes was pushing Ben's head down as he ushered him into the back seat. Bobbie had automatically reached for Spangle's lead with her left hand out of habit. Is this really happening? She thought as McNally gripped her forearm, ready to shoehorn her into the vehicle. The doors were closed quickly, trapping the lead, as the unmarked police car gathered speed along the Promenade approach road. The extra long extendable lead that had been bought to allow Spangle more freedom was now proving to be a rather inspired purchase. Although the unfortunate dog ran at increasing speed, it could not match the police car. Ben and Bobbie watch helplessly over their shoulders as the lead got longer and longer. It was buying Spangle time, but the inevitable would happen without a change of pace. Spangle needed a longer lead or a slower car, without either he would soon be dragged along behind the car, like a rapist in Soweto.

"Spangle, what about Spangle? You have to stop." Bobbie was getting visibly upset. Barnes checked his mirror and was greeted by the sight of the terror stricken dog at full speed. He slammed on the brakes and came to a halt as quickly as his ABS system allowed. The tension on the lead was released. Dogs do not have brakes. Spangle was trying manfully to slow down, but was running out of tarmac. He came to a shuddering halt against the back of the police car, causing considerable damage to the rear bumper and to himself. Bobbie was desperate to get out but had to wait for the security lock to be released.

"Are you alright, baby? He is not moving," she was beginning to panic.

DC Page was watching events unfold in the interview room from the anonymity of the two way viewing mirror. He could still see the smug faces on Barnes and McNally as he informed them that it was their case.

"I'll leave the interview to you two. It's your collar," he had said. What could he do? He was too embarrassed to see Bobbie; she hadn't returned his calls after that lunch date. He really thought that it may lead to something, something meaningful that had a future, a happy ending. That's all he really wanted; to live a normal life. There was also the issue of the injured dog. And him, that Thomas bloke, it didn't take him long to get over his wife's accident. He was always ringing about the case; any news? He was always pretending to care so much about her; and now here he is with Bobbie. He watched Barnes start the interview.

"Why did you start embracing after the car highlights were flashed on and off?"

"I, I mean we, were not aware of any flashing lights. We were just sheltering from the rain; enjoying the sunset." Ben was still furious about the whole business, but he had to be serious. The last time he acted vacantly in a situation like this, with the Local Authority assessment team, they had taken Tommy away.

"If people can't go for a bike ride on a public highway, I don't know what the world is coming to," he complained. He was genuinely furious.

"The point is you were not on a public highway. You were sat at a notorious 'dogging' site." Barnes was in full flow, "We have evidence."

"What is 'dogging?'" Bobbie asked in genuine innocence. "How can you say dogging when poor old Spangle may be dying for all I know." After it was explained to her that it had nothing to do with an actual dog, she calmed down slightly, but was still horrified that Spangle was anywhere near such a citadel of shame.

"Where is Spangle?' She asked.

"In good hands." Barnes was keen to return to the case.

On the other side of the mirror PC McNally was playing the footage back to Page.

"As you can clearly see sir, the couple sit and wait for the cars to signal. See, sir, he looks directly at the car flashing its lights. That's the signal to start performing. They then start the action, which was getting rather heated before we had to call a halt. It was getting too explicit."

Page watched the couple on the small screen attached to the camcorder. A part of him wished that he was on the bench with Bobbie instead of Thomas, quite a large part. He imaged himself in her embrace, smelling her hair, touching her cheek. Page watched the kiss. It was a natural kiss, reciprocated affection. How he longed to be on the bench with Bobbie. Was she seeing this Thomas all the time, even when they had lunch? He was confused and sad about the whole episode.

"It doesn't look premeditated to me PC McNally, the lights are coming on all over town; it is dusk after all. The way the cuffs are being roughly administered behind their backs is more suggestively erotic than

81

anything they are doing on the bench. Release them with a caution."

"Sir, are you serious?"

Page was looking increasingly agitated; his snake skinned left foot tapping repeatedly on the tiled floor.

'It won't stand up in court. Release them."

-.-

The police couldn't do enough. They collected their bikes and delivered them to the Vets where the dog had been taken. They left the Veterinary Surgery with Spangle in a basket. He had a sprained neck resulting in a restraining collar being draped around his neck, like an Elizabethan ruff.

"The police will be paying the bill; I'll make sure of it; and a compensation claim." Bobbie was still furious. "How dare they hurt my poor little Spangle."

"He seems better now he is sedated," Ben consoled, "let's pop into Simon's for a drink. Come on it's been quite a day." He needed a drink. He hadn't enjoyed their experience at the police station. It had too many bad memories. They pushed their bikes along the pavement in the dark, Spangle's basket resting on Ben's seat. Bobbie fussed all the way, worrying about the slightest little bump in the pavement.

. -.-

"You can't possibly bring that animal into my house." Brie greeted them at the door. For once Ben found himself agreeing with Brie. He still didn't like dogs, even injured girlfriend's dogs.

"But he is in a basket, sedated, what harm can he do?" objected Bobbie.

"OK, leave him in the hall," Simon was trying to act as arbitrator.

"I'll lock the bikes," said Ben.

"Stay Spangle darling; mummy won't be long." Bobbie kissed the dog's head. Ben started to recount the story of their arrest and the unfortunate incident with the dog. He left nothing out, gave a really animated account of the events. He was on top form; almost back to his old self, entertaining and amusing.

"Having a criminal record isn't that great, Ben," interrupted Brie.

"It was just a caution, their way of admitting they had misread the situation. A claim will be going in for the dog." Simon and Brie stood in muted response, not reacting to the twists and turns of his story.

"What's up with you two? You seem pretty glum." They looked at each other with sad eyes before Simon spoke.

"We have been to the Hospice. Things deteriorated quickly today. The doctors gave us all of the options. It was very difficult, but we..." He paused to look at Brie. They both looked at the floor.

"We switched Holly's ventilator off, she has gone." Simon was still inspecting the floor as he spoke. They

83

all descended into a group hug, staying there for minutes, swaying slowly for comfort.

"How devastating for you both," Bobbie eventually broke the silence.

"We knew it was inevitable. It's just so sad, so very sad, but life goes on." Brie was being brave, but the tear stains on her make-up were clear for everybody to see. She had had enough of crying for one day. She was desperate to change the subject. Simon took Bobbie into the kitchen to make the drinks. Ben was left alone with Brie, his fiercest critic. She reminded Ben that he is still a father; that he has a son, a son that is currently missing. Ben was mildly offended by the sudden switch of topic.

"Oh yeah, a dead wife and a missing son, life is just great. Who wouldn't want to be me?"

"Come on, come on, stop being so.." She looked around the room in desperation, looking for the right word. " ..so maudlin. Get back to basics. You have retired; not such a good idea really, too much time on your hands. You need to get some structure back in your life." She was talking sense, he knew that much.

"I'll get back into the poker scene. I was always ahead of the game," he said.

"Not exactly what I was thinking of Ben. I was thinking more of bike rides, walks in Snowdonia, swimming. You know, something healthy, something to get your blood pumping. Come on Ben, do you really want to spend your time in a sleazy casino?" She did her head to the side thing; the move that she thought was irresistible, the persuasive comforting Lady Di manoeuvre which always brought home the bacon. He hesitated just long enough for her to believe that he was considering her point of view but he had already made up his mind.

"Look Brie, I know you are upset and I'm really sorry about what's happened today, I really am; but you need to get off my case."

"And the casino, tell me you're not going back to that life". She hadn't given up on her Mother Theresa routine.

"It's what I do. It's what I do best." With that he walked out of the room. She didn't say another word. She knew he had been roused out of his lethargic depressive downer but she didn't much like where he was going.

-.-

DI Page had also had a bad day. It had really disturbed him seeing Bobbie in the interview room. He had high hopes that maybe something would come of their first date. Don't be stupid, their only date, he realised that now. But he still liked her, couldn't help himself, all he wanted was to go home to a partner instead of his mother. He loved his mother, of course he did, but caring for her did cramp his style somewhat. He turned into the freezer aisle, and ticked pizza and fish fingers off his list as the boxes joined the growing mountain of items in his basket. Once he had suffered the ordeal of the pinging checkout, he loaded the car and drove home without incident. He always tried to carry too many bags to the house, just to get it done quicker.

"Hello, I'm home. Hello mother." He was met by the accustomed silence. All the lights were on as usual, illuminating the hall. At the bottom of the stairs his mother lay motionless. He quickly checked her neck for a pulse. A faint beat greeted his probing fingers; a raspy sporadic breath was exiting her drooping mouth. She was having a stroke. He collected the rest of the shopping from the car and diligently emptied all of the bags into the respective cupboards. All the frozen items were stored neatly into the freezer. Once all the carrier bags were in the bin, Page returned to the hall and checked that his mother was dead. Only then did he call the Emergency Services.

"Can I have an ambulance please? Yes, I have just got home and found my mother at the bottom of the stairs. Please hurry." Page sounded panic stricken, hopeful and forlorn all at the same time. It would sound convincing on the tape recording.

Chapter 8

Freddie needed to get away. Needed to get off the ship and be free to breathe, to live, to kill. The desire was growing inside his body. It was a palpable addiction that had to be satisfied. He disembarked the ship and caught the first train into Dublin; blending with the crowd, his baseball cap concealing most of his hair under its prominent peak. Once in town he headed to the Temple Bar district to have a drink, listen to some live music and look for a victim. Anyone that didn't find him hilarious would do. He soon got chatting in a bar to a couple of girls. The place was heaving; standing room only, as a band played Irish music with those funny little rhythmical drums. People were dancing, having a good time. It was the weekend so people were letting their hair down. Crowds of girls dressed as nurses or in angel costumes were everywhere, along with groups of cheerful young men teasing their 'L plated' hero. There must have been at least six simultaneous stag parties filling the streets with colourful merriment. It was just a normal Friday night in Dublin's fair city. Freddie was at the bar; he ordered a Guinness and started chatting to two local girls. One was really stunning with scarlet curly hair. The other was unremarkable in appearance. Freddie gave 'curly' his best shot, but the two obvious lesbians weren't laughing much at his devastatingly amusing chat up lines; paying more attention to each other than to him. The plain one was getting on his nerves, she was a real dyke, not in a clichéd dungaree wearing, shaven headed way; but just not as attractive as the stunning one. She was larger, had a bonny farmers wife feel to her appearance. Freddie wasn't sure if she liked funny, strong men; or funny submissive women. Funny is funny. Make me laugh you can have me; one way or another he was going to find out. They made their excuses and left.

He followed them out into the narrow streets. One of them was going to pay dearly for the affront; one was going to take their last breathe before the night ended. They were so engrossed in each other that they did not notice Freddie following, carefully staying in the shadows. He blended in with the late revellers at a safe distance. The security on their ground floor flat was abysmal; he was inside within seconds. He savoured the smell of the incense as he hid behind the floor length curtains covering their bay window. He enjoyed eavesdropping. He had to wait for the right moment.

"What are we eating tonight honey," the big one asked without looking up from her 'Hello' magazine. The settee was adorned with empty crisp packets, dirty glasses and discarded newspapers.

"Look babes, why does it always have to be me that cooks, cleans and does the washing?" The pretty one was protesting. The big one remained on the settee stifling a yawn. Freddie loved a domestic squabble.

"It is your house Hun," the big one snapped with emphasise on the 'your'. She had always resented her partner's independence and ability to organise her life and remain genuinely funny.

"I could murder a pizza. Why don't you practice your hostess skills and pop one in the oven."

"What do you actually do in our relationship," exploded the slender blonde. "I provide the food, the comforts, the entertainment, and the …everything."

"One; I look good on your arm when we are out. Two; I'm great eye candy." The big one was unconsciously counting on her fingers, not realising point one and two were the same, the thick bitch.

"Three; You love me. Just do what you're good at, and eat my minge, you skinny fucker." The thin one was furious as she dropped to her knees, but did what she always did; she munched up a storm until her chin glistened. And she loved it, the dirty bitch.

Freddie was eying the scene with increased excitement. He was finding the lesbian love scene erotic, rather stimulating in a sexual context. It was, after all, every man's dream fantasy. He forced himself to concentrate on the kill. He was planning which one would get it, how to escape. Finally he was ready for action. He made his move. Without making a sound he was standing behind the big one as her petite partner continued her marathon munch at the business end.

They were both writhing around in the uncontrolled actions of orgasm.

"Oh, yes baby." The big one's head was thrown back as she lifted her feet onto the settee beside her hips. She was ready for the finale. The blonde was responding to her larger partner, getting deeper with her tongue. They were both engrossed in their session, eyes shut in their own private erotic worlds. Freddie got out his garrotte and pulled it tight around the big one's neck from behind.

"Oh," she was more frenzied, louder, her body thrashing around fighting for air. Her partner assumed that she was really going for it, so snuggled close; eyes shut, and pushed deeper. The big one finished her death dance. Freddie left before her partner came up for air. She continued to eat her still warm, but very dead partner.

The ship was docked overnight to enable passengers to enjoy the city. Freddie managed to get a train back to Dun Laoghaire in good time; he had to be back for his act, before they sailed to the safety of international waters. Once back on board, he mingled with the crowds that were spilling out of the main theatre. The garrotte had been discretely dumped overboard.

"Loved the acrobatic jugglers, how do they do that in mid air?" enquired a passing middle aged woman. There was a real buzz about the crowd. The ship was bouncing. Freddie needed a drink, but also needed to see Tommy before his performance. He was getting quite attached to him. Tommy was in the 'cyber zone' watching the teenagers surf the net. Dare he ask someone to use their keyboard to leave a message on Twitter? He couldn't risk it. He needed to stay anonymous until he could see his dad face to face. None of the trance like faces looked up from their screens; they were all absorbed in their virtual worlds. All except for the girl steward, her name tag displaying 'Kade' to the world. She was the cabin cleaner who had approached him during the fire drill. God, that seemed so long ago, but it had only been a few days. She was the only one that looked up to survey the room. He was really taken aback with her golden skin and constant smile. Tommy had never seen anyone from the Far East. He was rather smitten. But in this instance she looked puzzled, ill at ease.

"Are you OK," Tommy surprised himself with an involuntary question.

"Oh hello, I was just checking my e-mails."

"What's wrong with them?"

"Nothing, it is just my mother, she is having, how do you say; a bad day. Please sit down." She smiled politely. Tommy pulled up a spare swivel chair and buried his frame into it's comfortable padding.

"So, what's the problem?" Tommy was enjoying talking to her. She seemed so nice.

"I send most of my wages home to Indonesia, to Pulan."

"Pulan? I've never heard of it."

91

"Yes, it is my home. We live in a village outside of Palembang. My mother is there." Kade's face was brimming with happiness at the mention of her home; such a happy smile. The smiled faded when she introduced her mother into the conversation.

"Look at this e-mail. I am puzzled by it." They both studied the screen.

'I appresiate money you send. I love you Kade, beloved daughter."

"It doesn't sound right; not like my mother at all. She went to night class. She is so proud of her written English; that is why she practices it with the e-mails. The spelling is normally so meticulous; she just wouldn't make a mistake like that."

"She might just be having a bad day."

"No, it is not possible."

"Why don't you ask her a question?" Tommy was having a brainwave.

"A question?" Kade was looking puzzled.

"Yes. A question that has no right answer; something like 'how is cousin Alti? Is she still working at the hospital?'"

"But I don't have a cousin Alti."

"That is the whole point. You will find out if your mother is sending the e-mails or not." Tommy was pleased with his logic.

Understanding slowly dawned on Kade's face. It was with growing trepidation that her fingers began typing. She wasn't looking forward to the reply. Her fingers continued moving over the keyboard.

>*'How is cousin Alti, is she still working at the hospital?'*

A reply arrived in the inbox almost immediately. They were both impressed by the speedy technology.

>*'She is fine, asks after you my loverly daughter.'*

The spelling was still below expectations, but the chilling fact was that cousin Alti did not exist.

"Who could be sending these messages?" pleaded Kade; her face a mask of concern.

"I don't know, but maybe you should stop sending money home for now." Tommy said as sympathetically as he could.

"Try BBC News on Google." Her fingers were busy again.

"Why don't you try Indonesia?" She followed his suggestion and watched the screen come to life with a news headline.

>*'Indonesian soldiers stood by as mobs of ethnic Dayaks terrorized locals.'*

Tommy left her to read the story in private. He knew, even at his age, that it was not good news; that she needed some privacy to absorb the information. He had, however, made a mental note of her e-mail address.

He wondered who the other 146 were. He continued down the street and took the lift back down to the pizza cafe. Ron was still at the same table as before.

"Hi Ron," he said as he sat in the spare chair opposite his old friend. Ron was quickly into his life story. He was a permanent cruiser. He sold his house when his wife had died. Now he planned to jump from ship to ship until the money ran out.

"There's plenty of that; I've got lots of cruises to look forward to. Do you want a slice of pizza? It's free." Tommy had heard all this before, word for word. He was beginning to think that everybody he knew on the ship had a problem except Freddie.

"Don't you recognize me?" Tommy was searching Ron's face for any sign.

"I get a bit confused sometimes; my memory isn't what it used to be."

"Why don't we go and see Freddie at the Lounge, he will cheer you up."

"Freddie?"

"You know, my friend with the crazy red hair." Tommy wiggled his fingers above his head to indicate a frizzle cut.

"Oh yeah," Ron didn't remember. They arrived in the lounge just before Freddie was due on. Freddie was mumbling to himself, practising his act, as the pair approached.

"I'm a bit worried about Ron. I think he may have Alzheimer's; and Kade, she has problems at home," Tommy said in a concerned manner.

"Like I give a shit. Who are these people? I'm on any second, kid; we'll talk later."

The house lights dimmed as the invisible MC announced the next act on the public address system. He used the exaggerated extended syllable style used by the announcer at any boxing match.

"Please give it up for Frreddie Fuuugus"

Freddie bounded on stage aware that Fraser was watching his every move. He started safely.

"Did everyone enjoy Dublin? What a great place. Are there any Irish on board," Freddie had his hand cupped to his ear; abandoning his alternative comedy roots. A large proportion of the audience gave a vociferous affirmation of their nationality. The crowd were roaring their approval.

"Hello Ireland." Freddie shouted with his arms spread in crucifixion stance.

"I had a great day today. Temple Bar is amazing, but what is all that Irish music about. I mean, those little drums are a bit strange, don't you think." Freddie was wiggling his wrist violently. The crowd were laughing along.

"And the girls. My God, Irish girls are to die for." Another cheer cascaded from the crowd.

"My parents died last year." The crowd gave a collective Ahh, almost like a pantomime reaction.

"We bought a memorial headstone at £50 a month but only go to the grave once every two months, a bit like a gym membership." Freddie was struggling to concentrate; it was a good joke, the headstone thing, but it brought back memories of how his parents had died. He hadn't wanted much from them, only wanted them to come and support him in Edinburgh during the fringe. It was rumoured, at the time, that he may be nominated for the Perrier 'Best Newcomer Award.' His performance that night was crucial, everything hung in the balance. They hadn't turned up. This upset him so much that he bombed; possibly his worst ever gig. They had to pay for their negligence. He drove all night; back to Bradford, used the crossbow, and then returned; all in one night. Nobody missed him in Edinburgh.

"It's great to see you all enjoying yourselves on holiday." Freddie had pulled himself together. "My last holiday was at Centre Parcs. It was the best open prison I've ever been to. I hired a bike and ran into a wire fence within a mile. It was like a scene from 'The Great Escape.' I half expected Steve McQueen to overtake me on a motorbike." The drink fuelled audience were responding well to the act.

"Are there any students on board?" Freddie enquired with his hand cupped to his ear in a pantomime pose.

"Yes," a group of four replied in unison.

"What are you studying?" Freddie was fishing for information.

"Pharmacy," replied the blonde girl.

"My sister works at Boots too," Freddie smiled at his punch line.

"Only kidding love, what about you?" Freddie nodded to the tanned male sitting next to her.

"Psychiatry," he replied, fearing the worst.

"I used to wet the bed as a child and was afraid of the pet poodle, what does it all mean?" Freddie was in full flow. The student was smiling and clapping along with the rest of the audience; he knew better than to answer when a comedian was on form.

"I've seen a lot of wheelchairs on this cruise. There are plenty of people convalescing onboard. I bet there are even people with Alzheimer's. Well, they won't forget me in a hurry."

Tommy didn't like the joke. He thought that it was disrespectful towards Ron. Why did Freddie have to include that in his act? Did he have to be performing 24/7? He was becoming tired of Freddie's jokes. Freddie was in full flow on stage.

"What's with that Doris Day song - 'Que sera sera'- have you listened to the lyrics?

Freddie started singing.

'When I was just a little girl,

I asked my mother what will I be?

Will I be pretty? Will I be rich?

Here's what she said to me.

Que sera sera, whatever will be will be.'

The crowd were singing along with Freddie conducting on stage; he suddenly stopped; dropping his conductor's arms down by his side for emphasis.

"Now you would normally say to your daughter 'of course you will be pretty.' Not 'whatever will be, will be.' She must have been one ugly kid."

At the end of his act Freddie took his applause and wandered to the back of the room where Fraser was waiting.

"That was much better Freddie; much better. Keep it like that and we are in business." Fraser was smiling as he looked over Freddie's shoulder. He had other things on his mind. That's all he said before joining a girl at the bar.

"Come on Tommy, I need a drink." Freddie was feeling good after his performance.

"What about Ron?"

"He's a big boy he can look after himself." Freddie was already walking away expecting the boy to accompany him to the bar area.

"That the point; he can't. I'm taking him back to his cabin, but I'll be back." Tommy grabbed Ron's arm gently and ushered him towards the lift. Freddie watched him go until he disappeared into the corridor. Once they were away from the crowds Tommy started talking.

"What's your cabin number?"

"I can't remember."

"Let's see your card."

Ron took it out of his breast pocket and handed it over without objection. It had a three digit number but the cabins all had four digit numbers. They had to try each deck until they found the right cabin.

"How have you been getting back to your cabin, Ron?"

"Somebody always helps me. It's kind of slow with my crutch, but I always get there."

They got their bearings regarding the cabin number. It had to be aft on the starboard side. They started on deck six and worked upwards using the lift; they found his cabin on the ninth deck.

"Can you remember deck nine?"

"I'll try. Come in and sit on my balcony."

Inside the cabin was extremely tidy, with very little on display. The only personal touches; the objects that obviously belonged to Ron's, were a book on the bedside cabinet and a photograph of a younger Ron posing with a girl.

"Who is the girl, Ron?"

"You know what the answer is son."

"You don't remember?"

"Correct."

They sat on the balcony for a while. Ron talked about things he could remember. He recounted childhood recollections of climbing trees and playing in the streets until dark; things that Tommy knew nothing about, being a twenty first century teenager.

"I have to go Ron, it's getting late; but I'll see you tomorrow. I promise."

"Take the photo; as a memento."

"I can't possibly..."

"It's no good to me now." He was pushing it into Tommy's hands. "Take it."

"OK, as a friendship thing, goodnight Ron."

"OK son."

"What deck are we on, Ron."

"Nine." Ron smiled. Tommy smiled back as he gently closed the cabin door.

-.-

Freddie was having a good time at the bar; people had been backslapping him and buying drinks. It had been a great day. The tension had been released by his little trip into Dublin; tonight's gig had gone down well with the punters; Fraser was off his back, and it was the last night on board. There was a real party atmosphere in the Lounge, with holidaymakers determined to have one last frolic. Tommy spotted Freddie at the bar and sauntered over.

"Took your time, didn't you?" Freddie enquired like one half of an old married couple. Tommy was becoming wary of Freddie's possessive nature.

"I said I'd be back, and I am." Tommy's eyes flashed defiance.

"What's with the photo," Freddie asked as he nodded towards the frame in Tommy's hand.

"It's just a keepsake from Ron."

'Getting rather friendly with the old boy, aren't we?

"It's just a photo."

Freddie was surprised at how jealous he was feeling; it was putting a dampener on his evening. He had things to do. He needed to pack; to put his suitcase out for offloading.

"We need to think about how you are going to get off the ship without a pass Tommy. You don't want Security calling the Police do you?" Tommy's face visible dropped. An open mouthed, vacant expression dominated his features.

"I hadn't thought of that."

"How did you get on in the first place?"

"I just, sort of, sneaked on with the food delivery."

"Well it's not going to be that easy getting off, security will be tight. Let's go back to the room and think about it. Make a plan." Freddie was enjoying Tommy's discomfort as they plodded down the corridor to his cabin. Once back in the cabin Freddie started to pack his suitcase, which lay open on his bed.

"I could mingle with a family and just walk off."

"No good, everyone is screened as they hand their passes in at the gangway."

"I could try the food area again." Tommy tried again.

"Not so easy to hide on an empty pallet Tommy, rather exposed, don't you think?" teased Freddie.

"I could dive into the water and swim." Tommy was getting desperate.

"No, the best idea is if you hide in my suitcase and get delivered to the dock by the porters. I can collect you in the morning and we will be home free." Freddie was beaming, his green eyes flashing with devilment. Tommy didn't answer; he wasn't impressed with the prospect of being trussed up like a chicken all night.

"It is sheer genius, even if I say so myself. Hand delivered by the staff. I love it." Freddie was beside himself in self congratulation.

"I don't think I will fit in." Tommy objected, but he was weakening and Freddie knew it.

"Get in and try it out, come on; we can have a test run." Tommy duly obliged; if he doubled his knees up to his chest, his supple teenage frame easily fitting into the oversized suitcase.

"What about your clothes?" Tommy enquired from his foetal position.

"I will fill them in around you as padding." Freddie started to do just as he said.

"I don't want any dirty stuff near my head. This is the clean end." Tommy demanded.

"I've only worn them once," Freddie said as he stuffed his underwear around Tommy's torso.

"It's getting a bit of a tight squeeze in here."

"You'll be fine," said Freddie as he began pulling the big zipper that ran around the lid of the suitcase.'

"I feel like a ventriloquists dummy in this case."

"Oh no you don't."

"That's a pantomime not a ventriloquist." corrected a muffled voice from inside the case.

"But I'm funny aren't I?" Freddie's green eyes were twinkling with devilment.

"Yes Freddie, you are hilarious. I'm struggling to breathe in here."

"I bought a book once, an introduction to ventriloquism. It was entitled 'Ventriloquism for Dummies.'"

"That's not funny Freddie. I'm struggling to breathe."

103

Freddie picked up the knife from the tray left by room service and stabbed the suitcase in a quick fluid motion. It felt good, not as good as the last time he had stabbed someone, but still good.

"How is that Tommy? Enough ventilation for you?" Inside the case Tommy considered the knife inches in front of his face. Maybe Freddie wasn't as friendly as he had first thought. Maybe I had better not argue about the escape plan; keep on his good side.

"I need the photo, can you pass it in please."

The zipper was opened just enough for the frame to be slid inside beside his face. Freddie zipped up the case for the final time, removed the knife and dragged the case off the bed to test the weight balance.

"Are you OK in there," asked Freddie as he did a test drive to the door.

"I'm fine."

"It feels normal enough to me, wheels just fine. Tommy can you hear me OK," Freddie had his head against the cloth of the case.

"Yes."

"I'm going to put the case outside in the corridor for collection. It has to be there before midnight. Are you OK with that? You will have to be quiet until they offload the case. I will collect you tomorrow once the case is off the ship."

"I need the toilet."

"This is not the right time Tommy."

"But I really need it. I can't stay in here all night. I might soil your clothes." Freddie relented and opened the case to allow Tommy admittance to the bathroom. He was soon back in the case; neatly propped up against the wall outside the cabin. The photo frame close to his face, unseen in the dark, but close enough to his cheek for him to feel the cold glass against his face.

"Hello Ron, remember me?" whispered Tommy. Ron still didn't remember, but Tommy did.

"Kade147@Hotmail.com" he whispered to himself.

Chapter 9

Ben carried the tray into the bedroom and placed it on his bedside table. He had re-arranged the bedroom; gone for the minimalist look. Now that he had invested in wall mounted lighting, and ditched the alarm clock there was plenty of space on the table. The contents of the tray filled the room with delightful gastronomic aromas; nothing as mouth watering as a top notch restaurant, just honest to goodness steaming hot tea and toast.

"Eat it while it is still hot. I love hot toast." Ben was smiling, thinking that last night had also been pretty hot. For a first time they had been extremely compatible; being comfortable enough in their exuberant nakedness to try out a number of adventurous manoeuvres. Bobbie was sat up with pillows protecting her naked back from the wooden headrest, making short work of her first piece of toast.

"That is absolutely gorgeous." She was already half way through her first slice.

"Thanks very much." Ben was confident lying with his torso exposed.

"The toast, you idiot." They were both laughing.

"That was quite a night. Thank you for staying over," Ben was getting more serious.

"The pleasure was all mine." She smiled the seductive smile that had led them upstairs last night.

"You're pretty good at all of this," Ben swept his free arm to indicate the rumpled bed sheets and their exposed bodies.

"Oh come on Ben, do not do the 'I expected a virgin' routine; you have been married and we are both in our forties."

"Have you ever been in a serious relationship?"

"Are you offering?"

"I'm just curious, that's all." He adjusted his pillows to get comfortable.

"If you must know; my first love was when I was eighteen. Gary, that was his name, he went backpacking and never came home. I took some time to get over that. Last I heard he was working on a farm in Bolivia. Settled down with a local girl; but that was literally years ago. He could be anywhere now."

"Farming in Bolivia; is that code for drug baron?" Ben teased.

She pulled a scrunched up face that is universally recognised as meaning 'you are so funny' when, in fact, the face puller is always thinking the exact opposite.

"Any more?"

"In my twenties I was seeing Clive."

"Seeing?"

"We went out for five years; my longest stretch."

"You make it sound like a prison sentence."

Bobbie lay down again to get comfortable. She wasn't laughing; she had a serious expression, looking into the middle distance vacantly. She continued to speak.

"He was an Estate Agent; doing really well apparently. The problem was he was using empty premises to cheat on me. He would take his other women to empty properties for a viewing; there were lots of women apparently. Most of the time would be spent in the bedroom."

"How did you find out?" Ben was genuinely interested.

"His boss became suspicious; his sales were down. He went from salesman of the year to one of the worst within months. His boss started checking which keys he was booking out and eventually followed him. Apparently it was quite a scene when he entered the bedroom just as Simon was entering 'whatever her name was.'"

"That couldn't have been nice."

"For me or his boss?" Bobbie was trying to lighten the mood. "I'm well over that now. My last significant other was Leroy."

"Are you OK talking about all this? We can stop if you want; but he does sound exotic." Ben opened his eyes wide in mock surprise, urging her to continue as he stroked her hair.

"I was on holiday in Barbados with a friend. Leroy was crewing a catamaran that we used one day; such a wonderful day. The Caribbean is so seductive. Anyway, one thing led to another and a holiday romance resulted. I just couldn't bear to leave him at the end of the holiday so I brought him home with me."

"Really, you did that?"

"He was so charming; I had my own place, my parents had given me one of the florists, they figured 'why not now? Why wait until they were gone?' I was lonely and vulnerable. He didn't like Spangle, was really nasty to him."

I'm beginning to warm to Leroy, Ben thought to himself.

"He helped out with the florist shop; doing the local deliveries. He turned out to be a real waster. A friend saw him leaving a woman's house and put two and two together. He admitted it all; didn't fight at all when I confronted him. He was on the first flight back to Barbados."

"You haven't had much luck with men in the past have you?"

"What about you?" Bobbie dodged the question.

"I was strictly a one girl sort of guy until the accident; apart from Jane, but that was too soon after..." Ben looked away, out of the window at the middle distance.

"I didn't mean to upset you, I'm sorry." Bobbie rolled over to cuddle him again. Her left hand tucked itself under Ben's body, coming to rest under the pillow.

"What's this?" she enquired, as she produced a paint brush which had been nestling there.

"Oh, it was Mary's; a bit silly of me really, but it calms me down. It is a comforter, a bit like a child's blanket. Just stroking the brush ends reminds me of her, busy at the easel; as if nothing ever happened."

"I didn't mean to intrude, but I can think of better things to do with it in the bedroom." Bobbie started to stroke Ben's body with the soft smooth hairs, slowly up and down his stomach.

"Relax, turn over." Ben complied obediently.

"Get up on your hands and knees" Bobbie was getting bossy; Ben was still compliant as he assumed the position. She examined the paintbrush while Ben was expectantly waiting for her next move. The handle end of the brush had a metallic fixture, like a palette knife, which was used for oil painting; a multifunctional tool that Mary had found very useful. Bobbie started to gently stroke Ben's buttocks with the brush end.

"Do you like that Ben?"

"It is very nice, relaxing in a tickly sort of way." His rapidly growing penis indicated that it was far more than that. Bobbie reached through his legs from behind and started to brushstroke it to greater lengths.

"That is amazing," Ben closed his eyes; he was concentrating on controlling himself. Bobbie brought the brush slowly up his thigh and back through his legs, carefully caressing all that dangled, until she was back toying with his buttocks.

"Do you like that?"

"Oh Yes." Bobbie reversed her grip on the paintbrush so as use the other end to delve into his crack. She was pulling one cheek to the side to get a better look when she slipped on the silk sheets. The metal palette knife stabbed Ben in his left cheek, drawing blood.

"What the ..." Ben was confused. How could something so erotic turn so painful so quickly? "That's dangerous, it's a lethal weapon."

"Sorry, sorry." Oh God, he has sussed me out, Bobbie thought. This sort of thing is always happening to me.

-.-

The sisters discussed their plans whenever they got a few minutes together during quiet moments. Katrina longed to escape the confines of the brothel, that's what it was; no need to dress it up with exotic descriptions. They had become 'ladies of the night', except most of their trade was during working hours. She couldn't wait to get out, anywhere. Anna, on the other hand, had settled into a routine of regular docile clients who were only too willing to be humiliated by her. She loved her dominatrix bodice; all patent leather and thong ties. She really enjoyed playing the part.

"We cannot stay here forever Anna, we are no better than slaves, kept animals. We need to get out, to have control of our lives."

"I have control." Anna's strikingly beautiful face was set in a defiant posture.

"Not of your own life." Katrina had a point and Anna knew it.

"If we are to escape, we need some insurance; something to protect us." Katrina was beginning to formulate a plan.

"What are you talking about?" Anna was struggling to understand her sister's train of thought.

"You know the password to his computer." Katrina's eyes had a sparkle that Anna had not seen for a while.

"But we don't know the password to his personal files," Anna was not willing to commit to any foolish illogical plans.

"We can worry about that later, we just copy the files and take them to the police if we need to." Katrina was excited and afraid in equal measures.

"What if he finds out?" The first real signs of interest and concern began to show on Anna's immaculate features.

"We run."

"I see you have really thought this through."

"Do you have a better plan?" Katrina was met with compliant silence from her sister.

Anna was always ready for Roman when he visited the brothel. Every Thursday without fail he would expect her to be waiting in the office in her costume, but it was he who would be the dominant one during the ensuing activities. Frank always opened up the office to allow her to set the mood for Roman.

How easy is this? She thought, as she searched for a memory stick in the desk draws. She wasn't very computer literate, just knew enough to get by. She booted up the computer to save time as she opened the bottom draw. It contained mundane office equipment, a stapler, a hole-punch, pens; she could have been in any corporate office. A small black memory stick was nestling in the corner, the type that opens like a flick knife. The screen came to life with a welcome message and then waited for the start up password. Anna punched in the mixture of numbers and letters she had seen many times before, from a lower angle, and waited for the screen to come to life. The familiar screensaver of a snowy landscape soon appeared. Anna became busy with the instructions Katrina had made her memorise. She inserted the memory stick in the USB port; So far so good. Her hand began to move the mouse to select 'computer'; and then 'removable disc.' She quickly copied the file to the Desktop. She hurriedly copied the file and pasted it into the 'removable disc.' Anna was waiting for the blue bar to move from left to right. It was taking too long. 58% complete, come on. She could hear Katrina talking loudly to Frank outside the door. That was the warning signal if things were going pear shaped. 70% complete.

It seemed to be taking forever. At last it reached 100%, the bar disappeared to indicate completion just as Frank walked in.

"The boss has just arrived; he will be here in two minutes. Don't disappoint him."

"I never do," Anna smiled seductively as she placed her body in front of the computer screen. Frank left the room, his work done. He felt uneasy in Anna's presence; she had that effect on most men; except the boss. She switched off the computer and left the room to be met by Katrina.

"Have you got it?"

"Yes, no problem." Anna waved the memory stick in her left hand.

"You did everything I told you to do?" Katrina's eyes were searching Anna's face for any sign of doubt. Just then Roman waltzed past the pair and opened his office door. He turned towards them as his hand prepared to turn the doorknob.

"Anna we have an appointment," he said with a nod of his head, requesting her presence in the office.

"Did you do everything as I instructed," persisted Katrina.

"Yes, I copied the files from the desktop," whispered Anna. Through the half opened door, the office was illuminated by the glare of the screen as Roman booted up his computer.

"Copied? You mean cut don't you. I said cut. Please tell me you haven't left the file on his desktop."

"Sorry, but it was definitely copied. Why didn't you do it yourself, you are much better at this stuff than me?"

"You had access to the office Anna. We have to go; now." Katrina's face was a picture of annoyance and fear. Roman was getting impatient.

"Anna, hurry up, don't keep me waiting." He shouted through the door. He just had to check his e-mails and then he could get down to business. He clicked on the icon for his mail and noticed the file name on his desktop just as the screen opened up his mail. He minimised the e-mail quickly to double check his desktop. There it was in the top right hand corner. His most incriminating file copied to his desktop. He opened it and was met by the encryption code request. Any IT geek worth his salt could break that given time.

"Anna, get in here now." This time he was shouting at the top of his voice. The sound of his hysterical voice was almost as loud as the breaking glass in the foyer.

The gap in the smashed window was just big enough for a petite female figure. Katrina enlarged it by removing all remaining glass shards with the chair leg.

"Jump." Katrina was animated.

"Are you crazy?" Anna had no intention of making a move. Katrina had already done the calculation; the fall to the roof of the parked van was twenty feet, two storeys. The van roof would soften the blow slightly, it was time to move. She pushed Anna through the window and watched her fall onto the roof and roll off in to the street. She followed in a more graceful manner ensuring her knees were tucked up on impact. She straddled the side of the van and lowered her legs to the floor to find Anna spread-eagled in the middle of the narrow back street. She checked her sister for any injuries. All she could think about was how Anna had changed, how she had lost her innocence, her youth; become harder.

"My ankle; I think I have sprained it."

"Try to run, come on. We need to go."

Roman manic face appeared raging in the frame of the broken window; his short blond hair illuminated by the light of the room behind him. It looked as if he had a halo, but the girls both knew that he was no angel.

"You fucking bitches." He face was contorted in rage.

Katrina pulled Anna to her feet and started to drag her along the street but her injury slowed them down; she was limping badly. Roman aimed his gun and pulled the trigger. It may have been a lucky shot; he may have been an expert marksman; the end result was a direct hit on Anna's only fully functioning leg. She collapsed in a heap of patent leather; bleeding profusely from a thigh wound.

"We are going to get out of this, get up Anna. Come on." Katrina was reluctant to leave her sister.

"Take the stick."

They were both shocked by the crunching sound of Roman landing two footed onto the roof of the van. He stood there smiling triumphantly. He knew he had wounded his prey. He knew that he had time. He ran his hand across his throat in a symbolic gesture of impending execution.

"Take the stick and go." Anna repeated. "He will forgive me." Anna's eyes were imploring her sister to go. Katrina reluctantly took the memory stick and started to run, leaving her sister on the ground. Anna's eyes never left her sister as gunshots once again filled the night air. She watched until Katrina dodged into an alley twenty yards ahead. She remembered happier times in Slovakia when they were young girls, days picnicking by the river, innocent times. Roman was giving chase, disappearing around the corner into the alley. Anna heard gunshots again, followed by cursing from Roman. She took this as a good sign. All Roman found in the alley was Katrina's coat draped over the barbed wire covered wall at the far end. He searched all of the pockets and found nothing. He returned casually to the static figure of Anna in the back street.

"Hello Anna, where is the file?" Roman had a distant sadistic smile on his handsome face. He smoothed his short blond hair back on his head, a self massaging action that he often did in times of stress. He produced a knife from his coat pocket; He was really tooled up, ready for any eventuality.

"I'll ask you again, where is the file?" Anna looked up into his eyes with the sultry smile that had seduced all of her clientele.

"She made me do it. I am sorry." She did her best pout and eye flutter. She was wasting her time. Roman pulled back her hair to expose a pale slender neck.

"Such a pity, we had some good times."

"We still can," Anna still hadn't given up.

"Where will your sister go, Anna?" Roman played the blade around the surface of her exposed neck.

"I don't know, and I wouldn't tell you if I did." Defiance was returning to Anna as she realised the futility of her situation. Roman's face was a mask of malevolence as he stared down into Anna eyes. The only change to his appearance came when the arterial spray from her neck covered his face, giving him the appearance of a geisha girl wearing vivid Japanese make up. He searched her clothes just in case she had the stick all along. It didn't take long, her flimsy costume having no pockets. He left her in the back street half light, a pool of blood growing ever larger around her head. No passport, no I.D., an untraceable illegal working girl meeting an untimely end. He was more interested in the whereabouts of her sister.

-.-

It had been the longest night of Tommy's young life. His body had been cramped up in its foetal position for hours before the porters had moved him from the corridor. The numbing pains in his knees were

118

unbearable. He had been surprised by his worm's eye view of the corridor from his knife-hole perspective. The late night revellers provided him with some early amusement as they enjoyed their last night on the ship, but once the ship became silent the wait for any action seemed to go on well into the night. Tommy was relieved when he heard the porters chattering away in their native tongue, getting nearer as they loaded the suitcases onto a trolley. He didn't care that his case was at the bottom of the pile, compressing his body; any change was a good thing in his world, such was the pain from his cramped situation inside the case.

Once off the ship his case was loaded in colour code inside the warehouse. All the blue labelled case sat neatly in a row to the left of the green ones. It took three hours for all of the cases to be loaded into the warehouse; three hours for Tommy to stay silent. Once the loading was complete the lights were switched off, turning the storage area into a dark dungeon. The only sound was an open window flapping in the wind. The sound of the window frame banging relentlessly every five seconds was enough to keep Tommy awake for what seemed like most of the night. He had lost all feeling in his legs, but thankfully he did eventually drift off into some kind of sleep, but only after faint light began filtering through the window in the early hours of the day. It had been a very long night. Tommy was woken by the sound of passengers searching for their cases.

"Sonia, it's the grey one; there, you can't miss it. There." A man was shouting.

"They all look the same to me."

"If you want something doing, do it yourself, I say," said the irate man as he struggled to pull his case from the 'Blue' section. Tommy could almost smell him, he was that close. The morning continued in a similar vein as what seemed like the whole ship scurried around the warehouse in search of their luggage, like a turn of the century scene on Ellis Island. Tommy was becoming really worried about the lack of any feeling in his legs; he tried unsuccessfully to move them. He was beginning to have a claustrophobic panic attack when he heard Freddie's voice.

"Well, if it isn't my very own ventriloquist's dummy," he said as he poked a finger into the knife wound in the case. "Wakey wakey."

"Just get me out of here will you."

"Not until we are out of the port area." With that Freddie began wheeling the case behind him, joining the queue of departing passengers snaking its way out of the main door.

-.-.-.-.-.-.-.-.-.-.-.-.-.-.-.-.-.-.-.-

Ben and Bobbie were back out biking. He needed some fresh air to clear his head, but was very aware of the delicate condition of his buttock. He rode out of the saddle as much as he could. The extra effort was taking its toll on his already aching body, so they stopped at Vale Park for a drink.

"These flowers are beautiful," Bobbie said as she took in the horticultural splendour of the well kept beds that straddled the pathway.

"Have a day off will you. The world is not all about flowers." teased Ben.

"But they are gorgeous, just look at the colours."

Ben chose a quiet corner next to the neat tables dotted around the patio area to perform his usual ritual locking together of the bikes. He turned to Bobbie to offer a drink.

"Hot or Cold?"

"Hot," she replied without hesitation

"Tea or coffee?"

"Coffee." She was getting rattled by the quick fire cross examination.

"Inside or outside?"

"What's with all the questions?" She had had enough.

"Just trying to please." Ben was smiling, enjoying being out with his new partner.

"Inside." She didn't want the chill in the air to affect her chest. Ben led the way to an empty table and ordered the drinks. They chatted away about the night before, in whispered tones, like young lovers.

"What are you going do now that you are retired? You must keep busy. Supply teaching perhaps? Maybe you could even do private tuition?" In her own mind

121

Bobbie thought that she was being demonstrative, but to Ben she was seemed rather pushy. Pro-active was the latest phrase.

"No I'm finished with all that. I used to love playing poker until Mary stopped it. She didn't like the hours." When the drinks arrived they both took a sip. Bobbie was looking over Ben shoulder at the flowers through the window, and Ben was looking over her shoulder at the paintings on the wall. They were both lost for a moment in their thoughts. She was planning on asking the park manger what the beautiful little purple flowers were. She should know what they are; being a florist, but their name escaped her for the moment. Ben thoughts were focussed on the painting on the wall; the only painting that Mary ever sold. She had been so proud of herself. The thought of Mary brought back visions of the black car, dark, wet street, neon lights reflecting, electric window rising, shaven head, the tattoo on the arm. What was it? A building and an animal; come on focus.

"Hello Ben, fancy seeing you here with another woman. I thought that you wanted your life back; that you weren't ready for a new relationship." The woman was standing too close, almost touching their table. Her eyes were cascading feelings of hurt and betrayal.

"Look, if you are seeing someone else then I am out of here. I will not fight over you." Bobbie's face was set in a confrontational mask. She wanted this strange woman to disappear, she was spoiling the moment.

"Jane, this is not the right place for this." Ben took a quick glance at Bobbie to assess the situation. "We were never right for each other; you have to let it go."

"I hope things work out for you, I really do," Jane whispered as she struggled to stay in control of her emotions before walking across the park towards the river.

"That was awkward," said Bobbie. "What was it all about?"

"Just a fling I had months ago. She was obviously keener than me. Simon told me it was too soon after the accident, and he was right. Anyway, you said yourself, this morning, that neither of us are virgins. We are both experienced people in our forties; we both have a past."

"I don't like surprises. Promise me she is a part of your past."

"She was not even that; I promise." Bobbie seemed to accept his account of events and brightened up. She watched the bunny boiler reach the railings that ran along the promenade; watched her consider the river.

"Wow, that is really impressive," said Bobbie in a genuine manner. Ben thought she was talking about the brass band playing in the domed platform, but couldn't resist a tease.

"They are just flowers," he said.

"No. The ship on the river; it is massive." She flicked her dark hair over her right shoulder. Ben loved her hair; he suspected she knew this, as she often did it for effect. They both went outside to get a better view as the ship docked across the river in Liverpool. It had bright red letters along its side announcing its name to the world; 'Armistice of the Waves.' Ben thought that Tommy would have enjoyed the sight; he loved ships. But Tommy was still missing, a kid on the run. They both fell into silence as they looked out over the river.

-.-

Freddie and Tommy were both enjoying crossing the river on the ferry boat. It felt so small, in comparison to the cruise ship, as it traversed across the red lettering. It couldn't compare in size or splendour, looking more like a tug than a ferry boat. The crossing gave them a chance to inspect the exterior of the cruise ship; they both stood, elbows on the rail, hunched over in awe at the ship right in front of them. Tommy had come full circle since his first sight of the ship; he was beginning to think that it had been a huge mistake, getting on board. Without the stupidity of his stowaway escapade he would never have met Freddie. They had done nothing but argue since the suitcase had been opened.

"I can't believe you went for breakfast before getting the case, I was in agony."

"A man has to eat, start the day on a full stomach." Freddie was enjoying the sea air in his face; enjoying the seagulls as they circled the ferry, looking for food.

"But my legs are still tingling; they have been cramped up all night. That can't be good for my circulation."

"You will be fine. Where do we go once we dock?"

"It's not far. We can walk." Tommy was preparing to join the other passengers as they huddled by the gangplank. The ferry was being moored by the attendants.

"I have four days before I am due back on the ship in Southampton. You can show me the sights." Freddie was in a playful mood. Tommy was beginning to relent; maybe he was being too hard on Freddie.

"Thanks for your help, Freddie. I can't wait to see my Dad."

-.-

DC Page pressed the remote locking device on his car in his designated parking place. He enjoyed having his name stencilled onto the tarmac; the nearest space to the Police Station doors. His snakeskin boots made their familiar echoing sound as he paced purposefully down the corridor to the open plan office. As he opened the swing doors he was met by the familiar sound of telephones ringing and animated conversations in full swing.

"Sir, I think you should see this." It was Barnes beckoning him towards the interview rooms. Through the viewing window Page watched Katrina rocking silently backwards and forwards in her chair; the memory stick concealed in her cupped hands which were joined, as if in prayer, on the desk in front of her.

"Get McNally in there. It's a female thing, get her calmed down."

125

"Yes Boss." Barnes scurried away into the busy office. Page grabbed a coffee while he considered the case. She was claiming a connection with a guy called Roman; probably Chavic, but that would need corroborating. Page was beginning to get excited at the prospect of finally having anything substantial on him. I've been after this bastard for years. Page nodded to McNally as he entered the interview room before sitting opposite the girl at the table. He started the recording device on the table, not the cumbersome tape recorder that he was used to, but a small sleek electronic device in a docking station.

Katrina was not thinking of herself. She did not consider the consequences of not having a passport; not having a visa, having no authorisation at all to be in the country. All she cared about was making Roman pay for killing Anna ; repay him for all the harm he had caused since they had first set eyes on him when the van was emptied of human contraband; He had to pay; justice must be done. She hated him with a passion she didn't think was possible.

"What is your name?" Page's voice echoed around the interview room, shocking Katrina out of her torment. He had to repeat himself to get a response.

"What is your name?"

She looked around the cold sterile room to gather her thoughts; to remember all of the details.

"Katrina. Katrina Weiss." The interview continued in a question and answer fashion, detailing every event since she had entered the country. Page pressed her on the details of Chavic's dealings, but she was more intent on her sister's murder.

"Did you actually see him kill her?"

"He shot her in the leg. I had to leave her, to escape."

Page was taken by her anguished honesty. He knew it was a weakness in his personality to have his head turned by pretty women, and Katrina was certainly pretty. He was finding it difficult to concentrate when her piercing blue eyes burned into his.

"Did you witness the murder?" Page persisted.

"I can show you the street; show you the house that we were kept in like animals. I remember where it is, I can show you." Page looked at McNally who was sitting with her back against the wall. He nodded slightly, which she took as a request to organise a search of the area indicated by Katrina. She left the room.

"Is this the man you know as Roman?" asked Page as he slid a photograph across the desk. Katrina recoiled in shock, unable to hide her fear and loathing of the man.

"That is him," she said in a lowered voice, her eyes closed in submission. Inside her mind all she had were feelings of hatred and vengeance. He will pay for what he has done.

"That is him," she whispered again in confirmation.

127

"You are a witness to the shooting, but not the final act." Page was reluctant to actually say killing, or knifing, such was his growing feelings of protective concern for Katrina.

"Once we build a case we will be calling you as a witness, but we need to gather evidence; Hard evidence. Are you sure you didn't see your sister...." Page's voice tailed off unable to put Katrina through any more anguish.

"I have the stick." Katrina whispered.

"Stick? Was there another weapon used at the scene?"

"The memory stick," she was fiddling with it in her hands, "It contains his business files." She placed it on the table next to the photograph. Page was a bit slow on the uptake.

"Are you telling me that this," he picked the stick up for effect, "contains incriminating evidence?" He was aware that the interview was still being recorded.

"Yes."

"Let the records show that a memory stick was produced by Miss Weiss." He held it up clearly so that it could be seen on the CCTV.

"McNally," he shouted. She entered the room as if she had been waiting for the call, almost as if her hand was already on the handle.

"Yes boss."

"Get our IT boys onto this, pronto." Once the interview was over Page had the opportunity to chat to Katrina in the corridor. He felt sorry for her, liked her.

"So you were working for him?"

"I was forced to. He is an animal." Page was excited by the prospect of finally nailing Roman; I might just have the bastard this time.

"What will you do?" He was genuinely concerned for her welfare.

"I have some money. I will find somewhere." Page rang around the homeless hostels to find a place. He was very helpful.

"You will have to report here on a regular basis, you are illegal after all. Once your witness status is complete you will have to make some difficult decisions. Strictly speaking; you are illegal, but a witness. You will be able to stay until a trial date is set; if this ever goes to court."

"It will. I will make sure of it." Her cold glare left nothing to the imagination. She meant every word. He rang a taxi for her and made sure she got in it. Once back in the office, it was business as usual.

"Get a search warrant for the Krem. Get some surveillance equipment installed; rules sometimes need to be broken."

Chapter 10

The Chapel of Rest was situated in the centre of the cemetery. It's warm sandstone structure contrasting sharply with the bleak bare winter trees that surrounded it. It looked warm and comforting, resembling an exclusive country retreat hotel. Parking was difficult, resulting in the circular road that surrounded the Chapel being packed with mourner's vehicles. A space had respectfully been left at the entrance for hearses. A service was being administered in the imaginatively named 'Room One'.

"Our death is not an end if we can live on in our children and the younger generation. For they are us, our bodies are only wilted leaves on the tree of life."

The female vicar was on auto pilot. Her wild unruly hair contrasted sharply with her white robed rotund body, giving her the appearance of a Demis Roussos tribute act. She had done this a hundred times; to much larger congregations. DI Page was the only person in the church. He was the only person in his mother's life. He wanted this to be private. He wanted it to be secret. Nobody knew her in life, why should anybody care now she was gone? He could still see her contorted face looking back accusingly at the foot of the stair every time his head touched his pillow at night. He wasn't getting much sleep, colleagues at the station thought that grief was taking its toll on him, but the truth was simple enough. It was guilt.

"Death is simply a shedding of the physical body like the butterfly shedding its cocoon. It is a transition to a higher state of consciousness where you continue to perceive, to understand, to laugh, and to be able to grow," Demis continued soullessly, only pausing to smooth the long hair protruding from her chin.

DI Page was standing during the reading. Head back, ramrod straight, eyes front. His black suit and tie were immaculate above his shoes; his shiny black shoes.

Next door in 'Room Two' it was standing room only. It was packed to the rafters with Simon's and Brie's entire world. Ben and Bobbie were in row three. The vicar started the proceedings

"Love is kind; it does not envy, it does not boast. It is not proud, it is not rude, it is not easily angered, and it keeps no record of wrongs. Love does not delight in evil, but rejoices in truth. It always protects, always trusts, always hopes, and always perseveres. Love never fails. And now these three remain: faith, hope and love, but the greatest of these is love." He paused and then continued.

"The first song of today's service is to be sung by a close family friend." Ben strolled purposefully into the aisle. He ensured he kept his head up all the way to the raised platform. He nervously looked around the room for supportive eyes; his face showing signs of emotion.

"I don't normally do this sort of thing, but this was Holly's favourite song, so here goes." Everyone in the room was willing him to do a good job. He began to sing acapella, his words resonating around the ornate rafters. The unaccompanied sound of his voice was crystal clear, a pure Tenor in perfect pitch.

"Is it a kind of a dream? Floating out of the tide,

Following the river of death downstream,

Oh, is it a dream?"

Ben's voice was truly inspirational. If it had been included in the film 'Shawshank Redemption,' instead of the female opera singer, it would have still bought the exercise yard to a standstill. He continued into the chorus.

"Bright eyes, burning like fire.

Bright eyes, how can you close and fail?

How can the light that burned so brightly

suddenly burn so pale? Bright eyes.'

At the end of the song, Ben returned to his seat in silence. The family members seated in the congregation nodding silent approval of his efforts, as Bobbie shuffled out of her seat to allow him back into the aisle, patting him gently on his thigh with unashamed pride. The vicar was back on his feet.

132

"And now Holly's father would like to say a few words." Simon walked resiliently to the dais to face the congregation. He looked past the seated throng; unwilling to catch a familiar eye. He had to keep it all together.

"Seven years is a short life, but it was all Holly had. In that time she demonstrated a love for life and for her parents, that knew no bounds. When I first saw her in the hospital when she was born, it was love at first sight. She was simple the best daughter anyone could wish for. Then again, I am biased, being her father. I say 'being', using the present tense, because in my heart she is still her; will always be here. Before I go I would like to read a letter that Holly gave me. She made me promise not to open it unless we were all here today. They are, if you will, her last words."

Simon reached into his inside pocket and withdrew an envelope and ripped it open. In the silent tension of the 'Chapel of Rest' the sound was dramatically shocking, magnified by the echoing effect that had been designed into the structure for acoustic purposes. Her handwriting was neat but child like, she had tried her best. He began to read.

"Goodbye Mummy. Goodbye Daddy."

Simon paused to swallow hard. The pale winter light was slanting through the stained glass window, highlighting his moist eyes. He was trying hard not to blink in case it started a torrent of tears. Brie had already blinked; her face was covered in a shiny membrane of tears as she let them silently fall. She was the unashamed picture of motherly grief. Simon continued reading.

"I know you wanted to save me, to make everything better, but it wasn't your fault. Please don't be sad. I always listened to the doctors. I knew it was my time to ride into the sunset.

All my love, Holly."

Half of the congregation were smiling at the cowboy reference, feeling her love for her father. Brie was still tearful, but comforted herself by rubbing her hands together. Simon arrived back from the front and hugged her. The vicar had replaced Simon at the dais, winding up for his finale.

"And they were bringing children to him that he might touch them, and the disciples rebuked them. But when Jesus saw it, he was indignant and said to them, "Let the children come to me; do not hinder them, for to such belongs the kingdom of God. Truly, I say to you, whoever does not receive the kingdom of God like a child shall not enter it." And he took them in his arms and blessed them, laying his hands on them."

Ben had switched off. The service had been emotional but he didn't need this religious hard sell. He knew the score, he knew it was a church, knew there was protocol to follow but it sounded too impersonal. He rubbed his fingers on the paintbrush in his breast pocket to calm himself down.

The sight of the velvet curtains closing on a small white coffin, while Elton John informed the congregation about the circle of life, was too much for the majority of the gathered local community. Two male mourners made that involuntary noise that only a man trying, and failing, to hold back tears can make. They quickly covered their faces with their hankies to conceal their feelings.

Katrina was standing, in the cold, a forlorn figure near the 'Chapel of Rest'. Next to her was a humble wooden cross stencilled with 'Anna' across the horizontal piece. She fondled rosary beads as she mumbled quietly to herself in Slovakian. If only we had stayed at home. If only we had never come to this terrible place, full of evil men. The guilt was eating her up. If only I hadn't persuaded Anna to come in the first place; none of this would have happened. If only we hadn't escaped. If only I hadn't pushed her out of the window. She blamed herself for everything that had happened since they were abducted off the safe streets of their home town. She was sobbing gently, her fingers moving involuntarily amongst the beads. The cold had turned her hands a pale icy blue. The words of the female vicar could be heard drifting out from the window of 'Room One.'

"Do not let your hearts be troubled. Trust in God; trust also in me. In my Father's house are many rooms; if it were not so, I would have told you. I am going there to prepare a place for you. And if I go and prepare a place for you, I will come back and take you to be with me that you also may be where I am."

DI Page also had a house with many rooms; too many rooms for one person. The congregation was beginning to spill out of 'Room Two', quickly disappearing into parked cars that slowly taxied through the cemetery until they could join the main road traffic. Ben and Bobbie waited respectfully until the grieving parents had entered their hired black sedan before following in Bobbie's VW Golf. Peter Page was left standing in the grounds; a solitary figure. He noticed Katrina and was torn between leaving and wandering over. He chose the second option.

"I'm sorry about you sister, so sad. What will you do now? Have you sorted out your accommodation?"

"The hostel is OK, for people like me. Maybe I will go back home to Slovakia, but there is nothing really there for me anymore." She didn't take her eyes off the small cross while she spoke. They stood there for what seemed an eternity, both not really wanting to leave, both not knowing what to say.

"I have a spare room."

Page's face was a picture of boyish bashfulness. He was looking down at the cross, wishing he had not spoken. How could I have been so stupid? He was embarrassed.

"I like your shoes." Katrina was struggling for conversation herself.

"They are going straight back into the wardrobe when I get home. I usually wear the snakeskin."

"But you suit black; they are nice," smiled Katrina.

"Come on. It is too cold to stand around here. I'll give you a lift."

"To the hostel?"

"No, we are going to my place. It is warm and I have plenty of food in." She didn't argue. She fell in with his stride pattern all the way to his parked car. She was glad to be out of the cold.

-.-

The winter light was streaming in through the conservatory windows, making it difficult to talk without squinting. Ben was pulling a peculiar face, his head tilted to one side to avoid the glare, as he conversed with Simon. Funeral receptions are never easy, especially when the loss of a child is involved; the child of your best friend makes it even more poignant.

"It was a fitting farewell, Simon. Your speech was really moving."

"Thanks for singing, really appreciate it." Simon replied, trying to change the subject. Making the speech had taken its toll on him emotionally.

"It was the least I could do." Ben squinted.

"It must be years since you sang in public." Simon was smiling, remembering their student days.

"I suppose you are referring to 'Walrus'," enquired Ben as he altered his stance with his back to the window, so that they were both looking into the room.

"That's better, I can see you now."

"Don't change the subject Ben; we were talking about 'Walrus'."

"I still stand by my assessment that we were that close to a record deal." Ben put his thumb and middle fingers millimetres apart as he spoke to emphasise his point.

"You had a great rock voice, still have, but the band; they couldn't play a note in tune." They were interrupted before Ben could respond.

"You didn't tell me you could sing Ben, quite a dark horse." Bobbie said as she arrived with a tray of bubbly. They both took a glass.

"To Holly," said Ben as they all raised their fluted glasses in the air. Simon noticed a photographer through the window, organising a wedding group in the garden; getting the bride's father to stand up straight. He couldn't help but think of Holly as a radiant bride; a scenario that was impossible given the circumstances, but a nice thought all the same. His thought pattern was broken by Bobbie teasing Ben.

"So, you kept 'Walrus' to yourself; I didn't know I was dating a rock star."

"We were huge on campus; I accept that outside the confines of that enclosed environment we may have been somewhat anonymous."

"Let's get the facts correct; you were not huge on campus. You had three forgettable gigs in the Student Union building that were received with lethargic apathy," Simon pointed out.

"You did very well today in the Chapel, I was proud of you," said Bobbie as she playfully stoked his cheek.

"I never thought that I would ever be a groupie." Bobbie was smiling, Ben decided that it was best to go along with the joke and smiled back. Simon was looking out of the window again.

Brie was circulating amongst her family, aware of Simon's position by the window; she kept one eye on him at all times as she accepted condolences from the small groups that had formed naturally on arrival at the function room. She eventually prised herself away to join her husband.

"Are you OK, you have that far away look on your face?" Brie had her hand on her husbands arm; a look of sympathetic concern on her face.

"I'm fine," replied Simon looking far from fine.

"It's just sad thinking of all the things Holly will miss out on. You know; an education, a marriage, a life." Simon's eyes were filling up. He had held himself together throughout the service but was now hovering on breaking point. Brie put a comforting arm around his shoulder.

"I know it is hard honey, but we will get through this together. I've been thinking, maybe we should set up a charity in Holly's name for Hospice funds," Brie had been toying with the idea for some time.

"That's a good idea, what should we call it?"

"That's a tough one. Have you any ideas on the subject Ben? Help us out here," Brie asked.

"It's difficult to think when you put me on the spot, but how about 'Lolly for Holly'?

Brie's disapproving look was enough to indicate that there were better choices out there. Simon picked up on the look before announcing. "Try again."

"I didn't mean that the money would be for Holly, it would obviously go to support the great work the Hospice does; it just rhymed, was a bit catchy." Ben stopped talking realising that he was digging a bigger hole for himself.

"What about 'Brookes aide'. Your surname is Brookes and you would be supplying aide."

"That's even worse, it sounds like a soap opera," Brie cut in.

"What about 'Bright Eyes Trust'" Bobbie offered. They all looked at her for clarification.

"Ben sang so beautifully at the Chapel, and the words of the song, you know, bright eyes, implies both hope and health."

'That is a really good idea Bobbie, I can have rubber wrist bands made up, organise some events; I'm even thinking of having Holly's name tattooed on my wrist," Brie was already making plans.

The afternoon drifted off into smaller and smaller groups offering sympathetic condolences to Brie and

Simon. Ben and Bobbie stayed long enough to be supportive but eventually made their excuses and left.

Even though it was only three o'clock, it had been a long emotional day. The short walk home in the crisp afternoon air lifted their spirits briefly.

"Have you any more secrets that I need to know about?" Bobbie asked light-heartedly as they turned into Ben road.

"Secrets?"

"The 'Walrus' thing."

Ben's mouth was open, ready to respond to her teasing, but remained frozen like an inflatable doll. He was distracted by the site of a young boy sitting on the wall outside of their house. It looked like Tommy from a distance. As they walked nearer, the realisation that it was Tommy grew with each step. Ben began to run and sound came out of his doll's mouth.

"Tommy, Tommy," he shouted.

Tommy was off the wall and running toward his father. They met in an embrace outside of Mrs Hargreaves at No 34, her net curtains twitching as she took in the scene.

"Where have you been all this time? I've been worried sick."

"I'll tell you all about it when we get inside."

"It's good to see you son, it really is, but what are you wearing." Ben asked as he noticed the cut off jeans and 'AC/DC Tour' T-shirt.

"Don't be having a go at my clothes; I hardly recognised you without the beard, you have smartened yourself up haven't you." Tommy was getting back into the banter with his father.

"That's probably on account of me," interrupted Bobbie by way of introduction as she caught up with the action.

"Tommy, this is Bobbie. We are seeing each other." Ben and Bobbie stood smiling at Tommy awaiting acceptance.

"Oh, this has happened a bit quick hasn't it? I'm not being rude; it's just a bit of a surprise, that's all. It is nice to meet you." Tommy put out his right hand for a formal handshake.

'It's nice to meet you too, Tommy," said a smiling Bobbie as she took his hand for a long extended moment.

"So, talk us through the T-shirt. I didn't know you were into heavy rock." Ben was back into parent mode.

"I borrowed it off Freddie."

"Who exactly is Freddie?" asked a concerned Ben.

"That would be me" answered the red frizzle cut as he appeared from behind the privet hedge outside of Ben's house ten yards away. His piercing green eyes accompanied a huge manic smile.

"Freddie Fungus; lost boy delivery service a speciality."

Chapter 11

"Where have you been? I've been worried sick." Ben said unable to keep the smile off of his face; a smile of joy, pure happiness at having Tommy home at last.

"It's a long story Dad."

"But how did you get out of the Care home? And where have you been all of this time?" Ben had so many questions to ask, not least wondering where the crazy looking Afro fitted into the picture. Tommy launched into an animated account of his adventure since escaping the home. He didn't mention his encounter with Derek or his night in the suitcase. He didn't want to upset his Dad; all that mattered was that he was home safely.

"And once we got off the ship we came straight here." Tommy finished excitedly.

"So that ship, the one docked across the river; you have just got off it?"

"That's right Dad, have you not been listening?"

"That must have been exciting. All's well that ends well," said Bobbie; realising that she must have sounded ridiculously bland.

"And where do you fit into all of this? Why are you still here?" Ben said looking directly at Freddie.

"Look, ever since Tommy barged into my cabin on board, I have tried to look after him. I could have called the authorities and had him removed; he would be back in care by now. But no, I felt sorry for him and helped him get home; a knight in shining armour, if you will. You have a lot to thank me for." Freddie stopped for breathe, looking as if he was to continue his diatribe, but Ben cut in.

"That's all very well, but don't you have to be back on the ship?"

"I'll take that as a 'thank you'; but no, I have four days off; I have to be in Southampton for the start of the next cruise. I was hoping you could show me the sights for a day or two. I've always wanted to see Liverpool." His green eyes were disarming.

"Can he stay Dad, can he? It's only a couple of days, what harm can it do?" Tommy was pleading; just like when he wanted an ice cream at six years of age. "Can he?"

Ben was pondering things. He would have to report Tommy's appearance to the authorities, do the right thing. If he ever wanted him home in an official capacity, he would have to play it straight; but not just yet. Maybe he would call the social worker tomorrow.

"OK, he can stay in the spare room; just a couple of days."

"I'll get the bedding changed," Bobbie enthused in a motherly fashion.

"I'm popping out for an hour, got some flowers to deliver. You three will be OK here won't you?" asked Ben.

"We will be fine, see you when you get back." Bobbie was already rummaging through the airing cupboard for fresh linen under the towels.

"You two make yourself at home," She said over her shoulder.

She was too late with the invitation. Freddie was already lying, feet up, on the settee; TV remote in hand.

"Any chance of a coffee?" he enquired as he surfed the channels.

The spare room in the attic wasn't really a room. Freddie wasn't too happy as he manoeuvred his suitcase into the small space. The attic conversion did not include a dormer window, consisting of a basic plastered attic with sloping walls, centre to outside. It had been partitioned off into two rooms, cells more like. Tommy had called it the 'nanny room' but no nanny worth her salt would accept sure basic living conditions. The headboard was positioned against the wall in the centre, the roof tapering down to the foot of the bed. Freddie would have to be careful not to bang his head when he woke up. There was a real danger that he might head butt the sloping ceiling and displace some roof tiles. If he ever had a desire to swing a cat this was not the place. Freddie wasn't impressed.

Ben had already completed the first delivery, a wedding anniversary. The wife had been delighted with the roses; the husband even happier in the hall behind her as he watched her receive them. A young boy wearing headphones walked into the road without looking. Ben rang the bell on his bike; the bell that he had fitted to the basket on the front since he had started helping out at the florist. How things have changed. The boy didn't hear the bell, couldn't with the headphones filling his ears with his choice of music. Ben had to swerve to avoid him. Kids, who would have them, he thought. Once the last delivery was done; a much sadder occasion; delivering a wreath, he stopped for a quick coffee, to consider the day's events. Tommy was home. That was marvellous, but he would have to report it. And who was Freddie, why was he hanging around?

"Lovely day," said the man sat at the next table. He was with a woman, probably his wife; both smiling like Moonie recruitment officers.

"Very nice," replied Ben. This was all the encouragement the stranger needed. He was off into a one-sided conversation that seemed to carry on for ever.

"We travel a lot; been all over the world. Last year we were in Australia, such a lovely country." There's that word again, thought Ben; Lovely. It was beginning to grate on him.

"We stayed with friends in Cairns for a month. They were so lovely."

Ben smiled back at the couple, wondering how he was going to escape. He needed peace and quiet to think things through; not this constant babble.

"Once you have paid for the air fare it is so cheap out there. We moved on to Sydney and stayed with people we once met on holiday; Mabel and Roger. They said 'any time you are in Sydney just pop in.' Well, they were so surprised to see us; in a good way we think. We stayed for two weeks and had a lovely time."

"Mary," said his wife.

"What are you saying dear?"

"It was Mary and Roger, nor Mabel."

"Whatever. They were perfectly lovely. Marvellous hosts."

Ben was getting rather frantic, feeling a bit trapped. He had to get away from the terrible twins.

"Nice meeting you, but I have to go." Said Ben as he stood up, scraping his chair on the floor.

"But we haven't told you about Borneo yet." objected the man; the man who had not introduced himself before telling his life story.

"Look, if I stay any longer, you will end up moving in for a month. Do you ever pay for accommodation? Or do you just bum your way around the world."

They both looked hurt. Maybe Ben had gone too far, but he had things on his mind. He was under a great deal of stress; pressure from a new relationship, even though things with Bobbie were good; pressure from Tommy arriving out of the blue with a red headed afro freak, and pressure from still being no nearer finding Mary's mystery hit and run driver.

"It has been lovely meeting you." He said as he left to unlock his bike.

-.-

Page was taking the last Morrison's bag out of the boot of his parked car, still trying to carry all of the shopping in one trip. He struggled to the door, trying to insert the front door key into the keyhole while still laden with bags. He eventually succeeded in entering the illuminated hall, walked past the stairs; past the place where his mother took her last breathe, and distributed the bags over the kitchen floor. Katrina continued to prepare vegetables on the work surface.

"Chicken breast with vegetables, is OK?" She asked without looking up.

"That's fine, I have got the shopping." Things were rather forced between them. He had expected her to be more grateful about his offer of accommodation, but she had remained stand-offish since she moved in. He didn't really expect her to share his bed, have a sexual relationship; even if she had been working in that field of business. He was being unreasonable, he knew that, but he expected a bit more friendliness from her. He was, he knew, taking a huge risk having a witness in one of his cases stay with him; but he couldn't help himself. There was nothing going on between them, even if Page wished there was. He was such a fool where women were concerned. They continued a stilted conversation while he put the shopping away. Her clipped accent showed no warmth.

"Have you had a good day?" Page enquired as he stretched across her to put the cereal into a cupboard.

"It has been OK in the house. I do housework," she replied as she moved slightly to her right to avoid any physical contact. Katrina reasoned that she was in the safest place as long as Roman was still free to search for her. He must know the police have the memory stick, but his type never give up on justice; justice in his world was to track her down and kill her; that much she knew. She was also determined to dump the hateful red stilettos.

"Any news on Roman?" she asked.

"You know I cannot discuss the case with you. All I can say is that we are continuing with our inquiries," replied Page. He was disappointed at the pace of those inquiries. The IT people were finding the memory stick a tough nut to crack, quite a sophisticated encryption system, and Roman himself had gone to ground, had disappeared without trace.

"Food is ready." Katrina was placing a large steaming bowl on the table. They sat at the kitchen table and ate in silence. Page had no idea that Katrina had a part time job at the most unlikely location.

-.-

Ben locked his bike in the garage and entered the kitchen from the garden. He could hear conversation and laughter from the front room, Tommy and Bobbie seemed to be getting on famously. She was making a real effort to bond with Tommy. Freddie was in full cry with a story while the others laughed along. Ben was on his way down the hall to join them when he had an urge to go into the back lounge; Mary's art room which had been left untouched since her passing. He needed to stroke her paint brushes for comfort after his uncharacteristic outburst at the coffee shop. He needed to remove the stress that had built up. He touched the bristles with his fingers and flicked his thumb across the top of the brush, allowing the bristles to lightly tickle his fingers as they cascaded from right to left. He was starting to feel better, feel her presence, when he noticed the canvas that he always left standing upright on the easel.

The virginal white surface, which had stood there untouched for so long, now had a vivid array of colour swathed across its surface. Bright, bold strokes indented with grooves where the brush had made it's signature. Ben had been waiting all this time, subconsciously, for some kind of sign from Mary, a message to say she was OK; a message from the grave.

"Mary, Mary." He was shouting, looking around the room, at the ceiling; half expecting her to be still in the room in some form. His arms stretched out horizontally in crucifixion mode as he rotated like a carousel.

"Tommy, Tommy; come and look at this." All three raced into the back lounge to see what the fuss was about.

"Look, look, it's a painting; a message from Mary. I knew she would find a way if I left her stuff out. What does it mean, can you make out any shape." Ben was hoping that maybe it was a copy of the tattoo on the arm from the hit and run, after all Mary had a closer look that he did.

"Do you like it?" asked Freddie.

"What do you mean, 'do I like it?' I think it is marvellous." Ben was beaming.

"Thanks."

"Thanks?" Ben didn't understand.

"Thanks for the compliment. I did it." Freddie was proud of his artistic endeavours.

"You did it?" Ben was furious; feeling foolish about his outburst about Mary being the creative force in the room.

"Well it was just there on the easel when I came in for a look. I've always fancied myself as an artist; can put my hand to anything really; so I had a go. Not bad is it?" Freddie was displaying his best smile. He was looking for praise; totally misreading the situation. "Yeah, I did it this morning. Just saw all the stuff, like, and thought I'd have a go. It's not bad for a first effort, even if I say so myself." Freddie was full of himself; he started doing an impersonation of a pretentious London art critic at a gallery opening.

"Love the use of colour, the bold striking lines. They are absolutely delicious, darling." Freddie's hands were sweeping dramatically around the canvas. "Turneresque in their intensity," Freddie was almost impressing himself with his art knowledge.

"Turner was predominately a seascape artist; he never produced a still life in his life." Ben was furious that Freddie had touched Mary's equipment, her shrine. "I forbid you to ever come in here again. It is private. Do you understand me?" Ben was livid, in part because of the intrusion into the study, but mainly because he had allowed himself to believe such a wildly improbable scenario. Freddie just looks at him. Tommy had seen the look before, on the ship.

"He won't do it again Dad. Will you Freddie?" Tommy's eyes pleaded with Freddie; willing him to calm down.

"No problem. I will stay in my room. Did I say room? It's more like a cupboard." Freddie was letting it go. He could see that maybe he had been a little insensitive, but couldn't resist criticising the accommodation.

"It's just not on." Ben was livid.

"Sorry dude, I didn't mean any harm. We could wash it off the canvas if you want; it is only watercolour after all." Freddie grabbed a cloth and approached the canvas on the easel in a business-like manner.

"Don't touch it," Ben was still livid. He stepped forward to block Freddie's advance and accidentally knocked the canvas off the supporting easel. It seemed to take forever to hit the floor, spinning almost in slow motion; everybody was frozen in expectation; waiting for the inevitably impact. It smashed into the laminate flooring, filling the room with splintering noises. The frame was not as strong as Ben expected, losing its shape on impact. The original rectangular form changing into what Tommy's mathematical mind correctly identified as a misshapen rhomboid as it bounced twice. The backing tape came away at one of the corners to reveal the small cavity behind the canvas.

Looking at it on the floor, Ben hated the result of Freddie's work even more than when it was displayed on the easel. He picked it up, tapping the frame gently in an attempted to tease it back into its original shape. It rattled in time with his taps. Ben did it again to check that he wasn't imagining the noise. He tapped out a bit of Morse code that he had learnt in the Scouts, the frame reverberated an echoed response in perfect time, almost like a harmony duo. Ben removed the backing tape to reveal a mobile phone and a key nestling in the bottom corner; like trapeze artists that had landed into the comfort of their safety net.

"Ok, the show is over, you two go and grab some lunch," Ben wasn't in the mood for a discussion. Tommy ushered Freddie out of the room. They were both more than happy to leave Ben alone. Ben switched the phone on, a cheap serviceable model; no internet connection, just a standard phone. He checked the

154

contacts; none. He checked the 'in box' for texts; none. He ran out of things to check being a technophobe at heart. He forced himself to think straight; the phone obviously belonged to Mary, but she already had a phone, and why were there no contacts or text messages. He suddenly had the brainwave to ring his own number, punching in the digits as quickly as his panic would allow. His phone rang in his pocket; the screen displayed an unknown number. He was pleased that he had identified the number and the fact that it was still operational, but what good was that really? He could ring the provider and ask for contract details, past history of calls, but probably would run into confidentiality issues; it wasn't his phone after all. It obviously still had credit; or was it a contract phone, but that was unlikely as no standing orders were on the bank statements. What if Mary had a secret account; Ben's mind was racing.

What about the key? What was that for? Could it be a safety deposit box? Ben thought he had been watching too many spy films; but it had to be for something. He would have to enquire at Mary's old bank, check any holdings she had; he was the sole beneficiary from the will and had power of attorney over her estate. The bank should be no problem, but what was Mary thinking? They never had secrets from each other.

-.-

"We need to talk Tommy." Ben summoned his son to the kitchen with a nod of his head.

"I know what you are thinking Dad, but Freddie is OK; he helped me."

"Anyone who comes into our home as a guest and then behaves so appallingly, touching stuff he has no right to; I have issues with that."

"It won't happen again, I promise." Tommy was desperate to calm the situation, to change the subject.

"Bobbie seems nice; where did you meet her."

"Don't change the subject."

"Does she know that you play poker?" asked Tommy

"I haven't played for a while, but am going to get back into it." Ben's face relaxed as his mind turned to the world of the green felt tables.

"You were never that good at it anyway." Tommy teased.

"I could always read a player, pick up body language, sense when they had a hand." In his mind Ben was back at the tables, studying his opponents for any information they were willing to divulge.

"But the maths was a bit above your head Dad, you know, odds and probabilities. I am better than you at that stuff." Tommy was correct with his analysis.

"But you are too young to play. I rang Rob about the possibility of a game; he has invited me to a game tonight." Ben couldn't conceal his excitement at the prospect being seated at a poker table.

156

"What about the phone and key that was hidden in the picture frame?"

"There is nothing we can do tonight; I will enquire about the key at the bank tomorrow. Just have a word with Freddie will you, make sure he behaves himself in my house."

Chapter 12

'The Kreme de la Kreme' was a strange looking building nestling as it did between rows of neat semi-detached houses in a sleepy suburban road. White walled from top to bottom with the club name emblazoned across the front of the building in blue lettering. Local residents were amazed that it continued to get its license renewed every year; but it always did, despite numerous petitions and objections from the disgruntled neighbours. A gentlemen's club to all intent and purposes, but sometimes some unofficial activities took place there. Tonight was such an occasion; tonight Rob Garrison had organised a poker game, had invited all the usual suspects to bring their stashes for the biggest game to take place for a while. Inside, the club oozed its usual dark subdued ambiance. The recent police raid, led by DI Page proudly holding a search warrant, had found nothing or, more to the point, found no trace of Roman Chavic. It had, however, set up streaming of the CCTV cameras, enabling illegal surveillance of all interior cameras. If Chavic showed his face in his club DI Page would soon know about it.

-.-.-.-.-.-.-.-.-.-.-.-.-.-.-.-.-.-.-.-

Ben was nervous as he sat in the back of the taxi. Rob had said some regulars would be there accompanied by some big hitters. He had brought three thousand pounds from his severance pay out; he hoped he would not have to use all of it; he needed to get a good start and stay ahead. Once inside the Krem, he was ushered towards a tray of welcome drinks. He took a Diet Coke and joined a small group and proceeded to make small talk with two players that he vaguely knew. Khan, the owner of three local oriental restaurants, regularly donated a proportion of his profits into the poker world; Ben had never seen him win. Cocoa was also there. He ran a local security firm, protecting property from, well, from himself really. He ran a thinly disguised protection racket which stayed just the right side of legality. He was a good player.

"Good evening gentlemen. May I invite you to the table? The stakes are one thousand pounds minimum buy in, blinds of five and ten pounds." Rob announced as he held the door to the private back room open. Inside the green felt table was illuminated by a bright spotlight positioned directly above. The dealer had stacks of chips of all values neatly displayed in front of him. The players began taking their seats; Ben made a point of sitting to the right of Cocoa for tactical reasons.

"How much sir," the dealer asked.

"A thousand," replied Ben. A stack of different coloured chips was pushed in front of him. He went through his ritual of checking every one of them.

"Reds are a hundred?"

159

"Yes sir."

"Give me two thousand." Cocoa had come to play. His name didn't refer to any ethnicity or skin colour, but to his fondness of drinking hot cocoa. The table started to fill up with the other players, a younger crowd than Ben remembered.

-.-.-.-.-.-.-.-.-.-.-.-.-.-.-.-.-.-.-.-

"What have we here?" Page was talking aloud in front of his computer watching the footage from the Krem.

"Looks like a poker game sir."

"I know that Barnes, but who have we here? It's like a Who's Who's of local movers and shakers. Cocoa, Khan, Flanagan, Potter..." Page stopped talking as the camera slowly scanned the table.

"Go back; to the left." Page moved closer to the screen to get a better look.

"We have no control of the camera's movement, sir. We are just hooked into it, like voyeurs."

The camera swept slowly back to the left as if it had heard Page's request. What is he doing there? Page thought as he studied Ben's profile. I always knew there was something dodgy about him. Why had he suddenly appeared on the scene with Bobbie after our date had gone so well? Didn't take him long to get over his wife. He was always a suspect in her death; family and loved ones were always the first line of enquiry; but he was inside the restaurant when his wife was hit. We really pushed him on the case, even considered the possibility that he had hired a hit man, but in the end he was clean. He was also cautioned about the recent dogging incident; there was something Page didn't like about him, and here he was again, sat with known criminals at a private poker game. I'm watching you Thomas, I'm watching you.

The last chair to be filled was still empty opposite Ben. A side door opened to reveal two heavily muscled men who proceeded to check out the room and the players for any weapons, before allowing the final player to enter the room. He was a tall blond attractive man immaculately dressed in a dark suit. He sat in his allocated seat, swept back his neatly cropped blond hair with both hands and requested five thousand. He was here to bully people, something that he was very good at.

"I am here to ensure that we have a smooth friendly game; any disagreement will be settled by the rules. My word is final. Deal the first hand please" Rob announced the start of the game as he backed away into the shadows.

. -.-.-.-.-.-.-.-.-.-.-.-.-.-.-.-.-.-.-.-

"I'm going to show Freddie the sights, the usual tourist stuff," said Tommy as he jumped up and down on the spot. He was trying to act grown up but was failing lamentably.

"I want to do The Beatles tour," said Freddie, he hadn't been this excited since he was a young boy.

"You haven't eaten. Let my rustle something up for you," fussed Bobbie.

"We'll get something when we are out," replied Tommy as he took the money off the mantel place, where his father had left it for him. "Oh, no."

"What is it Tommy. What's wrong," asked Bobbie in a worried motherly manner.

"The angel is still here."

Freddie thought that some kind of spooky thing was going on again. The dead mother, the painting; things were a bit weird around this house.

"What are you talking about?" Bobbie was starting to get worried herself.

"Dad's glass angel is still here, on the mantel place. It is his lucky charm. He never wins if he hasn't got it with him at the poker table. He always places it on top of his chips."

"I thought it was all about maths and probability." Freddie always had to make a point.

"It's just routine, superstition; but I think my Dad will miss it."

"I can drive. Where is the game" Bobbie offered.

"The Krem."

"We can be there in ten minutes," she was already picking up her car keys.

"I will sit in the back," said Freddie as they scampered to the car.

"Where are you going now Tommy?" asked Bobbie as he turned to run back to the front door.

"No point in going without the angel is there? It's still on the mantle place."

. -.-

The game had started slowly. Ben hadn't really got involved, had folded most hands. He was intent on watching people's betting patterns. The only pattern from the blond Russian was to raise every hand.

"Raise to fifty," he was at it again. Everybody folded again.

"What is the matter, why does nobody want to play with me? Are you all pussies?" Roman was goading the table, trying to get some action. Ben turned up the top left hand corners of his two hole cards, a routine he always went through. It was better to act exactly the same with every hand. Two black ladies stared back at him. He stroked the brushes of the paintbrush in this breast pocket where they protruded slightly like a dress handkerchief. He had a feeling that it would bring him more luck that the glass angel. He called the ten pounds convinced that the Russian would put in a raise again. Cocoa was next to act and was considering getting involved in the hand. He was singing under his breathe.

"I believe in miracles...you sexy thing." Cocoa was singing Hot Chocolate without a hint of irony. "Fold"

163

he said eventually as he tossed his cards towards the dealer.

"Raise to fifty," Roman said for the eighth time since the game began. He planned to keep up the aggression until somebody stood up to him. Ben considered re-raising but decided to see a flop; a flop he hoped would not include an Ace or King.

"Call," Ben tossed the extra four chips into the pot; each of the green chips representing ten pounds.

The dealer placed the three cards face up on the table. It was a dangerous flop; The Ace and King of Spades accompanied by the lovely queen of diamonds. Ben wondered if the Russian could really have Jack ten, or even pockets aces or kings. It was very unlikely, but possible.

"Check," Ben wanted to trap him.

"Eighty." Roman had not had anybody get involved in a big pot; he wasn't in the mood to slow down. Ben was getting an uneasy feeling that maybe his queens were losing; there were plenty of hands that could have him beaten. It was one of those hands were he was miles ahead or miles behind.

"Call."

The turn card was the seven of spades. If the Russian was on a flush draw, he just got there. Roman was getting nervous, straightening his hair with his hands, giving enough signals for Ben to believe that he was ahead. He could, of course, be acting.

"Three hundred." Roman tossed three reds in a small arc. All the players watched them splash into the pot.

"Call," Ben was committed to his hand. He slid his chips silently across the line on the felt. He checked his cards again, something that he didn't usually do, maybe it would look weak. The queen of spades looked back at him. Dark hair and jet black eyes, just like all the cocktail waitresses in The Krem. Real or wigs they were all dark haired lovelies, just like his dead wife. He could see Mary's dark eyes looking at him and had to blink, to focus. Mary made a metamorphic change back into the queen of spades; how he loved her, how he misses her.

"All in."

The dealer had placed the river card on the table while Ben was drifting. It was a harmless red four which had produced the ultimate response from Roman, who now sat smiling at Ben.

"Have you got the balls to call that?" Roman was a snarling pit bull.

The regulars at the table all knew that Ben was strange, had a flawed history, wife died, hadn't played for a while; but he was a respected player. He had to fold, there were too many monster hands possible. Ben was thinking. Come on, compose yourself. You have trip queens. Roman had a confident smile, the smile of someone who always gets what he wants, a killer smile. I'm losing, I know I am. But I have put four hundred and thirty into this hand. A hand that involved Mary;

OK that might have just been my mind playing tricks, but it felt real. I play by feel. He stroked the bristles on the brush in his breast pocket again for encouragement. I have a hand. Against all the mathematical and probability theory that Tommy had reiterated in an endless mantra, Ben found himself going on instinct and with Mary.

"Call." Ben heard himself say as he slid all of his remaining chips into the middle.

Ben tossed his queens face up onto the table, he wasn't into waiting games.

"Can you beat that?"

Roman mucked his cards and the dealer swept the chips towards Ben. A thunderous look of hatred that came from deep within his dark soul clouded Roman's face.

"You think you can fuck with me?"

Ben ignored him and stacked his chips into neat colour co-ordinated piles; both of his hands fishing out the red ones to begin the structure. Ben was relieved that he had won the hand; all logic suggested that he was lost.

"Ace King?" asked Ben. "Or were you just bluffing?"

"How can you call that?" thundered Roman.

"I was just playing my hand." Ben was still stacking chips.

"The games has just started my friend, it is just warming up. It will be a long night before you take those chips home." Roman nodded towards Ben's chip stack as he removed his jacket and placed it on the back of his chair.

"Let's play. Next hand," He snapped as he began rolling up his shirt sleeves. It took a few second for Ben to notice the tattoo on Roman's right forearm. It was a tattoo of a camel standing in front of The Pyramids.

. ‾.‾-

Bobbie had parked the car in a side street and they were all at the main door of The Krem. The girl on the reception desk was talking on the phone.

"I know; what a cheek. She has only known him for a week." She was twiddling with her hair as she noticed the trio in front of her. She twitched her head forward while holding an outstretched hand towards Freddie; silently asking for a membership card to swipe through the electronic system that would open the entrance door.

"We are not members. We need to get inside." Freddie gave her his best smile.

"Gotta go; speak to you soon," the brunette reception said, as she hung up. "You need to fill out this membership form. Have you any ID on you?" she was back in business mode as she slid the paperwork across the counter. Freddie began filling in the boxes on the form with the pen she had slid towards him along the desk; it had the cheap company logo emblazoned down the side.

"It's best that I go in. You are too young Tommy, and you are not a gentleman," Freddie smiled towards Bobbie as he continued to write. "It is a gentleman's club after all." He turned his attention to the receptionist. "Driving Licence OK?"

"That's fine sir, just sign and date the bottom section." She busied herself on her computer, eventually producing a plastic card with the garish club logo proudly announcing itself across the top.

"That will be twenty pounds."

"Twenty pounds?" Freddie was indignant at the sudden cost of being a Good Samaritan.

"This entitles you to full annual membership and a welcome drink. Single not double." She was on auto pilot. Freddie was considering arguing about the charge, but the receptionist had still not handed the card over.

"There you go," Bobbie said as she placed a twenty pound note on the counter. The girl swiped the card producing an electronic beep from the machine and a small click from the door.

"Welcome to the club, sir."

"I'll be out in five minutes," said Freddie as he opened the door.

"Freddie, you'll need this," said Tommy producing the angel from his pocket.

"Good luck," said Bobbie.

"I don't need luck, what can possibly go wrong?" Freddie said over his shoulder as he disappeared into the club; the door clicking shut behind him.

. ⁻.⁻

"OK, we have all the exits covered; there is no way Chavic can leave without being picked up. We will just wait him out, keep watching the screen."

"Why don't we just go in sir and arrest him?" Barnes suggested.

"A search warrant takes time, and we have only just done the club last week. The camera link was a punt on my part. but anything we have would be inadmissible in court, not to say illegal. He can't stay there forever; we will monitor his movements and pick him up when he leaves. Keep watching."

. ⁻.⁻

Ben was still on a high from winning a big hand, but the tattoo in front of him was bugging him. The pyramids could, if he scrunched his eyes, look like a building; a Dutch farmhouse. The camel obviously was an animal. Could this really be the arm that disappeared behind the electronic window on that rainy night? The night Mary was killed. Ben studied Roman, studied his face; the look that he must have had on his face when Mary lay dying, wedged beneath his BMW. The look that indicated 'how do I get this piece of shit off my car?' How could he drive away and leave her to die in the gutter. She did make it to hospital, to die on a cold slab in front of inexperienced staff .They couldn't have saved her at the top of their game, no-one could have.

"It's on you sir," the dealer said to Ben, who hadn't even looked at his cards. He folded them without a glance. He was too distracted to play.

"Not playing? Now you have won a hand?" Roman goaded. Ben body felt like ice. He was hot and cold simultaneously; in shock. He had to confront this Russian, but he owned the club, had minders watching from the back of the room. He decided to play on and hurt him with the cards. He could identify him to the Police later. Ben had a plan but his emotions could not allow him to follow the sensible course of action.

"Been to Egypt, have you?" asked Ben aggressively.

"No, I just like camels," Roman joked. "Raise to fifty."

The table folded in a clockwise direction until it was Ben's turn. He wanted to dive across the table and throttle Roman such was his intense hatred for him, but Ben had no physical prowess, Roman looked like he could handle himself without the assistance of his minders, and the situation was too public. He needed to calm down; calm down and follow his plan.

"Re-raise to one hundred and twenty," Ben heard himself say. He had never played this way before, especially with 'queen four off suit.' Some players go on tilt because they are losing, or running into incredible bad luck. Ben was steaming as a result of pure hatred.

"You think you can bully me? You think I will back down to you?" Roman was losing it.

"How is your BMW? Running OK?" Ben was pushing buttons he didn't know existed.

"All in." Roman pushed all of his chips forward. He started with five thousand, had lost a thousand when Ben doubled up; so he still had Ben covered. It would cost Ben all of his two thousand to make the call.

"Call," Ben said rather too quickly. This was no longer a poker game, it was personal.

"On your backs." the dealer requested both players. Roman showed a suited Ace King, Ben defiantly showed his Queen four. The other players were shocked at Ben's hand, at how weak it was.

"They're both live," said one of the young Asian players. The flop and turn produced nothing of significance but when a red four appeared on the river Roman exploded with rage.

"You call me with that shit. What is going on here?" All the other players kept their heads down, watching Ben stacking chips.

"I am talking to you," Roman was in Ben's face across the table. Ben continued to stack his chips and didn't see Chavic grab him by the lapels and drag him across the table, spraying chips everywhere. The first punch broke Ben's left cheek bone and was enough for him to almost lose consciousness. The ensuing beating that the assembled players had to witness was unnecessary from a competitive point of view; Ben lay

171

lifeless on the floor as Roman proceeded to kick him relentlessly. The others players looked away, shocked at the severity of the attack. The paintbrush that was supposed to bring him luck flew from Ben's breast pocket and slid across the floor, settling at the feet of the blonde cocktail waitress. Ben lay motionless on the floor. His cheek bone was dislocated and both eyes were closing rapidly.

"Let's play" commanded Roman as if nothing abnormal had taken place. The others meekly sat waiting for the next hand.

. -.-

Page sat staring at the screen, thinking. Thomas has got what he deserves. It is a case of 'wrong place, wrong time'. He is the least of my worries, it is Chavic I am after.

PC McNally was watching events with an ever growing sense of unease. Her skills with the camcorder at the dogging arrest had come in useful, enabling her to set up a simultaneous copy of the streaming coming from the 'Krem' CCTV system.

"He looks pretty bad sir, should we call an ambulance or go in."

"No. Keep watching. We will have Chavic when he leaves."

Chapter 13

Freddie scanned the room to get his bearings. The bar to his left was busy with men holding ten pound notes above their heads to attract the attention of the barmaids.

"Two pints of lager, love," a young shaven headed punter attempted to jump the queue. Nothing new there thought Freddie; it's the same the world over. The music was loud; The B-52's banging on about the love shack while a dozen girls gyrated on the small dance floor. The men stood on the side watching, waiting for their drinks to be delivered by their mates. It could have been any club in the country such was the clichéd scenario. Freddie was looking for a poker game, a private room. The well dressed tall man standing on guard by a side door gave the game away. Freddie was no private detective, but it was glaringly obvious to anybody with a brain. He approached the guard with authority.

"I'm her for the poker; invitation from Rob."

"Name?" The guard produced a card from his inside pocket.

"Freddie."

"There's no Freddie on the list," he replied without looking up from the card.

"I'm more of a delivery boy than a poker player. I need to see Ben Thomas to give him this angel." Freddie flashed his best smile, holding up the glass cube with the angel hologram inside.

"You're not on the list." The guard's voice hardened as he put a restraining hand on Freddie's shoulder.

"Look, it is his lucky charm. Give me a break. I'll be in and out in two seconds."

"Have you not been listening mate? You are not on the list, end of." His final rebuke was accompanied by a gentle push, a show of strength to bring the exchange to a close. Freddie took a step back to ride the impact and then stood thinking with a vacant look on his face. Why doesn't he just let me in? What harm can it do?

"Are you sure I am not on the list?" asked Freddie. As soon as the guard looked down towards the card Freddie crashed the corner of the glass angel into his face, sending him staggering backwards. Freddie opened the door and strode in.

"Freddie Fungus, lucky charm delivery service a speciality," he beamed. The scene that welcomed him was not what he expected. There was a poker game in progress, the chips were scattered over the floor, but where was Ben?

"Who the fuck are you?" snarled Roman as he stood, holding up a retraining hand to his two minders, who had started towards Freddie. They stepped back to their

174

position against the wall. Freddie finally noticed Ben motionless on the floor behind the tall shaven headed figure of Roman Chavic. Freddie was confused. Ben looked in a bad way. What had been going on in here? He obviously was in need of some luck and medical attention.

"I said who the fuck are you." Roman was standing face to face with Freddie in intimidating fashion. Freddie noticed the clenched fists of Roman, ready for action; clenched fists with grazed knuckles; fresh blood. Again, Freddie's powers of deduction reasoned that this was as a result of a fracas with Ben. Freddie had the angel in his left hand, one of the corners of the glass cube bloodied. His right hand was in his pocket tightly clasped to the handle of the knife that he always carried.

"I do believe that I announced myself on entry. I am not in the habit of repeating myself," Freddie was ready for the inevitable confrontation, was almost encouraging it.

"Think you are funny? Do you?"

"Well yes I do. I almost consider myself to be hysterical."

Roman was still on a high from Ben's beating. He was more than willing to continue inflicting pain on the slight framed red headed freak in front of him. He swung his right hand in a wide arc, aiming for Freddie's left temple; Freddie ducked slightly and countered with a glancing blow with his knife across Roman's bicep. It

175

was a flesh wound, but a deep flesh wound. Blood began to flow down his arm, down between the pyramids, along the hind legs of the camel, between Roman's clenched fingers. Finally the blood dripped off the knife in his hand, onto the floor.

"You have just made a big mistake my friend," Roman said with certainty. He was an accomplished knife fighter; he had never met anyone better. Freddie wasn't intimidated by Roman; now that he had his knife he was also at home. Coincidence had conspired to have the two best knife fighters in the country confront each other. Sky Sports would have paid a fortune for the exclusive rights; the ultimate 'pay per view.'

Roman had switched his knife to his left hand because of his injured bicep. Both men began circling each other. All on lookers stayed in their seats, the minders waiting instructions from Roman. He didn't need any assistance; he was Roman Chavic. They continued to circle.

"So, you know this guy?" Roman nodded towards Ben's motionless body, trying to distract Freddie. Freddie didn't answer. He kept his eyes on Roman; his piercing green eyes staying locked on Roman's ice blue counterparts. In his mind, Roman was back on the streets of Kiev gaining a ferocious reputation for violence, back in Anton's bed waiting for a chance to finish their relationship with his blade in the dead of night. He knew the moves to make but his injury was slightly disabling. They both tried a quick stab forward but both efforts were easily dodged. Freddie was also in the zone; this wasn't his usual stalk and kill strategy, more a confrontation; a very public confrontation. I am defending myself surely? Freddie reasoned with himself. This is self defence. The situation appeared to be something of a standoff until they both lunged forward at the same time, torsos colliding, as if they had 'gone into hold' during a ballroom dance; right hand gently resting on their partner's left shoulder.

The only difference was that they both had a knife lodged in their respective ribcages. They stayed in hold, faces close together, breathing heavily. They both realised that they were impaled; both were assessing the extent of the damage. Could they breathe properly? Where their lungs damaged? In their close proximity Roman had flash backs to his younger days. Days spent with Anton, nights in his bed, before he killed him. He had an overwhelming urge to kiss Freddie. No, no. I am not gay. He was struggling to shake the impulse from his brain. Freddie was enjoying the dance, another chance to feed his frenzy. He was concerned about how public it all was but he was defending himself, surely. Freddie sensed Roman's weakness and withdrew his blade to inflict further injury. Two more quick stabs sent Roman reeling backwards across the room to land on his back at the feet of the blonde waitress. She bent to assist him but he pushed her away. The movement sent blood cascading across the magnolia wall, and him back onto the floor where he stayed motionless. Freddie walked over to the prone body to check that Roman was truly incapacitated before coming back to Ben.

"Looks like you need this," he said as he placed the angel into Ben's pocket. "Come on, we are getting out of here," he continued as he attempted to drag Ben to his feet.

-.-

"Sir, we have no choice. We have to go in." McNally was insistent. They had all watched the last few minutes' action from 'The Krem' with increasing incredulity.

"OK, OK. Go in." Page gave the order, but only after he had made an anonymous noise complaint about 'The Krem' from an untraceable mobile he kept for such purposes.

The police had the emergency exit into the small car park covered as the main door was crashed by three helmeted officers wielding batons. The receptionist buzzed them through once their warrant cards had been flashed.

"Cut the music," the lead officer ordered. The club seemed surreal without the sound of music pounding out an incessant rhythm. The dance floor slowly emptied as revellers realised that something serious was happening. The house lights came on, the normal signal to get your coat or go for the girl. What was going on?

"Is it a bomb scare? A hoax?" a girl enquired of her scantily dressed friend.

"Move along, move along." The police were taking control.

"To where?" The drink fuelled youths were beginning to get agitated. Freddie appeared from the side room dragging the semi conscious body of Ben. He was sweating profusely from the pain and effort. He noticed the heavy police presence, checked all exits with a quick darting glance. There was no way of getting out of the club. Freddie knew the game was up so let gravity assist Ben in finding a comfortable position on the floor. Once free, Freddie raised both arms in submission. It did not take the police long to get the two injured parties into a police van and take them to the hospital. Roman was put into a different vehicle bound for the morgue.

-.-

"Oh my God; that was your Dad they just put into the police van. The other body has to be Freddie, the red hair was unmistakeable. What is going on?" Bobbie was in a real frenzy. It was only five minutes since Freddie had walked into the club, a bone fide membership card in his hand; and now they have both come out horizontally, looking the worst for wear.

"We'll have to follow them." Tommy was being logical, but he was worried for his Dad and for Freddie. Bobbie was quickly into the flow of traffic, her Golf overtaking any cars that got in her way. She caught the police van up on the motorway and stayed behind it all the way to the hospital, trailing in the glare of the flashing blue lights. Once there, the problem was parking. The police van had stopped at the main door and both bodies were already being carried into A&E;

179

Bobbie had to park the car; not an easy task in the overpopulated expanse of tarmac that confronted her. Finding an empty space was similar to spotting a leopard on the Serengeti Plain.

"You go Tommy. I'll catch you up. You have my number." He didn't need asking twice; he was out of the passenger seat and racing towards the hospital door in record time. Bobbie started her second lap of the car park hoping that somebody would leave and vacate a space.

"Two men have just been brought in by the police. Where did they go?" Tommy was at the Triage Desk, searching the nurse's face for any signs of sympathy.

"Please take a seat." She was playing the official line.

"Please. He is my Dad, the one without the mad red hair." Tommy was pleading.

The nurse gave a small almost involuntary nod towards the corridor on the left. Tommy was gone, a brisk walk taking him quickly down the brightly illuminated corridor. Coloured stripes on the wall indicated pathways to Paediatrics, to Oncology but there was no colour for his missing Dad. This was worse than being on the ship, he thought. He resorted to opening doors randomly. The first two had complete strangers occupying beds. Tommy apologised quickly and backed out of both. The third door revealed medical activity around two beds. There was a police presence at both beds even though both patients were in no condition to affect an escape. The white coated doctors were busily assessing injuries.

"Penetration wound between ribs. We need to stop the bleeding." Two medics were busy at 'bed one'.

"There are contusions to the face and head; a possible concussion. Call radiology." Bed two seemed to be under control. Ben in 'bed two' was still drowsy, but Freddie in the other bed was lucid if still in some pain.

"Well, if it isn't little Tommy, come to see his injured friend." Freddie was pleased to see Tommy; he was getting quite attached to him. Tommy walked past Freddie's bed as if he didn't exist.

"Are you alright Dad? Can you hear me?" Tommy was at his father's bedside, stroking his forehead. Freddie watched with the vacant stare of a jilted lover.

"You can't be in here. You will have to wait outside," a uniformed policeman ushered Tommy gently by the arm. "There are seats in the corridor." Tommy duly obliged, walking out backwards, never taking his eyes off of his father. He stayed there for what seemed like hours, but in fact was only fifteen minutes. The wild mental imaginings of serious injuries to his father that were flying around Tommy's head were only disturbed by the sound of shoes clicking on the rubberised floor. Bobbie was hurrying along, trying to put the car park ticket away safely in her handbag while carrying a polystyrene cup of coffee. She was closely followed by a pair of brown snakeskin boots.

Once Page had been debriefed he came back into the corridor. He wasn't relishing the prospect of talking to Bobbie, especially about Thomas, but he had to be professional. He informed her that Ben's injuries were not serious and that he would be interviewed as soon as he was fit enough.

"Thanks Peter," responded Bobbie with an appreciative hand on his arm. Freddie; however was being detained. He was being charged with murder.

-.-

The winter light coming through the conservatory roof reflected off the empty bottle of Chardonnay on the wicker table, causing Brie to scrunch up her eyes to focus. Her efforts to focus were compounded by the contents of the bottle which were racing around her blood stream.

"You should take it easy Brie, slow down just a little." Simon comforted her.

"Let's get on with this shall we?" Brie nodded to the cluster of papers on the table. "A charity doesn't organise itself; and get me another bottle out of the fridge." Simon was concerned about her increasing dependency on wine, but he didn't have the balls to say no, so he subserviently padded out into the kitchen. The chink of glass could be heard as he opened the fridge door.

Brie was busy sorting out Charity events. The school had been brilliant; dedicating the Spring Fair to Holly's Charity; 'Bright Eyes Foundation.' The local free paper had run a story on the launch which had kick-started donations. Soon they would have their first thousand pounds to donate to the Hospice. She was looking forward to holding the big cardboard cheque and attending a theatrical handover. Things with the charity were running well, but the big event of the year was to be the concert in the park. She had to get attractive acts booked, acts the local populous would want to hear. Three up and coming bands were confirmed, youngsters who knew Holly, who wanted to help; but Brie needed a headline act, someone to bring in the older crowd.

"Here you are honey." Simon was back with the wine. "Make it your last glass." Maybe he was growing a pair.

"Can you get my medication?" Brie asked as she prepared to take a sip.

"You shouldn't be mixing them with alcohol."

"What harm can it do?"

Simon tossed her bag over and watched as she placed two pink pills alongside a yellow and white striped oblong tablet. Each pill was washed down with a sip of Chardonnay.

"Let's get back to work. We need a band."

The phone rang and was answered quickly by Brie. "Hi, Bobbie."

She sat with the phone at her ear, listening intently, her face a picture of concern.

"No way; the hospital you say? We'll be right over."

The doctor had reluctantly given Page clearance to conduct an interview.

"He needs rest, but as it is a murder inquiry, you can see him. But the nurse must stay."

"Ok, we won't be long. Come on Barnes." The pair entered the side room as the nurse was administering some painkillers.

"I will be right here," she said as she retired to a chair in the corner.

"Getting a bit of a habit isn't it? Being interviewed by the police?" Page opened smugly. Ben was remembering the interview after Mary's death; remembered how hard Page pushed him down the 'you are the prime suspect' route. He made no attempt to hide his contempt for Page.

"You have just been involved in the 'dogging case.'" Barnes offered out of the need to be involved.

"I hope you are not suggesting that I had anything to do with Chavic's death."

"You do have a habit of being in the wrong place."

"I was on the floor injured; attacked by Chavic. I cannot deny that am glad that he is dead. He was driving the car that night. Check his arm. You know the tattoo that I have been describing? It is on his arm."

"That is a line of enquiry that we will be following, but for now we are investigating his murder. Did you see Mr. Fungus stab him?"

"I was on the floor, out of it. But there was a fight going on, I remember that. They both had knives."

"Did you see him stab Chavic in the neck?" Page was pushing for an answer.

Ben could remember the scene from his low viewpoint. Wounds were inflicted on both combatants, but he couldn't recall a wound to the neck. That seemed to occur when Chavic pushed the waitress away.

"Did you?" Page repeated.

"Yes," Ben said reluctantly. He wanted Freddie out of his life, away from Tommy. Freddie had an unhealthy attachment to Tommy that was unsettling.

Page missed Ben's whispered answer. Page had never liked Ben, these feeling intensified once he had pinched Bobbie, yes he had pinched her. I know one date, a coffee really, doesn't constitute a relationship, but it was going so well. At least there was still Katrina.

"Did you?" Page was louder.

"I said yes, and don't forget my money. I had £4,032 worth of chips in front of me before he attacked me."

Despite all that he had been through; the beating; Mary's death; Tommy being missing for so long; a new blossoming relationship with a attractive florist; numerous police interviews, harassment really. Despite all this, his first thought was for his winnings. What was wrong with him? Was he addicted?

"I want those chips."

"I didn't do it. OK, I stabbed him, for sure, but it was self defence. He started it. I definitely did not kill him; no way." Freddie's interview was rather more intense than Ben's. There was more at stake. Freddie knew very well that the initial bicep wound and the rib shot were not fatal; he could see it in Roman's eyes. He knew the last two wounds were also not life threatening, they were intended to slow him down. Freddie knew very well how to kill; he had done it many times. It was tempting to say just that to get Page out of his face, but he controlled himself; dug deep.

"I didn't kill him. Check the footage, my knife never goes near his neck."

"We have a witness that said it did." Page was enjoying his discomfort.

"Who would say such a thing? Who would lie?" Freddie was breathlessly agitated in his bed. "It is a lie."

"You are the only person, apart from Chavic, who had a knife. We have footage from the CCTV and a witness. You are to be charged with murder."

Chapter 14

Brie was engrossed in 'Brighteyes' paperwork at the conservatory table, gentle sunlight highlighting small hairs on her cheek. She visited the salon every month; paying good money to look her best. But now, in the sunlight, her appearance was not up to her usual immaculate standards. She was letting herself go. She was not stunningly beautiful; attractive certainly, in an appointment at the hairdressers every two weeks, expensive clothes, sort of way. Money can't buy good looks but it can transform plain into attractive. She was drinking too much, getting way too familiar with Chris the reporter at the Globe. The phone rang with the annoying "Yellow Rose of Texas' ringtone, how she hated it. It was Chris from the 'Globe.'

"Hi, Chris." Brie looked around sheepishly, worried that Simon could hear from the chair where he was reading 'California Gold Rush.' "I can't talk now. Yes, that will be fine. I will see you there."

"What did he want?" asked Simon looking up from his book for the first time.

"Just another meeting to run through the article on the charity, you know, to keep it in the public consciousness."

"That's good of him; very friendly." Simon didn't know what to do. Was he losing her? Was their marriage falling apart?

Brie hated herself for getting involved in a casual fling; Chris wasn't particularly attractive, certainly wasn't an improvement in the bedroom. She had just hit a low point, was drinking too much. She could stop this at any time, she was in control. She did what she always did when she was feeling guilty; she went on the offensive.

"You are such a stupid, stupid cowboy. What is all that anyway? Why the strutting around in that ridiculous waistcoat and those pathetic cowboy boots. I just don't get it. I'm going upstairs to change." Brie stood to leave the room, but turned to finish her glass of wine in one mouthful, tilting the glass vertically with her head thrown back in receptive mode.

"Need to change do we? Making an effort for Chris are we?"

"What's with the 'we'? I am changing for a meeting to represent the charity. We have to keep the profile up, need to raise money. Any publicity is good publicity." She ran her hand through her hair as she strode towards the door.

"This is the third meeting you have had with this

reporter. I'm not stupid, what is going on Brie?" He almost didn't want to hear the answer."Right; get your coat. You are coming along as a chaperone; just to see for yourself that it is a perfectly innocent business meeting."

"There's no need for that." He was still in the chair with his book in his hand, finger inserted to mark his page.

"I will go on my own then." Brie swept out of the conservatory and up the stairs to change, relieved that her bravado had subdued Simon.

Simon stayed in his chair. There was no need for him to accompany Brie; he had seen enough on the texts Chris had been sending; Brie not being quick enough, or sensible enough, to delete them immediately.

-.-

Tommy was picking at his roast chicken and vegetables at the dining room table. The neat garden looked immaculate through the freshly cleaned glass of the patio doors; that reached from floor to ceiling. He felt uncomfortable being stared back at by twelve garden gnomes. Mr Fletcher was into gnomes whereas Mrs Fletcher preferred china owl ornaments. It was that type of house. Mrs Fletcher, his foster mother, was talking at the other end of the table.

"We have apple crumble for dessert; made it myself. There's nothing like home made crumble."

Tommy wasn't really listening. He was miles away, wondering when he could go home to his Dad. Mr & Mrs Fletcher were very nice and friendly, too friendly; but he would rather be at home. The evening meal;

served on owl motif plates, was edible; but he just wanted to be left alone.

"I said 'we have apple crumble,'" Mrs Fletcher raised her voice to attract Tommy's attention without letting her fixed grin leave her face. The grin seemed to be a permanent fixture, Tommy believed that it remained on her face throughout the night, even when she was sleeping. Did she think there was some kind of secret assessment going on? Did she not realise that she had got the gig; that she was being paid for the foreseeable future. She could drop the pretence, but she kept on smiling like a Notre Dame gargoyle.

"That sounds really tasty." Tommy eventually replied with as much enthusiasm as he could muster; he tried to compete with her scary smile, but he was wasting his time; it was unbeatable.

"When we have finished and washed up we can play scrabble again." Mr Fletcher was joining in. Tommy remembered last night, the disagreement over his high scoring word. It wasn't a disagreement as such, more of a smiling competition, but they were both obviously unhappy at his word, which he knew existed.

"Catechize" he had displayed across a triple score square.

"Challenge." Mr Fletcher had announced.

"How very ironic," Tommy had replied smugly.

"Ironic?"

Considering that it means 'To question or examine closely' I think it is ironic. After the dictionary was consulted and Tommy was exonerated, his score was accepted, putting him in an unassailable lead.

"Well done Tommy," they both congratulated him through gritted tooth smiles, but he was soon sent to his room. He had spent the evening reflecting about his present situation. His Dad had let thing slip initially, resulting in him being in that care home, and now Dad just can't keep out of trouble. Dad just needed to keep his nose clean for a while, get reassessed and I will be home. He had smartened himself up and was in a new relationship, it's just the stupid police stuff that keeps ruining everything. Fancy my Dad getting arrested for dogging and then being beaten up in a gambling den; not to mention being a witness to murder. No wonder Social Services had put my return home on hold. Life is so unfair. The only person who has been good to me was poor old Ron. Tommy hoped Ron was OK, stuck on that ship.

Mr Fletcher was rummaging through the letters bag, giving them a good mix before picking seven. He just couldn't wait for the return match.

"Can't that wait until after the crumble, dear," Mrs Fletcher smiled.

"I'm just getting things ready for the big game, sweetie," Mr Fletcher grinned back. Tommy had been there four days and never heard them address each other with their Christian names. Mr Fletcher was sorting his seven tiles, moving them around his tray in an attempt to form a large word.

"Come on Tommy, pick your letters," Mr Fletcher was determined to start the game.

"We can eat dessert during the game," Mrs Fletcher conceded. Tommy plunged his right hand into the bag, rustled the letters around to ensure a good mix, before withdrawing a handful. He lined them up on his tray neatly. He looked at his selected letters; N C I T R E S.

"You have first go Tommy," Mr Fletcher beamed. Tommy didn't really want to play, it only led to trouble. He was well aware, after only one game, that the Fletchers were very competitive; hated losing. Tommy didn't really care about the stupid scrabble game. He was wondering where the crumble was, Mrs Fletcher being totally distracted once the game had begun. He studied his letters again and realised that he had a seven letter word. After last night's game he didn't want to antagonise them, they were desperate to win this time. However, starting with a seven letter word would be impressive; the problem was the word was CRETINS. Tommy was worried that they would take it personally, as an assessment of their characters. He took the diplomatic route to smiley happiness, placing five tiles on the board to spell NICER.

"Good word, Tommy." Mr Fletcher grinned manically. Tommy couldn't wait to get to his room for some privacy. He was looking forward to the weekend with his Dad.

Ben had recovered enough from his beating at the Krem to get out and about. He was still bruised and battered but mobile. He had traced the key that was hidden in the picture frame to a safety deposit box at the Nat West; his appointment with the branch manager was in ten minutes. He sat in the waiting area inside the bank wondering what he would find. He had brought all the requested documentation, death certificate, marriage certificate, and passport. He was inspecting the marriage certificate, staring at Mary's name. What had she been up to? Why the secrets?

"Mr Thomas?" enquired a smart female teller.

"That's me."

"Mr Chapman will see you now." He felt like a contestant on 'The Apprentice'. Once the paperwork formalities were concluded, Chapman entered a four digit pin to enter a secluded room containing wall to wall strong box compartments. Chapman stopped at number 177.

"This is it. I will give you a few moments of privacy," he said as he backed away and pretended to inspect other strong boxes in an attempt to look busy. The key slipped into the locking mechanism easily. One turn to the right produced a click and the door opened on a spring loaded device. Ben couldn't believe what he saw inside. Resting on the removable tray were varying sized stacks of twenty pound notes; all bound by elastic bands. Ben withdrew the tray and placed it on the table in the middle of the room to begin counting the money. As he was counting, Ben's mind was racing with thoughts of how Mary had accumulated such a large stash. He was so distracted that he had to begin counting again, three times, as he lost count. He was thinking of the red shoes Mary was wearing on the night she died. Could there be a link with Chavic? He was running a prostitute ring, where has the money come from? The thought were driving Ben crazy. He remembered Mary going out at night.

'Just popping out' she had said, but she was gone for hours. The thought that she may have been working, and then coming home to him the same night, was driving him demented. It was all too much for Ben to contemplate. He tried hard to erase negative thoughts from his mind and to concentrate on the counting. Where was Tommy when you needed him? He would have had this done in minutes. Once he concentrated, he quickly completed the counting; sixty thousand pounds lay neatly on the table.

"Can you deposit this into my account please," Ben gave his instructions to Chapman, who was still continuing the pretence of not being there.

"Certainly sir, will that be all?"

"Yes thanks. We are finished here."

"Was there anything you can think of that Mary may have said about any money?" Ben was giving Brie the third degree. "You two were close, she must have said something."

Brie put her pen down on the conservatory table and considered the question. She pushed her sunglasses into her hair, forming a temporary headband which scrunched her hair into a peculiar shape. There was no real need for the sunglasses on the dull November day.

"All I know is that she was planning a big surprise. I was sworn to secrecy. That's all I know Ben. I'm sorry if it is not much help."

"What's going on in here?" Simon demanded as he swept into the conservatory unannounced. "Oh, it's you Ben. I heard voices and thought that.." he let his statement drift away as he realised the male voice he had heard belonged to his best friend. He looked rather sheepish.

"Do you know anything about any money Mary may have been saving, Simon?"

"Sorry, can't help you on that one." Simon was embarrassed about his intrusion. Brie didn't look happy at all. Ben thought that there was an underlying current of animosity in the room, so made his excuses and left.

"OK. Thanks. I've got to go, things to do. Thanks again," Ben left with his hand raised in thanks. Once he was home, Ben starting tidying up the house to keep his mind off the money. Where did it all come from? He was trying to remain positive but he kept returning to the red shoes and the late night scenario that was freaking him out. He had spent months agonising about the tattoo; and now that was resolved another puzzle presents itself. How could she accumulate so much money? He kept the phone that was with the hidden key on the dresser in the back room; permanently charged, just in case, even though it lay dormant and unused. It was some sort of anal retentive compulsion.

"Let's get this place tidy; Tommy is coming round for his weekend visit," Ben instructed Bobbie. They both busied themselves with putting things into cupboards, fluffing up cushions, vacuuming. Social Services could arrive unannounced at any time for the reassessment. They would be ready next time. It would look like a show home; something out of a magazine. Ben was more than annoyed. Making so much effort for your own son, he should just be able to chill out and relax in his father's home. But no, we have to be scurrying around to make it perfect just in case we are inspected by the 'Child Police'. Bobbie began to feather dust the ornaments on the fireplace, giving them a gentle caress with the pink feather duster she had bought for the clean-up. She was too heavy handed with the photo of Ron, the one he had given Tommy. It fell onto the marble plinth that surrounded the base of the fireplace, smashing the frame and glass.

"Sorry, sorry." Bobbie was truly apologetic.

"No problem; we can clean it up."

The back of the photograph had become exposed, revealing some writing. Ben picked it up and began to read.

'To Dad, love Sally' followed by an address in Huddersfield.

"Tommy is going to love this. If I know my son, we will be having a day out at the weekend; a road trip. We must go and see her, show her the photo, tell her where her father is. Tommy will love it."

"Would Ron remember her?" Bobbie asked reluctantly, pulling a winching face.

"What? You think that he might not remember his own daughter?" Ben's arms we spread out horizontally in an appealing manner. As he was getting the dust pan and brush from the cupboard under the stairs he was disturbed by the post landing on the laminate wood flooring in the hall behind him. Three official looking envelopes nestled on the welcome mat. The first one was from Social Services informing him that Tommy would be placed with Foster carers until a re-assessment could be organised at some future date. It was nothing he hadn't already been informed of by his Social Worker personally. It was just officialdom putting it in writing; keeping records. The second letter was an invitation to 'The Class of '92 Graduation Anniversary'. He struggled to believe that it really was twenty years since he graduated. Bobbie had silently appeared by his side.

"I'll get on with the clean up," she said as she took the dust pan from him.

"I'm not sure that I want to go to this," Ben said; almost to himself.

"What is it?"

"It is an invitation to the twenty year anniversary of our graduation. A room full of people I haven't seen for years, apart from Simon and Brie; all asking how Mary is. I don't think I can face it."

"But it is part of your past; an important part of your life story. You must try and face it; you will regret not going." Bobbie was talking good sense.

"We'll see," said Ben as he began opening the third letter by inserting his thumb and ripping the flap off.

"It's another invitation."

"You are mister popular today aren't you," Bobbie teased.

"It is more of an order than an invitation. Ben began to read the letter out loud. 'I have been subpoenaed to appear as a material witness at the murder trial of Mr Freddie Fungus.' Ben's mind was racing. I lied about Chavic's death, after all. I just wanted Freddie out of our lives. I was almost jealous of him for killing Chavic after my pathetic showing; now I will have to commit perjury in court or admit I was lying all the time.

"12th December; at Liverpool Crown Court."

Ben stared at the date; he wasn't looking forward to it at all.

Chapter 15

Bobbie parked her Golf outside of the neat semi situated in a leafy suburban Upton road on the outskirts of Chester. It was only thirty minutes from home but it felt like the other side of the world. The houses were larger; the gardens neater, it was altogether more upmarket.

"Why am I so nervous about taking my own son out for the weekend? I should be excited." Ben was apprehensive about meeting his own son.

"You'll be fine, just go and knock on the door," encouraged Bobbie as she applied the handbrake. Ben got out of the car and stretched to his full six foot, rotating his head to click the small bones in his neck. Why did this feel like a job interview? He walked down the path, noticing the immaculately manicured lawn and the proliferation of gnomes. The Terracotta Army sprang to mind. He had seen gnomes before, usually they were sitting on a toadstool holding a fishing rod or smiling like a friendly Santa; but these were weird. Two were arm wrestling, one was eating with a knife and fork and another was juggling fruit. Ben had to look twice to notice the detail. The fruit had been wired to appear in mid air. He pressed the doorbell and could hear the chimes inside the hallway. What he wasn't prepared for was the welcome from the gnome on the tiled stoop.

"Welcome to the Fletcher home," announced the smiling porcelain figure. Ben almost shit himself, but heard himself answering.

"Hi there." The door opened to reveal more smiling porcelain figures. This time they were human. The Fletchers had been watching Ben's every move from behind the net curtains and now stood, side by side, smiling their spooky welcome.

"Is Tommy ready?" Ben heard himself say. No 'Hello, nice to meet you, you must be the Fletchers. How is Tommy settling in?' Ben realised that he had said nothing like that, no social awareness; just a blunt 'Is Tommy ready?'

"Here he is," said Mr. Fletcher, as Tommy appeared from the front room, "Quite the Scrabble player is your Tommy." Ben didn't understand what he was talking about but recognised the look on Tommy's face; the 'I'll explain later' look.

"We expect him back on Sunday night; eightish. Mrs. Fletcher was stating the conditions of the placement.

"We won't be late," promised Ben. They were quickly into traffic on the A41.

"Scrabble? You never play Scrabble."

"I know Dad, but they were really persistent about it, you know; it was their thing."

"And the gnomes?" Ben was still surprised by the obsessive display in the garden.

"They're OK Dad. It's only for a while. I'll be home soon." They all sat silently in the car, watching the delights of Eastham pass by their window.

"I have some great news, son." Ben finally broke the reflective silence. "Do you remember the photo of Ron? The one with the woman in it?"

"There is only one photo of Ron, Dad." Tommy was getting impatient.

"Of course, well on the back of the photo there is a message. Have a look." Tommy took the photo and sat staring at it.

"Why did you take it out of the frame?"

"That was me. I broke it while dusting. Sorry." Bobbie offered without looking away from the road. Despite being clumsy, she was a careful driver.

"The point is; do you want to go and see her? Maybe reunite her with her father. We could be there and back in a few hours," Ben was watching Tommy closely for any sign of excitement.

"Too right; let's go."

"Get on Google Maps on my I Phone and enter the address," Bobbie offered helpfully.

"Road trip!" Ben said excitedly.

"Grow up Dad. We need to turn around and get on the motorway," said Tommy without looking up from the small screen in his hand.

-.-

DI Page was in the kitchen chopping onions. He had gotten into a routine where he prepared the vegetables while Katrina cooked the chicken or fish, whatever she felt was healthiest. He had become rather domesticated since Kat had moved in, the chopping board matching the china containers that held the coffee and sugar along the side of the work surface. Kat was busy spraying the frying pan with a low fat aerosol.

"There's something I would like you to look at after we have eaten." Page announced. Kat looked up suspiciously; startled like a rabbit in the headlights.

"What is it about?"

"It can wait." But it spoiled the meal; an oppressive silence hanging over each mouthful. Halfway through her low fat peach yoghurt Kat caved in.

"OK, what is it? Have you reported me to the authorities as an illegal immigrant? Do you think I should perform sexual favours to keep you quiet? I know I was in a brothel, but I am not like that. You let me live her day after day; you must want something in return. What is it? What do you want?" It all came out quickly; in a rush, her heavily accented East European tongue making it all the more endearing.

"OK. Let's do this. I'll get my laptop." He quickly logged on and opened video footage. It was a close up

202

of the fight at the Krem, the sequence where Roman Chavic fell against the waitresses. Page pressed the 'pause' button.

"Is that you?" he asked as he watched her reaction. He zoomed into the face on the screen. If you mentally removed the wig it was unmistakably Katrina. She watched the screen, her eyes dancing trying to think of any believable reason why she could be there.

"OK. It is me. I got a job there as a waitress, to be near him. I swore that I would get revenge for Anna; but when I got there I couldn't do it. The security was too tight. He had minders everywhere, not to mention that he was a brute himself. It was not possible for a girl like me." Page pressed 'play'. The screen came to life again. She could be seen clearly bending down to help Chavic, but as soon as she was near him, a blood spray cascaded against the wall. He pressed 'pause' again.

"Can you explain what happened there?" He was in interview mode. Kat's face was beginning to crumple with emotion; her lips making an involuntary movement, minute muscles out of her control.

"I still don't understand it." She looked genuinely puzzled.

"Understand what?"

"I remember picking up the paintbrush that had slid across the floor when the first fight was taking place. It was more a beating than a fight. The point is that I had the brush in my hand. I was looking at the metallic end, wondering if I could use it. Then, suddenly, he was

203

there in front of me; on the floor. When it came to the crunch, I just couldn't do anything. I honestly had intended to kill him, but the opportunity arose I just froze. It sort of just happened. It was as if the brush had a life of its own. I honestly don't recall using it; it just happened." Her eyes were pleading, burning with a deep intensity that Page thought was difficult to manufacture. Either she was one hell of an actress or she was telling the truth.

"I swear on Anna's life. You have to believe me."

Page was struck by her vulnerability, he understood the heartache and pain she had suffered travelling to Britain; being used and abused; having her sister die in the gutter. He understood all of this; it was part of the reason why he had acted in such an inappropriate manner. It was bad enough that he had given her a roof, against all police protocol, but his latest act was much more foolish, but he couldn't help himself, it was an obsession.

"I have deleted all of this from the official footage that will be used in the Chavic murder trial."

"Why would you do such a thing?" Her eyes were dancing; looking for any semblance of logic in his words.

"I want to help you Kat." Page had an earnest look on his face. Kat just stared back at him, not knowing what to say.

McNally was also looking at the footage from her copy of the fight at the Krem. She had rewound it to the place where the paintbrush slides towards the waitresses. She 'paused' the footage to get a closer look at the waitress. Even with the wig, it was obvious that it was Katrina. McNally compared it with the mug shot she was holding; the mug shot taken during her interview regarding her sister's death. There was no doubt, it was the same girl.

McNally fast forwarded the screen until Chavic was lying on the floor in front of Weiss. She watched the next sequence in slow motion. The blood spray only hit the wall as Weiss bent down towards him. She paused again and zoomed in; the paintbrush could just be seen in Weiss's hand, protruding over Chavic's shoulder. McNally was puzzled. Why would Page remove this part of the video evidence? Why would he remove the part that could corroborate Fungus's defence regarding the fatal wound? This girl, she was on record in the interview room, saying she would exact revenge on Chavic for the death of her sister. It was too blatant a piece of evidence for Page to miss. What was he up to? She would have to consult her superiors.

-.-

The Motorway drive was taking its toll. He would have to stop at the next service station to rest and grab a bite to eat. The sign informed him that 'Knutsford Services' were only one mile ahead. He took one hand off the steering wheel to gently smooth his cropped blond hair; his finely chiselled cheek bones protruding out of his smoothly shaven face, giving him a skull like appearance. The gentle Cheshire countryside flashed past on his left. It's a lot nicer than I expected up North, he thought. He took a quick glance at himself in the mirror. It still amazed him, how after all these years, he was still so similar to his brother in appearance. But then again, that's what twins do. They look identical.

Stefan hadn't seen his brother for years; not since they had both came to England from the Ukraine. He had always looked after Roman; always teased him that he was the baby, Stefan having been born one minute earlier. Roman had, in truth, always been the baby. He always needed looking after. Roman was the soft one. Stefan was stronger, more resilient. He didn't like his nickname; 'Chavic the Savage', but it was accurate. He was ruthless. He parked up away from the food outlets and checked the equipment in the boot. The case with the gun and silencer were still hidden in the spare tyre well. The wig and make up neatly stored in a canvas bag. Stefan had made a good life and a comfortable living as a professional assassin, but this time it was personal. This time he would listen to the evidence in court and delivery his own justice; his own retribution.

-.-

The M62 snaked over the Pennines, eating up the miles quicker than they had expected. The last signpost had indicated that it was only eight miles to Huddersfield. A light drizzly was giving the rolling landscape a miserable damp backdrop that was totally undeserved. On a clear summers day the view was amazing, but today, in the rain, it was a damp depressive grey overcast blur. They took the next exit and were soon surrounded by stone houses, Asian food outlets, and satanic mills. Tommy was giving directions from the I Phone.

"Next left and then straight on for four hundred yards." Bobbie followed his directions meticulously, keeping to the speed limit and indicating in good time.

"This is it; number 14." Bobbie parked up neatly under a tree. Ben was looking at the photograph, checking the details of the house behind the father and daughter portrait. The windows had been renewed, white PVC; and the tree had grown to its full height. The undisputable conclusion was that it was definitely the same house. Ben took a deep breath; he knew how important this was to Tommy.

"OK, let's go and knock on the door."

They all got out and wandered up the path, a varnished hardwood front door with brass fittings was waiting their attention.

"This is your project Tommy, use the knocker." Tommy duly gave the brass fitting a vigorous hammering. The door was opened by a woman.

"Hello can I help you?"

Ben looked at the photo. He could see a resemblance; she had put on twenty pounds, her hair was slightly greyer; Brie would have died of shame to be seen like that in public. She looked sadder. She had become a middle aged frump, but looked pleasant enough. The biggest change in her appearance from the photograph was the wheelchair. Ben wasn't sure how to begin so he said the simplest thing that came into his head.

"Sally?"

"I'm sorry, I don't know you."

Bobbie took control, speaking calmly and soothingly as she handed over the photograph.

"We don't mean to worry you, but is this your father?" she asked.

Sally sat staring at the photograph deep in thought.

"Where did you get this from?"

"Ron gave it to me, as a memento," Tommy piped up. Sally softened in her attitude. "Since Mum died, he sort of disappeared; I didn't know what to do. I reported him missing, but after a while the police lost interest. There were no bank records. He sold the house and emptied the account; do you think he could be out there, a vulnerable old man with that much cash? It is frightening."

"We think we may know where he is," Ben informed her. Tommy was already on the I Phone, checking the itinerary of the ship.

"The 'Armistice of the Waves' is in Southampton; due to sail to Norway tomorrow morning."

"What are you talking about, I'm confused," interrupted Sally.

"I was on the ship with him, he gave me this photo. He is still on the ship now."

"Do you want to go and see him?" asked Bobbie.

"I would love to, but I am house bound," she replied with both hands on the wheels of her chariot to emphasise her predicament.

"We will bring him here," announced Ben.

-.-

Stefan had two days to kill. He had booked into 'The Hilton' using his fake identity and was now getting accustomed to the area; strolling around the shopping areas that surrounded the Court building. Liverpool was a lot nicer than he had expected; modern buildings piercing the sky on the waterfront, giving it an international flavour. He was enjoying a coffee at a window seat across the road from the court buildings. Which way would prisoners arrive? Was there a loading bay for prison vans? He had to plan this properly; stay detached. He needed to check out the interior of the building; he would probably attend the case out of morbid curiosity; he wanted to see Freddie and listen to the evidence. However, his professional instincts were telling him that it was far safer to complete the business at hand in the street to enable a quick exit.

He left his cappuccino half full and wandered over to the court building, the large letters on the front informing anyone who was interested that they were dedicated to 'Queen Elizabeth II'. He started climbing the steps to begin his scouting mission; to anyone watching, he was just a neatly dressed, curly headed anonymous court official going about his daily business.

-.-

The drive down to Southampton had been uneventful; the only stop had been for refuelling at Watford Gap accompanied by an overpriced lunch being the only delay. They were all checking road signs for the cruise port as they snaked their way past the numerous hotels and restaurants that populated the streets adjacent to the seafront.

"How are we going to get on the ship Dad?"

"You are the expert son."

"I'm being serious, this is a major international port; security will be tight."

"We don't have to go onboard. All we need to do is ask them at reception to escort Ron to us; make an announcement on the public address system," suggested Bobbie as she took the next left turn.

"Sounds like a plan. We should have Ron in no time at all," announced Ben.

"It will be great to see Ron again; and tell him about his daughter," Tommy said with as much enthusiasm as he could muster, but he was more concerned about Kade, wondering if she was still onboard, going about her cleaning duties on Deck 9. Why didn't she reply to his e mails? He tried again on the I Phone. His thumb selected the 'Email' logo. He began to type. Kade147@Hotmail.com. He wondered if there were a lot of girls named 'Kade' in Indonesia or whether she was a very good snooker player. God, it sounded like something Freddie would say. He was sort of missing him in a strange way. He started his e mail message.

'Hi, it's Tommy. I have been wondering what you have been up to lately. How is your Mother? I am in Southampton today with my family; it would be really great if you could meet us. We are in the embarkation lounge.'

His thumb hovered over the send button for a second before he applied enough pressure on the screen for the message to appear as a sent item. It sat there below the other six messages he had sent lately, six messages with no replies. A one sided conversation. Bobbie switched off the engine after parking neatly in the massive car park literally yards from the dockside; the impressive 'Armistice of the Waves' dominated the skyline.

"Ok let's get Ron," said Ben ask he strode purposely towards the 'Embarkation Desk.' "Come on Tommy, put that phone away."

-.-

Stefan was sat in one of the four chairs that were neatly secured against the wall outside of Court room No 4. The sports pages of 'The Telegraph' seemed to occupy his full attention, but he was observing the interior of the courtroom as two court officials talked whilst holding the door open. Access was restricted to the door that was being held open and also the stairway to the holding cells below, located near the witness box.

All corridors were heavily populated with CCTV cameras. It would be almost impossible to exact revenge within the building; he would have to take action outside. He imagined Freddie leaving the building, a blanket over his shamed head. Baying crowds would be calling for his blood; there would be opportunity enough to strike.

A security guard had begun his patrol of the corridors, strutting self-importantly through the throng of humanity that was busily looking for their respective courtrooms. It was time to leave. He folded his newspaper under the arm of his neat suit and casually strolled to the exit, stopped to adjust his eyes to the changing daylight and then disappeared down the stairs into the shoppers on their way to Liverpool One. Tomorrow was another day. Tomorrow he would honour the family name. Nobody disrespects a Chavic.

-.-

"Hello I'm Ron Pickering; there was an announcement on the tannoy for me." He was standing earnestly facing the receptionist behind the desk. Her name tag announced 'Francesca' to the world. Additional information on the name tag indicated 'Puerto Rico' as her country of origin. Ron wondered why this was necessary.

"It is not a tannoy it is a public address system," smiles Francesca.

"OK, but why do you want me?"

"Can I see your 'Sea Pass' please?" Once she had verified Ron's identity in the system, she was all businesslike smiles. "There are people on the quayside waiting to see you on a matter of some urgency," she informed him as she flicked her short hair behind one ear.

"Raymond will escort you," she added nodding to a steward on her left. Raymond was from 'Haiti' and was smiling broadly.

"Shall I get you a wheelchair sir?"

"No, no I can manage," replied Ron as he secured his right arm into his metallic crutch. "I wonder who wants me?" he asked out loud.

"This way sir, we can disembark on Deck Five."

-.-

Kade was already on the quayside, making her way to the taxi rank. Her tour of duty was over, and due to her Mother's situation in Indonesia, she had decided not to renew her contract. She was going home to sort out her family business. She walked behind the brass band, all decked out in red and gold uniforms, preparing to start the 'Sail Away' concert. Trombones and clarinets were making random sounds as the band members tested their instruments.

"Is there no way we can get on board Dad?" asked a forlorn Tommy as he watched the happy cruisers board the ship through the security system.

"No need son, Ron is on his way to us."

Tommy continued to scan the ship, mentally counting decks down from the top. He knew the swimming pool was on Deck Fifteen, so nine must be six down from there. His gaze scanned across the ship, taking in all the balconies. Kade must be up there somewhere, it was her patch.

The band had started up with 'When the saints go marching in,' giving the quayside a party atmosphere; Ron was making his way slowly down the inclined gangway, assisted by Raymond.

"There he is; that's Ron," announced Tommy excitedly as he pointed at the gangway. He was barely audible above the noise of the band playing ten yards away and had to repeat himself as he tugged on Bobbie's sleeve. Ron was having a great time, taking in the colourful scene in front of his eyes. He had always enjoyed parades or musical events; he couldn't remember when he had enjoyed himself so much.

Kade took one last look at the ship out of the taxi window before it pulled away from the kerb. It was hard to believe that it had been her home for the last seven months; so many memories; so many friends, but she had to get home to her mother. The taxi driver edged slowly past the band, careful not to hit the tuba player, and then disappeared into the traffic leaving the port area. She turned to watch the ship out of the back window of the taxi. She still, after all this time, got excited at the sight of the majestic craft. The taxi stopped in heavy traffic at the gatehouse, giving her an opportunity to study the ship, her face completely filling the back window.

"Ron, Ron, it's me, Tommy." Tommy was waving his arms manically above his head. The band had moved on to 'I Am Sailing'; people in the queue to board were getting in the party mood, singing along.

"Ron," Tommy continued to shout above the noise of the band.

"To be near you, to be free...," a young couple passed by, out of key.

Raymond was following orders. He was told to deliver the old man to the 'Embarkation Desk'; and that's exactly what he did. Once there, Ben's group was ushered over by the girl behind the desk.

"Nice to see you again Ron," said a smiling Tommy.

"Hello son, how are you doing?"

"Do you remember me?" The pause from Ron, which lasted over ten seconds, told the group all they needed to know.

"Do you remember this photograph?" asked Bobbie, holding it gently in front of his face.

"I gave this to you didn't I? You were on the ship." Ron was pleased with his brainpower. He was having one of his momentary flashes.

"Do remember which deck you are on Ron," asked Tommy hopefully.

"Nine?" answered Ron with a smirk.

215

"The woman in the photograph is your daughter Sally," whispered Bobbie.

"Sally," said Ron wistfully, a flicker of recognition in his eyes.

"Do you want to see her? She is desperate to see you. She is in Huddersfield." Ben was taking control.

"Huddersfield," repeated Ron with the same wistful look. "I think I do, I need to visit my past to know my future."

"You need to board the ship, sir; we are sailing in ten minutes." Raymond was getting nervous.

"That will not be necessary; I am going with these good people." Ron had a determined look on his face which Raymond wisely recognised.

"Ok sir, have a nice day. What about your luggage?"

"I'll be back for the next cruise. Hold it." The band had finished their latest number and began turning pages on their music sheets ready to swing into 'Rule Britannia.' They made their way slowly to the car park. Once in the car Bobbie joined the queue to leave the port terminal.

"We have to get Tommy back to the Fletcher's before eight tonight; he is with foster carers on a temporary basis at the moment. And tomorrow I am in court, as a witness. Would you do us a big favour and stay with us for a day or two. We will get you to your daughter eventually." Ben stressed the word 'will' to appease Ron.

"I have all the time in the world, son; All the time in the world." Bobbie left the port and joined the traffic heading for the A36.

Chapter 16

The fork incision caused fat to ooze out of the sausage. Ron tucked in heartily to the first cooked breakfast that he had tasted in a long time. He was enjoying being with people, the ship was full of people, but this time he was actually with people that acknowledged him. He didn't feel lonely anymore. The toll road service station on the M6 motorway was proving popular with everybody. Tommy had a toasted bacon sandwich, Ben was devouring a triple pack sandwich, and Bobbie was picking at a bowl of fresh fruit. They were all deep in thought; enjoying their food.

"What are you thinking about Ben?" asked Bobbie as she popped a small strawberry into her mouth.

"Nothing much, it's just the Mary thing. It is driving me crazy; the thought that she could have been working for Chavic. Could it really be possible? You know, the red shoe, the money in the safety deposit box. What else could it be? He being a know gangster, dealing in prostitution." He was talking quietly at the far end of the table. He didn't want Tommy to hear any of the conversation.

"That doesn't have to be the only explanation. There could be any number of reasons why things happened the way they did." Bobbie realised, as she spoke, that she did not sound very convincing. Ben was still struggling with the facts; he needed to change the subject.

"What's up son? You have been very quiet; I would have expected you to talk to Ron. I thought that you would be pleased to be getting him home," he asked in a louder voice.

"I am Dad. Don't get me wrong. I really appreciate what you have done today. It's just.." Tommy's statement tailed off into silence as he examined his toasted bacon sandwich. All four of them watched the brown sauce drip out of the base as he held it with two hands; shoulders hunched in readiness to take a bite.

"It's just what? I know when something is bothering you." Tommy considered whether to talk about his concerns as he watched the sauce continue to drip, forming a small brown rivulet on his left hand. He started to speak in small staccato sentences.

"It's this girl. She works on the ship. I really like her."

"What's her name?" asked Bobbie, concern showing on her face.

"Kade," answered Tommy, smiling for the first time since they had left Southampton.

"That's nice," Bobbie continued in soothing tones. "Is it French?"

"I thought she would be there today. I thought that I would see her; that I would be able to speak to her." Tommy sounded crestfallen and forlorn.

"Sometimes it just doesn't work out the way you want son. Life's not fair, people come and go. It hurts sometimes." Ben was being kind, he knew only too well about lost love.

"God, I remember some of my old flames; they really cut my heart out at the time, but time is a great healer. Life and love; it gets you every time." Bobbie was trying to ease the situation, but wasn't really helping.

-.-

"It was just a moment of weakness. I was feeling so depressed and desolate over the loss of Holly." They both looked down at the mention of their daughter's name, trying to keep the tears at bay.

"He was sympathetic and caught me at my lowest ebb. It is you I love Simon, you must realise that. You have to believe me." Brie's eyes were burning with intense passion, searching her husband's face for a connection.

"This is going to take some working through. You have betrayed my trust." Simon was firm but wounded at the same time.

"I know, I know. We can work it out."

Simon was in no mood for the silly game he played with Ben; the one where they sang songs when the title came up in conversation. But he was tempted.

"Yeah, we can work it out," he echoed.

-.-

Page held the letter in his hand. It had been on the mantelpiece when he had arrived home, but he didn't want to open it. The writing was unmistakably Kat's, childlike in blue biro. 'Peter' in block capitals across the middle of the envelope. He feared the worst but realised that he had to know what she had written. He opened it with an inserted thumb, making a tearing sound that seemed louder in the quiet house.

Dear Peter,

Thank you for your kind hospitality. A lot of bad and sad things have happened since I came to your country. It is time for me to go home. I hope you have a good life and find happiness, but for me, it is a return to Slovakia.

Thank you again

Katrina.

Page looked at the letter with sad eyes. All he could think of was that there was no kiss after her name. He went to the kitchen and burnt it on a gas ring, holding it up until it was completely burnt. Only when his fingers began to tingle, did he put it under the tap and then into the bin.

-.-

"There will be others son," encouraged Ben, but his words fell on deaf ears. Tommy sat staring at the growing pool of sauce on the table below his untouched sandwich.

"I don't want there to be others." He was obviously at low ebb, lovelorn.

"I remember those times. Love can be really rough," interrupted Ron.

"You do? You remember?" asked Tommy, perking up a little.

"No, I am just trying to cheer you up," replied Ron as he continued to eat his sausage.

-.-

Freddie ate his mashed potato in silence. The accompanying sausage lay untouched on his plate. Any attempt to eat it had been met by baying wolf whistles from other inmates at his table in the refectory. The overpowering sense of danger in the prison could be felt everywhere; it was stifling. The sausage thing was bothering him; he knew that it was a homosexual reference but wasn't sure how far things would be taken. Were the other inmates joking around or were they really deranged slavering psychopathic homosexuals.

"Not hungry pretty boy?" asked a large West Indian inmate on the next table to Freddie's left. A huge vindictive grin accompanied the question; they would not let it go. Freddie was beginning to worry a little; his roughly cropped hair was showing signs of moisture causing it to stick flat on his head. The unwelcome attention continued.

"Do you want a real sausage to chew on?" The Rasta continued with malicious intent. The baying crowd responded with a knowing cheer. Freddie knew he was in a difficult situation, being the new boy on the block, so he decided to move tables. He picked up his tray in both hand and stood up, making a loud scraping noise on the tiled floor with the metallic legs of his chair. The noise attracted the attention of the remaining tables that were not initially intent on his humiliation. He began to walk towards a table two down which had an empty chair. He didn't make it. A leg flicked out in front of him as an arm pushed him in the back. His tray flew in a parabolic curve as he released it, trying to steady himself with his arms but he could not prevent himself from falling face down on the cold tiled floor.

A crowd immediately formed around his prone body, pushing and shoving to get closer. Freddie tried to get up but was restrained by a size nine boot pressing on his shoulder blades. How did I get in this position? The large Caribbean inmate that had been mercilessly goading Freddie at the table was now standing in front unfastening the buttons on his prison issue trousers. Freddie looked away as his tormentor inserted his right hand into the unbuttoned fly to present his rapidly growing penis. As it was forced towards his mouth Freddie moved his head from side to side trying manfully to avoid penetration, but a punch to his stomach caught him off guard causing an involuntary grunt which opened his mouth just enough to allow entry. It was Freddie's worst nightmare. He kept his eyes tightly shut; he didn't want to remember anything of his ordeal; didn't want to make eye contact with the hysterical crowd that was ringed around the action, like a playground fight. He hated the hand on the back of his head, pushing rhythmically, hated it more than he hated the owner of the cock in his mouth. He switched off mentally, trying to go to another place in his head; the cheers of the crowd fading away as he was transported to happier times, to his first few days in prison.

The Induction Wing had been a breeze; it couldn't have been easier, caring professionals asking lots of questions. He had a nice cell with a decent bed. Freddie thought prison life while on remand was going to be a doddle. Once the assessment process was completed he became a 'Category A' prisoner and was promptly transferred to C Wing.

"Now you are with the big boys," teased the guard as he unlocked the large barred entrance gate and led Freddie to cell 47. He could hear the welcoming taunts as he ran the gauntlet.

They didn't come any bigger than Freddie's tormentor, whose rhythm had increased as he approached a climax. The incredibly annoying hand was still operating Freddie's head like a master puppeteer. Freddie forced himself to think of anything to distract himself from his ordeal.

The crossbow was on his shoulder, his finger on the trigger. It was dark outside his parent's house; he had waited over an hour for them to return home. He knew it was extreme behaviour to kill his parents, but they deserved everything he had planned for them. They should have come to Edinburgh to support his big night, his 'Perrier nomination night.' The sight of his father writhing on the floor with a bolt in his neck was almost as pleasing as the look on his mother's face as she looked around despairingly for help and realised that she was the next helpless victim. He enjoyed his slow walk towards his mother, who was paralysed with fear; enjoyed her pleading; enjoyed pulling the trigger again.

"Ok break it up; the show's over," Officer Powell shouted as he broke into the circled crowd. Two other officers accompanied him with batons drawn. He had watched the action from the main door from the beginning; had allowed Clarence to have his fun for a while out of respect to his 'Wing commander' status. He was top dog. But enough was enough; the new kid's humiliation had to be cut short before the top brass became aware. Powell didn't want any trouble on his shift. Clarence wasn't happy about the sudden interruption.

"I ain't finished here yet boss."

Powell pushed him aggressively in the chest, forcing him to take a step back to balance himself. Freddie was only too grateful to have his mouth back to himself without any deposits.

"The party's over, back to your rooms." Powell insisted. The crowd started to meander to their respective cells, noticing the growing presence of guards on the periphery of the Refectory.

"No hard feeling bro," said a half cast with short dyed blond hair. He shook Freddie's hand in a slow rhythmical manner. Freddie recognised the rhythm; how could he forget it?

"No problem," Freddie heard himself reply, but there was a problem, a big problem. He would deal with it some other time when the conditions were right.

-.-

Back in cell 47 Freddie was gathering his thoughts. All this was Tommy and his Dad's fault. Why had he lied about the fatal wound to Chavic? He just didn't understand. Then there was 'Blondie' to deal with right here in prison. Freddie looked around the cell. There was a poster of Madonna on the wall, looking a lot younger than she does today, a throwback to her rebellious teenage years; a classic pose. His cell mate, sitting on his bunk without a shirt, was tattooed like crazy. He would not have been out of place in a Texas state penitentiary.

"Are they the plans to the prison?" joked Freddie as he nodded at his cellmate's chest. All he received back was a blank stare; the dude obviously didn't watch Prison Break

"Think you are funny?"

"Actually, I do." Here we go again thought Freddie; Me and my big mouth.

"My name's Frank," said his smiling cell mate, extending his right hand. Freddie shook it quickly; relieved that he had not offended him.

"Hope the initiation back there wasn't too distasteful," enquired a smiling Frank.

"I suppose I asked for that," conceded Freddie as he started to brush his teeth in the small corner basin. "Who was the blond kid?" he asked through frothing lips.

"You mean the guy giving you a helping hand? That was Winston. Winston James."

Freddie wiped his face clean and sat on his bunk nodding; committing the name to memory.

"So, what are you in for?" Frank sounded genuinely interested.

"I'm being tried for murder, but I'm innocent."

Frank laughed out loud, causing his tattooed body to ripple like a cartoon animation coming to life.

"That's what we all say."

"But I am," insisted Freddie. "What are you in for?"

"Armed robbery; and I did it." Frank had stopped smiling. The bolt on the door was suddenly slid to one side, followed by the opening of a flap.

"Mail," said a low male voice, as a couple of letters were thrown into the cell, sliding on the floor to come to rest at Freddie's feet. They were both for Freddie.

"I'm use to getting no mail, man. Go ahead enjoy," Frank encouraged. Freddie opened the letters. They were both from complete strangers. One woman was from South Shields and another was from Devon; both stating their devoted love. Death Row groupies, the type that are in touch with Texas penitentiary scum. Two letters already; Freddie thought that it didn't take long; one news item was all that was required to flush the idiots out of the woodwork. Freddie threw them both in the bin. There was nothing from Tommy. Freddie thought that there would be a thank you at least; after all, he did save his Dad. He may not want to keep in touch with Freddie, but he will certainly be keeping in touch with the boy. Yes, he must keep in touch with Tommy.

"I heard you are handy with a blade. I can get you a shank, jugetme."

Freddie thought that Frank was talking to his someone else. Maybe there were three to a cell. He thought it was a Nigerian name, and then realised what he was saying.

"Yeah yeah I get you," Freddie made a hand signal with his fingers bent at strange angles, like a finger puppeteer. He was really down with the boys.

"A shank is a piece of sharpened metal with cloth tightly wound at one end to act as a handle."

"I know what a shank is."

"If you are thinking of getting revenge on Clarence, I can help." A conspirator's smile lit up Frank's face.

Freddie didn't answer right away. He thought that, maybe, he was being used in some sort of gang war.

"Yeah, a shank would be good," replied Freddie eventually. But it wouldn't be Clarence feeling the blade. The cell door opened.

"Fungus, you have a visitor. Let's go."

Collette Singleton was young to be a barrister. She had been top of her class and headhunted by 'Taylor, Fritz and Giles'. She joined them straight from University and was now taking the lead in her first trial at the tender age of 25. Freddie was sat opposite her in the room reserved for meetings with legal teams.

"I didn't do it. Ok I stabbed him but no way did I get him in the neck."

"The problem we have here Mr Fungus."

"Freddie." He was keen to be on first name terms.

"The problem is that there was no one else in the room with a knife." Collette was being logical, dealing with the facts.

"I know it looks bad but..."

"The self defence argument won't wash, you pulled a knife first." Collette was being very businesslike.

"What are we looking at?" Freddie was beginning to realise the seriousness of his situation for the first time.

"If only you didn't carry a knife." He realised that she wasn't criticising him; was only constructing a defence.

"If I didn't carry a knife I would be dead now." It was the truth. They both acknowledged the fact with a moment of silence.

"The problem is that Chavic is dead. OK, we can claim extenuating circumstances. Maybe eight years. That isn't too bad. With good behaviour you could be out in five."

Freddie was thinking. Five years for an innocent man. OK I did stab him a couple of times. Then there were my parents, and that club owner, and the girl in Dublin. They are all dead. Five years with good behaviour. What about Winston? Doing him with a shank is hardly good behaviour. I need to get out of here soon.

"OK, I can go with that," he finally replied.

"OK, I will see you in court."

Back in cell 47 Freddie was horizontal on his bed with his hands clasped together behind his head.

"You still up for the shank?" Frank asked.

"I'm thinking about my court case. I have just seen my brief and she reckons on eight years. But yes I am still in."

"You know that Chamberlain, the court escort officer; he is always on his phone, following god knows who on Twitter. He can get very distracted at times." Frank gave Freddie a knowing look. A half smile with his head tilted to one side.

"What are you saying?" Freddie looked at Madonna, on the wall, for guidance.

"That he can get distracted sometimes, is all."

.-.-.-.-.-.-.-.-.-.-.-.-.-.-.-.-.-

"OK this room is yours Ron. I will change the sheets before bed time." Bobbie was being the perfect hostess. She was getting accustomed to Ben's neat semi in leafy suburbia. "Come down and eat before we take Tommy back to the Fletcher's." She opened a cupboard and threw a clean set of linen on the bed as a reminder.

"Life seems to be a bit complicated around here. Tommy's Mum is dead. He doesn't live with his Dad. You two are a new couple. It must be hard for the kid. I thought I had problems," Ron said as he reached for his arm crutch. Bobbie was taken aback; seemed a little flustered by his plain speaking, but recovered her calm persona.

"I am a very positive person. I really believe everything will work out well for all of us. That includes you Ron."

"I hope so, I really do."

"Are you coming Bobbie, it's time to get Tommy back to the Fletcher's," Ben shouted up the stairs.

"Scrabble time," said Tommy as he hummed the tune to a well known MC Hammer song.

"I'll be down in a second." She turned and continued. "Will you be alright on your own for an hour Ron? We won't be long; Ben has to be in court tomorrow. Help yourself to a snack."

Chapter 17

"All rise," the sombre tone of the court official filled every corner of Court 4. Everyone assembled in the court duly obeyed; the cushions making a strange friction sound as numerous polyester suites disengaged themselves. Judge Johnson entered from a side door and took his place in the magnificent chair below the carved wall mounted wooden eagle that dominated the bench. 'The Queen Elizabeth II' Court rooms had spared no expense; it was a truly impressive room, all dark oak and sweeping arches. He was a commanding presence with a reputation for heavy sentences. His strong jaw line and grey curly wig contrasting in styles. One was impressive; the other rather foolish. He swore in the jury; twelve people that were to determine Freddie's future. There were five females and seven males. They consisted of three of African origin, four Asian, and five Anglo-Saxon; just a typical cross section of modern British society.

Freddie sat next to his brief, the young and attractive Ms Singleton. He was dressed in a sombre grey jacket; his short cropped hair dyed a light brown. It was a last minute decision on his part; nobody liked a ginger. He looked nervous. Ms Singleton, on the other hand, was businesslike and composed as she leafed through the neat pile of papers on the desk in front of her. At the other desk sat the DPP representative, Raymond Matthews. He was slick, charming, and very persuasive. He had never lost a case in the five years since he began practising. He wasn't interested in the papers on his desk. He was studying the jury, looking for any signs of sympathy or animosity towards the defendant. He had had his chance to reject jury members, as had the defence team, and was reasonably confident that the twelve people in front of him could be manipulated, together with the overwhelming evidence, to return the correct decision.

Reporters filled the press section; fingers poised ready to relay the breaking news. The public gallery was packed to the rafters, rubberneckers not wanting to rely on artists impressions on the evening news; wanting to see the drama first hand. On the second row, in the forth seat from the left, sat Stefan. He was dressed in an open necked white shirt, his expensive curly wig looking natural in the artificial light. He was watching the defendant. He noticed that Freddie was enjoying the attention of the public gallery. He observed the sly smile on his face as his young female council whispered something in his ear. Stefan was filled with revengeful thoughts. He will pay the ultimate price, poor Roman will be avenged. His heart was filled with hate but his face did not betray any emotion; he was just another member of the public with one of the hottest tickets in town.

"Call witness number one," ordered the court official. The public Gallery, which had been a sea of bubbling conversation, gradually subsided into silence. The trial had begun. Ben walked nervously to the stand and was sworn in. He looked around the packed courtroom, aware that every eye was trained on his every move.

"Mr Thomas, is that you at the poker table?" asked Matthews as he clicked a device in his right hand. CCTV footage from the 'Krem' came to life on the big screen mounted on the wall. The action was frozen, the word 'Pause' flashing in the bottom left hand corner. The question was rather unnecessary, as it was obviously Ben; but for legal reasons he had to be asked.

"Yes, that is me." The sight of himself at the table with Chavic opposite him, the tattoo fully visible, came as a shock to him. All the feelings of hatred returned, and even though he had taken a beating at the poker table; he would do the same again, the feeling was so intense. The questions continued from Matthews and were duly answered calmly by Ben, until he arrived at the crunch question.

"Did you see Mr Fungus stab Mr Chavic in the neck?" Ben had watched the footage with the rest of the courtroom. There was no visible neck wound inflicted by Freddie. This was the moment. Did he continue the lie or not?

"You were on the floor at the time, were you not?"

"Yes I was." The questions were closing in on Ben. He would have to face the dilemma soon enough.

"You viewed events from a different angle; perhaps a better angle."

"Objection."

"Sustained." Judge Johnson was wary of Matthews.

"I will re-phrase the question. From your position on the floor, did you see Mr Fungus stab Mr Chavic's neck?" Ben sat in silence in the witness box, reviewing his thoughts. He had acted hastily at the time to protect Tommy, but this was a court of law.

"I really can't be sure; I was semi-conscious at the time." He was looking straight ahead, making no eye contact as he answered. Ben sensed that he sounded unconvincing but remained statuesque; willing the moment to end.

"Exhibit A; My Lord." Matthews passed a sheet of paper to the Judge.

"This is a police statement you made on the 13th November. It states 'Yes I saw the knife go into Chavic's neck.' What has happened since that date, Mr Thomas, to make you change your mind?"

"As I said I was semi-conscious at the time and on reflection I can honestly say I cannot be certain. The CCTV footage would appear to back me up." Ben sat stony faced waiting for the next question.

Stefan had watched the footage of his brother's death in shocked silence. He had come to the courtroom to corroborate the facts; to make certain he had the right man. There was no doubt in Stefan's mind that Freddie

235

had stabbed Roman to death. There was nobody else involved in the fight.

"Further CCTV footage shows Mr Fungus attacking a doorman to gain entry to the poker room," Matthews continued in full oily mode. "This is yet more evidence of his vindictive temper. I suggest, and I will produce evidence to prove, that he had a premeditated mission to attack and kill Roman Chavic. All the poker players in the room were interviewed by the police but they saw nothing. They were counting chips. How very convenient. Only you Mr Thomas saw anything, and now you are not so sure." He turned to pull a face to the jury, a puzzled expression which exuded doubt about anything the witness had said.

"I saw him stab Chavic twice, but not in the neck." Ben remained still in the witness box. He knew that it was a controversial moment, but had to see it through.

"No further questions," said Matthews through tight lips. It was not a good start for him.

"Call the second witness, Call Detective Inspector Page." Matthews questioned Page about the CCTV Footage. How he had obtained it from the Krem system.

He confirmed that Ben's statements were obtained legally at the police station and that he was clear that all evidence was valid.

"Have you any reason to believe that anybody else was involved in the confrontation on the screen?"

"No. From the CCTV evidence and witness statements we are certain that Mr Fungus is the only person involved in Mr Chavic's injuries." Page was wearing black shoes to give his evidence more weight.

PC McNally was sitting in row three with a smartly dressed male representative from Internal Affairs. She was whispering in his ear. He stood and addressed the court.

"I know this is totally against procedure my Lord, but I really must interject at this point. I believe the CCTV footage to be tampered evidence. I have the full, uncut tape here in my hand. If the court could play it, it may provide a fully picture of events."

"Objection." Matthews and Singleton said in unison.

"This is most unusual. Council, approach the bench," ordered Judge Johnson, looking flustered for the first time in years.

"I am calling a short recess while I view this new evidence in private. I will decide whether it is admissible or not. Mr Smith set up a screening in my chambers."

"Yes my lord."

After a short conference behind closed doors, during which the public area was awash with speculation, Judge Johnson watched the new evidence with both councils, who sat incredulous and silent as the events unfolded on the screen.

"Can this footage be verified?" Has it been tampered with?" Judge Johnson was covering all angles. He had not encountered such unprecedented events during all his time on the bench.

"Our most qualified IT people have checked it out. It is authentic. It would appear that the footage that you have already seen, this morning, has been edited," the un-named representative from Internal Affairs said in an authoritative tone.

"I will need signed statements to verify all of this." Judge Johnson was in control again.

"We will have them to you this afternoon." Internal Affairs were nothing if not efficient.

"Send the jury for an early lunch. Tell the court we will extend the recess until one o'clock."

"Yes, my Lord." Smith was already opening the door.

Back in the Court room The Press were busy on their I-Pads, keeping newsrooms abreast of the situation. The room was buzzing with expectation. The talk during the recess had been dominated by speculation regarding the uncut footage. What did it contain? Did it incriminate or exonerate the defendant?

Freddie had been taken down to the holding cell during recess. Chamberlain, the guard, was in the process of accessing the cell through the intermediate room. Once in there he was obliged to lock the door behind him, before exiting into the holding cell area through another door. He was on his phone checking his messages. Freddie was aware that he had not yet

238

locked the door to seal the room. He could see the key to the handcuffs hanging from Chamberlain's belt. They were swaying gently from the movement of his thumb as it moved across the screen of his phone. Could Freddie make a move here? His heart was racing. The door back to the corridor was still unlocked. Chamberlain had made a mistake in protocol. Freddie could hear the voice of his prison cellmate echoing in his head. 'He can get distracted sometimes. He loves Twitter.' Five years with good behaviour. It would be a lot more if he got caught in the building after attacking a guard. Freddie was beginning to waiver. Page was stitching him up in the court room, the CCTV footage was pretty damning. This just isn't fair; I didn't kill him. Can I trust my brief? She says five years, but she might be trying to pull the wool over my eyes, they might be all working together. He was getting frantic. Chamberlain was still looking at his phone, smiling. He was totally engrossed with the small screen.

Freddie used all the pent up emotion that had been building during the day. It happened so quickly once he had decided on his course of action. His head flicked back and snapped forward to spread Chamberlain's nose evenly across his face. There was a crunch of bone accompanied by a spray of blood that left the wall behind the guard splattered with a random red pattern. Freddie was struggling with the key to the handcuffs. It wouldn't reach the cuffs. He would have to take the guard's belt off. Chamberlain was groaning in semi consciousness, he wasn't totally out of it. Freddie allowed him to slump to a sitting position with his back to the wall, but the key chain was still too short. He felt vulnerable taking off the belt; he might recover and start fighting or call the alarm. He had no choice. Freddie butted him again to make sure he was not a threat. He butted him four times in a bloody frenzy; each one crunching bone further into the wall. Within seconds Freddie had the belt off the still body of Chamberlain. He struggled with the key, taking frequent glances over his shoulder, until his hand was free. His jacket was now splattered with blood from the attack. He removed it and discarded it into a corner. He quickly emptied the guard's wallet of any money before joining the crowds through the unlocked door.

Everyone was leaving the court building for an early lunch, rumours abounded about the new developments in the case. The local eateries were going to be busy today. Freddie joined the crowded corridor and walked as casually as he could. His recently dyed brown hair combined with his white shirt to allow him to blend into the excited crowd un-noticed, but he felt conspicuous. He ducked into a charity shop; Cancer Research, to browsed the menswear section. Freddie was mildly impressed by the quality of clothes on display. He spent twenty pounds on a new outfit. It consisted of a new white shirt, the collar too big for today's fashion. The trousers had a neat crease down the front; old man's style. He could almost smell the urine. They were just a bit too short making his socks fully visible. He looked like a Harry Hill impersonator. He was quickly off to the ferry terminal happy that he was less noticeable amongst the Christmas shoppers. He was back in the pale winter light, walking into the ferry terminal watching the waiting boat bobbing gently on the tide. He felt calmer with each step. He half expected a hand on his shoulder to end his short spell of freedom, but it never came. He tried to remember the way to Tommy's. Just get across the river, he told himself.

"Single please," he requested at the ticket window, handing over a five pound note. He put both the ticket and his change into his pocket as he continued down the sloping gantry to the waiting ferry. He knew he should keep his head down now that he was on the run, but he had unfinished business with the Thomas family.

"All rise," the court official announced for the second time today. Judge Johnson reappeared to a far more attentive gallery than at the start of proceedings. The silence was deafening.

"I have reviewed the new evidence and am allowing it to be shown. Please bring up the defendant." The court room watched the stairs, waiting for the sinister young murderer to appear. He had looked far less dangerous in the flesh than the photographs that had appeared in the press. The photographs had exaggerated his large red afro hair to almost caricature Freddie. Since his transformation, his appearance in the morning session had almost been 'boy next door'. After ten seconds the public Gallery sensed something was wrong, excited chatter began to resonate around the arched ceiling, amplifying the sound. A court official appeared at the top of the stairs in a flustered confused manner. He approached the bench and whispered to Judge Johnson, who had leant forward to receive the news. He obviously was not happy with the message.

"Court is adjourned until we secure the prisoner." He actually gave his gavel a tap for emphasis.

All hell broke loose. There were loud shouts from the Public Gallery, The press section were tapping away at their screens updating their news desks. Nobody was clear whether Freddie was at large in the building, or had escaped completely. Stefan was furious; he had seen enough of the trial to be convinced that Freddie was his man. He had planned to return later in the trial, set up his sniper rifle and pick him off as he left the building, as he boarded the prison van. He had already visualised Freddie's face under a blanket to protect him from unwanted attention. He had imagined him in the cross hairs of his sights. In his mind he had felt his finger on the trigger and enjoyed the sight of Freddie's head exploding like a melon. He would not be denied his family retribution. He left the building in an attempt to verify Freddie's whereabouts.

Back inside the court room officials were trying to keep control of events.

"Witnesses will have to stay available. The trial may be recalled at any time. Can you all please sign the paperwork?" Ben was happy to oblige. He walked over to the desk and grabbed a pen. Page was not far behind him; waiting behind the forensic expert and the doctor.

"Can we have a word, DI Page?" asked the man from Internal Affairs, who had crept up silently to appear by his side. He held his I.D. in full view for verification.

"Is it important?" asked Page, knowing the answer.

"It is official business. We need to start formal proceeding regarding tampering of evidence. We have a room prepared over here," he said as he gently but firmly guided Page's elbow to an open office. Inside was a desk and recording device. McNally sat in the corner. She wasn't enjoying this at all. She was just following procedure. A bent cop is a bent cop, even if it is your boss; the man you had looked up to as an inspiration. The man in black started the recording device in front of him on the desk. His hand gesture invited Page to sit.

"We don't need to do this," said Page. "I will resign."

"That is all very well, but there are criminal charges to be answered."

"I admit that I edited the tape." His head was bowed in submission.

"The tattoo on Chavic's arm; it was referenced in a prior interview with Thomas. Did you just forget about that? And why did you let the beating continue for so long? So many questions need answering." The man in black was thorough; calmly asking relevant questions. Page sat in silence. He could feel his whole world closing in on him, squeezing the life out of his body.

"Let's start with the girl in the film. You have interviewed her before haven't you?"

"Her sister was killed." Page was on autopilot, almost glad that he could talk about it.

"Can we trace her?"

"Not yet, we are making every effort."

McNally was staring blankly from her position in the corner. She was not enjoying watching a man hang himself in public. She had already reported her finding and evidence to Internal Affairs. They knew that Chavic was implicated in the death of her sister; knew that she had vowed revenge. They knew that Page had not questioned Thomas about the paintbrush in his pocket. It was sloppy police work. Or was it more sinister? Was he trying to frame Freddie? Was he trying to protect the girl? Where was she?

-.-

The planes were taking off from Heathrow Airport almost every minute. Katrina was mesmerised by the sight of them through the window. How could such heavy planes take off so easily? She couldn't help but recognise the irony of her exit from this country. A place, she now realised, that had brought her so much pain and anguish. Here she was waiting for a flight, a situation far removed from her arrival. Then she was a drugged captive, huddling with her younger sister, not knowing what fate awaited her. Now she knew her future was back in Slovakia.

Kade was ten yards to Katrina's left, looking out of the same window at the same planes. She loved her job with the cruise line but loved her mother more. She had to return to The Philippines to sort out her family business. She took a sip from the coffee in her hand, the polystyrene cup protecting her from the heat. She was getting nervous about her flight and wandered over to the departure board. It had updated. She scanned the screen for a few seconds to accustom her eyes to the scrolling information. There it was, just above 'Bratislava - gate 32 now boarding.' She was glad to see her flight information, 'Singapore - gate 17 now boarding.' She grabbed her hand luggage and walked down the corridor and turned left under the 'Gates 1 – 25' sign. Katrina turned right under 'Gates 26 – 50'; following directions.

Within thirty minutes they were both receiving a coffee from their respective flight attendant as the seatbelt sign allowed passengers to stand. Passengers were already scrolling through the in flight movie options.

-.-

Stefan recognised Ben from the courtroom. He watched him sitting at the base of a statute of a woman; the plaque read 'Queen Victoria.' It was surrounded by ornate stonework. The metalwork on the plinth had become stained green by the rain as it ran down the outside. It looked rather unsightly, even though the council had attempted to clean it. A woman walked across the paved area in front of the court building to join Thomas. They embraced and held hands as they began to walk down the street.

He was Stefan's only link to Freddie. The evidence in the morning had informed the court that Freddie had gone to Roman's club to give Thomas a lucky charm. They must know each other. Where else would he go? Stefan's was meticulous in his preparation when he was working, but this time things had not gone according to plan. This time he was going on instinct, and it was telling him to follow the couple. Stefan fell in with the crowds, keeping twenty yards back, ready to window shop if they ever turned around. He followed them to James Street train station, boarded the New Brighton train in the adjoining carriage, and expertly tracked them back to their cosy semi detached house in the tightly packed suburban sprawl that was Wallasey. Freddie had escaped, but somebody had to pay for the death of his brother. He watched as the daylight slowly faded and the lights in the surrounding houses began to illuminate the evening.

Chapter 18

Hello Ron, have you been OK on your own?" asked Bobbie as she hung up her coat.

"I have been watching a bit of television, a re-run of 'Colombo.'"

"OK, I'll leave you to it." She left to join Ben.

He was in the kitchen, drawing the blinds while he boiled the kettle.

"I'm a bit worried about Freddie being at large."

"Do you really think that he is a threat to us?" asked Bobbie as she settled at the oak table.

"I did give evidence that was a major contributory factor in him being charged with murder, and he is friendly with Tommy for some reason. So yes, I think he is a threat; he will come here, I'm certain of it."

"What can we do?"

"We need to get Ron back to Huddersfield. Tommy should come with us; get us all out of the area for a while."

"What about Spangle?" The dog was the least of Ben's worries, the very least.

"We could ask Simon and Brie to mind him. You know, feed him and let him out in the garden to do his business. I will ring them." He was punching numbers on the wall mounted phone by the freezer. He leaned back, knocking off a couple of fridge magnets from the metal door. A ceramic flip flop from Skiathos and a smiling Jamaican Rastafarian lay on the floor by his feet as he began speaking on the phone.

"Hi Simon, I know this is short notice but can you dog sit tonight? Come round for a drink and I will show you the ropes."

"No problem my old mate. We are on our way."

"That was easy," said Ben as he replaced the magnets on the door. "Now for the difficult call." He opened the address book and leafed through a few pages before punching more numbers into the phone, his lips whispering the numbers as he read them from the page.

"Hello, Mrs Fletcher. I know this is totally against the conditions of Tommy's placement. I know I should only have him at weekends, but could you do me a big, big favour." He was met with silence, so decided to continue talking. "We have a 'Good Samaritan' duty call that Tommy would love to be involved in; we promised him we would include him. I know the timing is awful but we would have him back to you by tomorrow evening. I promise."

Mrs Fletcher was smiling into the phone. This didn't particularly indicate anything favourable; she was always smiling. She probably would be smiling on her deathbed. Finally she answered.

"As it happens, we were planning a day out. It would be rather nice to have some time together, without Tommy."

"That is brilliant. We will come and get him."

"That will not be necessary; we will deliver him to you. We were planning on seeing the new developments in New Brighton; they are supposed to be very impressive."

"It is very nice there now since the place has had a facelift."

"We will be there as quick as we can"

"Thank you very much. We really appreciate what you are doing." Ben was talking to himself; Mrs Fletcher had already hung up.

Stefan watched the house from the top of the hill. He planned to wait until it was completely dark before approaching the house. He was certain that Freddie would turn up at this house. Stefan wanted to be inside, waiting for him. The disappointment of not having him in the crosshairs of his weapon outside the courthouse was still burning inside his brain. He would not let him escape again. A couple turned into the street, there was nothing particularly strange about them apart from the fact that the man was dressed in a cowboy outfit complete with Stetson, spurs on his boots, and a gun holster; very odd. Stefan watched them walk down the hill and knock on Ben's door. They were greeted warmly and disappeared behind the closed door. Stefan did not want complications. There were beginning to be too many people involved; Stefan preferred things simple, manageable; but if he had to deal with a crowd he would; he was determined to get Freddie.

Freddie had enjoyed the ferry crossing; the walk along the promenade had been invigorating. He had enjoyed the fresh air in his face. However, he was now lost and getting colder by the minute. The white shirt he had obtained from the charity shop was too thin to offer any real protection from the wind that had increased in strength as it whipped up moisture on its journey across Liverpool Bay. He was looking for a landmark. He had passed the 'giant clown' on the roundabout and was now looking for the dark imposing church on top of the hill. Where was it? It had large gold fingers on its clock face which dominated the skyline. As he rounded the bend by the sand hills he saw the top of a flagpole slowly appearing, displaying more of the Union Jack as he made progress against the wind. It looked familiar. As he climbed the hill, more and more of the church tower appeared over the horizon, until it was completely visible; the gold clock almost luminous in the fading light. Freddie continued uphill along the sloping road, the church getting larger with every stride. When he arrived at the lych-gate he read the notice board. 'St Hilary's'; this is the one. Freddie was pleased with his navigational prowess. Who needs a 'Sat Nav' when you have natural flair? He walked into the graveyard; impressed by the ornate stonework of some of the headstones. Some had been there since the eighteen century. He was really feeling the cold from the wind; he needed some shelter. He decided to sit on a grave with the headstone against his back as protection from the chilly blast coming from the Welsh Hills. 'Thomas Francis Williams' born 1822 died 1866. The headstone informed Freddie that poor old Thomas had left a loving wife and two doting children. This will do perfectly he decided, as he nestled down, making sure that his head and shoulders were properly sheltered by the headstone as he sat upright on the grave. Thomas wouldn't mind, Freddie convinced himself. The reason he had chosen Thomas's grave was that it offered a perfect view down the hill to Tommy's house. It only seemed like yesterday that he had hid behind the hedge on the day he delivered Tommy home. Now here he was watching a cowboy knock at Tommy's house and be welcomed inside. He would have to get nearer after it was completely dark.

"The dog food is in this cupboard here," directed Bobbie as she opened one of the many oak storage cupboards that lined the wall of the kitchen.

"He has one tin now and another at bed time. He likes to settle down at about nine o'clock." She wandered off into the lounge, still talking. "He normally watches TV with us from that basket in the corner. I'm not sure whether he will do that if you are on the settee, you'll have to play it by ear." she was talking very quickly, excited to be discussing Spangle.

"What about toilet time?" Simon was trying to move things along.

"OK. He will stand by the back door, spinning in circles, chasing his tail, when he wants to go. If he gets desperate he will start whining. Just open the door and let him into the garden. Make sure the side gate is closed before you do that. I don't want him running riot around the neighbourhood."

"What's with the nappy?" asked Simon.

"Since the accident with the police car Spangle has worn the neck support, the thing that looks like an inverted collar. But lately he has developed a gastric problem. He needs to wear the nappy all the time."

"So why does he need to go outside?" Brie was being logical.

"It's just habit. He finds it almost impossible to do it in the house, even with the nappy." Bobbie was a bit embarrassed about the subject.

"Will we have to clean up his business afterwards?" Brie enquired.

"No, no Ben will do that when we get back." Ben pulled a face in mock horror. It really was his job. Cleaning up dog shit for an animal he didn't even like. It must be love.

"It's best to let it dry out and get crusty," he said for effect. They all laughed, but he wasn't joking.

"It's all covered by the pet insurance," said Bobbie.

"You have Pet insurance?" Simon was incredulous. "What next? Do you insure your dog to drive your car? Do you have 'Dog, fire and theft.'?"

"Time for that drink I promised you. Beer?" enquired Ben in an effort to move on from Simon's terrible joke.

"That would be great."

"Brie?"

"Orange juice for me please."

"Not for me, I'm driving," said Bobbie.

"I drove all night, to get to you," Simon was doing his associated song game, where he sang any song that was remotely linked to anything anybody said. It was annoying, but Ben loved him for it. They had done it since University. The door bell rang, ding dong, a standard model.

"I'll get that," said Bobbie as she raced down the hall. She opened the door to be confronted by the smiling face of Mr Fletcher. Tommy, standing next to him, had an even bigger smile.

"We expect him back tomorrow as agreed," Fletcher said through a smile. How does he do that? His lips hardly moved. It was like a ventriloquist dummy, most unnerving

"We will bring him back tomorrow. Thank you for agreeing to this change," said Bobbie. Fletcher turned on his heels and returned to his car. Mrs Fletcher had been watching proceeding through the passenger window. Her smile had never left her face. Tommy had joined Ron on the settee talking excitedly about the trip.

"The woman in the photograph is your daughter Sally. You remember the photograph don't you?"

253

"Yes. Sally" Ron played along.

"Mustang Sally now baby…" Simon started into a rendition.

"So will you be OK with the dog; with the arrangements?" Bobbie interrupted; she was still fussing around.

"Just go and delivery Ron, will you. We will be fine," Brie tried to reassure her.

"Do do Ron Ron Ron, do do Ron Ron," Simon sang again.

"Will you stop doing that, it is so childish," Brie had had enough. Ben started collecting stuff for the drive; wallet, money for petrol. He was going through a mental list.

"Come on you two get in the back of the car."

Bobbie had backed her Golf off the drive and was waiting for everyone to get in.

Ron was slower that the other two, but once his rear door clunked shut she was off towards the M53.

"Are you two OK in the back?" Bobbie asked.

"We're fine." Tommy was pointing things out to Ron through the window.

"What about you in the front? Are you happy?" she gave Ben a quick sideways glance.

"You know what. I really am. I spend my days writing messages on the cards for your flowers, you know, when people phone up and dictate the message. Then I deliver them on my bike. I just might be getting bored with the standard messages that we offer. I could write much better messages than 'Best wishes' or 'Sorry for your loss' or 'In loving memory'. How about, 'Things can never be the same again. You were my rock, my life, my love. I will never forget you.'

"The cards are business card size not A4," teased Bobbie.

"We could get bigger cards. Allow my creative juices to flow." They both smiled at the idea of a giant envelope, like a garish valentine, attached to one of their flower arrangements.

"My crutch." Ron suddenly shouted from the rear seat. "I've forgotten my crutch."

"Do you really need it now?" asked Ben.

"Yes, it has all of my money inside the tubular frame."

"Your money?" it was Ben again.

"I got it from the house sale. I'm sure I told you." They all understood the situation immediately.

They were on the roundabout, almost on the motorway. Bobbie continued round completing a full circle to head back to the house.

"We will be back in a few minutes. That's not much of a delay." Bobbie was taking control.

Stefan had watched the car leave. There were only two people in the house now; the cowboy and his woman. Two was a manageable number; not too many to control. The sight of his gun would be enough to scare them out of their wits. It was now dark enough to make his move. He wandered down the road, underneath the bare branches of the trees that lined both sides. He imagined it would look splendid in full bloom during the summer. He attached the screw fitted silencer to his gun before ringing the door bell. The cowboy answered and backed away when confronted by the barrel of the 'Walther P99' hand gun.

"Get against the wall." Stefan ordered. "Both of you."

"How dare you barge in here with .." Brie was indignant, but was shocked into silence by Stefan striking Simon across the cheekbone with his gun, drawing blood.

"Now."

They both cowered against the wall and allowed Stefan to tie Simon's hands behind his back intertwined in the panels on the back of the dining chair. Simon's face was already bruised and swelling fast.

"What do you want?" Brie had recovered some of her fighting spirit.

"I am waiting for somebody. You must wait with me," Stefan answered calmly in his slight accent. "I will have to tie you up also."

"I am not being trussed up like a Christmas turkey," Brie was insulted.

"It was not an option. It was a statement of fact. I am not afraid to use this," Stefan waved the gun in her face for emphasis. The sound of a key turning in the front door interrupted their conversation. Bobbie and Ben burst into the hall, followed by Tommy holding Ron's arm.

"Where did you leave your crutch Ron?" asked Bobbie, keen to get back on the road.

"I can't remember."

"It must be downstairs somewhere," said Ben as he strode purposefully into the lounge where he was met by the shocked face of Brie, cowering in the corner.

"It's only me. I'm not interrupting anything am I?" he joked, but she wasn't laughing. He followed her eye line to take in the rest of the room. Simon was sitting bound to a chair in the other corner. Was this a sex game? He looked back to Brie for some clarification. She was still in a state of shock, her right hand over her mouth. Bobbie, Tommy and Ron had arrived in the doorway.

"What's going on? Have you got the crutch?"

"All of you please join the cowboy in the corner," Stefan ordered. None of the new arrivals had noticed him next to the display cabinet. He pointed to the corner with a sharp motion of the gun, glistening in his right hand. They all slowly shuffled subserviently into the corner to join Simon and Brie. Who was this guy? Ben thought that he looks vaguely familiar. Why was he here?

257

"What are you doing in my house? You have no right to be here." Ben was taking the lead.

"This gives me all the right I need," replied Stefan holding the gun menacingly towards the group.

"You cannot shoot all of us," Bobbie pointed out.

"Yes I can." Stefan meant every word.

"What are you doing in my house? Ben repeated.

"I believe Freddie Fungus will come here. I have unfinished business with him. If you intervene or try and stop me I will have no choice but to take you out of the equation. We sit and wait."

-.-

Freddie had seen the car return and park on the drive. He had seen Ben go into the house and be followed in by Tommy and Bobbie. He couldn't wait to confront them. What had surprised him was Ron, the old guy from the cruise ship. Why was he here? How did he get here from Southampton? He did a head count. According to his calculation there was Ben, Bobbie and Tommy; Old Ron, the cowboy and the woman. Then there was the stranger who had arrived quietly in the dark. That made a total of seven people in the house, too many to confront. Freddie stood up from his position on the grave; he was getting stiff in the cold wind. He couldn't resist taking a look and surprise them all. Maybe he could look through the window and check out what was going on. Perhaps he could try the back door. The temptation to get involved was growing. He started walking down the hill, excitement growing with every stride. He had a quick look round behind him; the road was deserted. The porch light of the Thomas's grew brighter in the dark as he got nearer.

-.-

"You cannot keep us all here indefinitely under house arrest. Someone will miss us," Bobbie was testing his resolve.

"How can anybody miss you in your own home?" Stefan was thinking clearly. He needed to get organised. He threw the rest of the tape he had used on Simon towards Tommy.

"Tie your father up." He was keen to disable the male adults. Tommy began the task determined not to do it too tightly.

Spangle was getting agitated in the kitchen, spiralling around on the tiled floor waiting for somebody to open the back door for him. He turned as he heard the door handle crank, but was puzzled to see it moving without a hand on it. He whined a little dog noise. Freddie tried the handle again but it was locked. He would have to go around to the front. The door bell rang; the chime resonating around the house, cutting through the tension.

"Are you expecting anybody?" asked Stefan.

"We don't even live her. We are babysitting the dog," answered Brie.

"Not you. You" he said, pointing the gun at Ben. The door bell rang again before he could answer.

259

"We can't just ignore it," Brie sensed that Stefan's was wavering.

"See who it is. Get rid of them." Bobbie was only too happy to open the door; for any distraction from the situation they found themselves in.

"No funny business. I am watching you."

Bobbie could make out the shape of a body through the opaque glass that dominated the top half of the front door. The shape stepped back to take a look at the house, checking out the upstairs windows before stepping forward to ring the bell again. Bobbie opened it and the shape barged in.

"Social Services," announced Joan as she flashed her I.D. card. She was already taking notes on her flipchart.

"This isn't a good time," Bobbie said as she tried to block the entrance into the packed lounge.

"I have authority to complete a habitat assessment at a minutes notice. Can I see the kitchen?" she asked even though she was already opening the door.

"Yes, yes, don't mind Spangle. Move boy." Joan had the fridge door open, taking notes.

"Fruit? Is there any fruit?" she asked as she eyed the work surfaces.

"In the bowl on the table," offered Bobbie relieved that she had been to Morrison's only yesterday. Joan continued to complete her paperwork.

"Can I see Tommy's bedroom?"

260

"Follow me," said Bobbie only too glad to get her upstairs. Once they were upstairs Bobbie made her excuses.

"Help yourself to the bathroom. You are welcome to inspect anywhere upstairs. Do you want a drink?"

"Coffee would be nice."

"I'll be back with it as soon as the kettle is boiled." Bobbie raced down the stairs.

"Who was it?" Ben asked from his bound position next to Simon. He noticed Simon's injured face for the first time. They both looked dreadful.

"That Social Services woman; she has come to do the assessment. She will be a while upstairs. We may be able to get her out of the house without her coming in here."

"Perfect timing," whispered Ben.

"It's got to be – perfect," Simon hummed the tune under his breath. He always got worse with his silly game when he was nervous.

"OK back to business. Tie the women up," ordered Stefan. Tommy continued with the tape.

"I will deal with our visitor when she comes down. Tie them tight, I will be checking when you have finished."

"What unfinished business have you got with Freddie," Brie was prying again. Stefan was beginning to feel the pressure. This situation was getting out of

261

control. There were way too many people involved, and they were all annoying him in varying degrees. They were all dispensable. The wig had been itching since he had arrived; it must be the central heating. He had an uncontrollable urge to remove it. What harm could it do? These people cannot hurt me. The men were tied up, the women almost done. There was only the boy and the old man to deal with. He took his wig off. The tight black curls falling to the floor. It felt good to be free.

"Oh, my god. I thought you were dead," Ben was visibly shocked.

"It is Roman who is dead. I am here to avenge his death. We have all heard the evidence in court. We wait here until Freddie arrives. He will come I know it," Stefan was raging; his short blond hair, slicked back, making him the mirror image of his brother. It was unnerving. "And when he does, I will kill him."

"How did you get here?" Brie was still probing despite the shocking revelations.

"We both arrived from Ukraine. We went our separate ways. Roman up here and me in Basildon," it felt good to talk; it was a release for Stefan. "Why are you smiling?"

"It's just Basildon, you know. It is in Essex, and your name is Chavic," answered Simon nervously. Ben stared at Simon, willing him to catch his eye so he could stop him, but he continued despite his facial injuries.

262

"I don't see the connection," Stefan said. "Please explain."

"Well, Essex apparently has a high percentage of 'Chavs.'" Stefan looked mildly interested, but the rest of the group were dreading any further explanation. This couldn't end pleasantly.

"So it is rather amusing that there is a Chavic in Essex," Simon concluded. Stefan's face was pure evil. It was a contorted red mask of hatred.

"You make fun of my family name? The Chavic name is well respected in Ukraine. My parents were killed by the authorities. My brother was killed by Fungus; and now you disrespect me." He was shouting, eyes blazing. "Since my parents were killed we had looked after each other, Roman and I; and now he has gone. Somebody in this room will die in redemption. It is an eye for an eye and a life for a life. Somebody must die for the death of my brother."

Ben could hear Tony Christie in his head, singing about his wife Maria. But it was Simon who spoke first.

"Tony Christie."

"What?" Stefan demanded, his gun waving wildly around the room from person to person.

"A life for a life, somebody must die for the death of my wife; not brother," Simon did the quote mark mime with two fingers of each hand as he said 'brother'. "But close enough." Stefan was so furious that he didn't notice that Simon's hands were free.

"Are you disrespecting my family, cowboy?" demanded Stefan as he pointed the gun in Simon's face. Simon's hands were up in defence. "No, no. It's just the song. I sort of recognised it. No offence."

"He is nervous. We all are," said Ben. Stefan had lost his composure. He was steaming; pointing his gun at all of them in random order.

"So, who is to die?" he asked as he swept the gun around room. "Shall it be you? What is your name?"

"Tommy," answered the teenager as he cowered away from the barrel of the gun. Stefan placed his gun against Tommy's temple; his finger was on the trigger.

"Give me one reason why I should not pull the trigger?"

"He is just a boy," said Ben softly. Tommy was terrified. He could smell the gun. It had a metallic aroma, as if it had been recently cleaned. Bobbie spoke up.

"Look, we're all really sorry about your brother, but nobody here in this room is responsible. It was Freddie that killed him; and he has been arrested. Let the law take its course."

"But he has escaped. I was there in the courtroom. It has been on the news. So somebody must pay," Stefan responded. He was being irrational, eyes wild like a crazed animal. Ben joined in the debate.

"Look, I was there when your brother was killed. He attacked me. If I could, I think I would have killed him myself, but I wasn't strong enough." Ben looked down; ashamed of himself, but still wanting to protect his son. "So let the boy go. If anyone is guilty of wanting him dead, it is me."

"And why would you want to kill him?" Stefan asked.

"Why? He was responsible for the death of my wife. Ben's eyes were blazing, but he gave Simon a quick look to discourage any more references to Tony Christie. This was too serious."

"Let the boy go," Ben pleaded "Let him go." Ben gave Simon another nervous glance, hoping that he wouldn't start into a full rendition of 'Bohemian Rhapsody.' The gun moved from Tommy's to Ben's temple.

"Do we have any more volunteers?" Stefan asked as Ben flinched in his chair.

"Kill me. I deserve to die," interrupted Brie. She was sobbing gently. "I miss Holly so much. It was me that switched off the ventilator, not Simon. Holly could have lived for weeks, months even; as a vegetable. But it would have been a horrible existence for her and for us. I just couldn't face the trauma of the daily visits, the eventual loss. I like order in my life. Things have to be neat and tidy. You all make fun of me; I know you do. I am not stupid. There is not a day goes by without me thinking of her little face. And now I am drinking too much and having a pointless affair. I'm just a terrible, terrible person. So kill me. I deserve it." She continued to sob quietly with her head bowed. The gun barrel moved slowly from Ben to Brie. Simon walked across the room to where Stefan was holding his gun to Brie's head.

"She doesn't mean any of that. Surely you couldn't contemplate killing a pregnant woman. If someone raised a gun to you, you would have to shoot him, am I right?"

"What do you mean?" asked Stefan. Simon took his replica gun out of his Wild West holster and held it dangling at the side of his thigh.

"If this were real, you would have to shoot me before I shot you. A duel if you will."

"Simon, don't." Brie was worried.

"This town ain't big enough for the both of us." Simon continued in a strange western drawl. He raised his silver plastic model of a Colt 45 and placed it at Stefan's temple.

"Remove the gun or I will shoot you," demanded Simon.

"Do you think I do not know the difference between a fake gun and a real one, cowboy?"

"Can you be sure?" Simon continued the pretence.

"That is a fake; Do you think I would allow such a thing to be held to my head?" declared Stefan as he casually shot Simon in the thigh; the silencer ensuring that his gun only made a slight muffled sound. Simon made considerably more noise as he collapsed onto the floor screaming in pain. He lay still, clasping his leg with both hands, taking short sharp breaths. Nobody else made a sound except Brie.

"Are you OK, darling? Why did you do such a crazy thing?"

"A man's gotta do what a man's gotta do," he whispered between breaths.

"You know I still love you don't you?" Brie was still crying.

"I know."

-.-

Freddie sensed that there was some kind of confrontation going on in the house. There were raised voices, shouting and he was sure that he had heard a noise; a quiet muffled shot, he was sure that it what a gun. He tried the kitchen door again but it was locked tight. He avoided the green bin by the drainpipe on the corner of the house and decided to try the downstairs toilet window.

Mrs Hargreaves at number 34 had been watching the comings and goings at the Thomas's house all evening. She was sure there was somebody in the garden. There he was again fiddling with a window. She picked up her phone and rang the police.

"I don't want to kill you, you stupid cowboy; and even I can't kill a defenceless woman. So that leaves one of you four," Stefan said as he swept his gun around to the others. He had the gun against Ron's head.

"Why should you live?"

"Do something good for once in your life, son. My life is already over. So, go ahead, pull the trigger. No one will remember me. I certainly won't," Ron was serious. Tommy had recovered his composure and was desperate to help Ron.

"We have all experienced loss. You have lost your parents and brother," he pleaded as he spoke directly to Stefan. "He has lost his memory," he continued, pointing at Ron. "I have lost my mother; his wife." Tommy nodded at his father for clarity. "They have lost their daughter," his open palm indicated Simon and Brie huddled on the floor, where she was inspecting his leg.

"And who have you lost?" Stefan asked Bobbie.

"Well, my first dog died because I couldn't afford the injections. I felt so guilty."

"You stupid woman, we are talking about real human loss, and you compare it to a dog." He stepped closer to her and placed the barrel of his gun against her temple.

"We have a winner." He had run out of patience and was serious in his intent to make an example of somebody. He had had enough of these weird misfits. Freddie could wait.

Spangle had been spiralling in the kitchen all the time. The sound of his owner's voice crying out in distress caused his ears to prick up. He had always been fiercely loyal to Bobbie; doted on her. All his life, all he could remember was being spoilt with good food, a warm house; Bobbie had nursed him back from his serious injuries with the police car. It was time to repay her generosity. He scampered into the lounge to witness the scene. Bobbie was cowering with the gun against her head. All the others were frozen in fear; he could sense it. He didn't break his stride, but continued at speed, taking a giant stride to launch into a jump. He aimed at the menacing blond man, hoping to sink his teeth into the forearm that was holding the gun. He had seen police dogs do it on TV as he sat in the basket enjoying a film with his owner. It should be easy. The ruff around his neck and the nappy around his backside made control of his flight more difficult than he had imagined. Once he was airborne he had to just go with the flow. He sailed through the air, narrowly missing Stefan. The exertion of the leap caused the nappy to become dislodged enabling the contents to spray across Stefan's face.

He recoiled in shock, eyes closed instinctively as he felt the heat on his face. He wiped his face with his free hand to clear his eyes. He looked like he had been let loose in a chocolate factory. Spangle was still travelling across the room planning his landing. His leap had been considerable longer than he had intended, adrenalin resulting in a personal best distance. He landed on the table amongst the painting equipment that belonged to Mary. The landing caused paintbrushes and tubes of oil paint to scatter across the table. One paintbrush in particular shot up into the air like a missile and sped back across the room towards Stefan. He was still rubbing his eyes as the metal end of the brush lodged itself into his eye socket. It was an extraordinary coincidence. He lay there; screaming in pain. Ben took the opportunity to break free from the loose fitting tape and take the gun.

Just as everyone was catching their breath from the incredibly stressful scene they had witnessed, the door handle cranked and the door opened. In waltzed Joan, clipboard in hand.

"I have finished upstairs. Everything seems fine. I am gasping for that coffee you promised me." She wasn't often lost for words, but this was one of the few occasions that left her speechless. The scene that met her eyes left her open mouthed. Mr Thomas' partner, the woman who had shown her upstairs, Bobette or something like that; she was tied to a chair. Tommy was here on an unauthorised visit. There was a man writhing around the floor covered in dog shit with a paintbrush stuck in his eye. A cowboy was holding his bleeding leg complaining that he had been shot; and then there was Mr Thomas, standing in the middle of the room with a gun in his hand.

"This is not what it looks like. I can explain," said Ben above the sound of the police car stopping outside of the front window. The noise of the siren filled the room through the window, as flashing blue and red lights shone into the room casting strange patterns on the far wall behind Ron and Tommy.

Chapter 19

"Where did you get the gun?" asked the neatly dressed plain clothed officer. McNally was in the corner observing. She had not really expected to be promoted after Page had been removed, but had always felt that maybe there would be some kind of recognition for the work she had produced during the trial. She had blown the case wide open.

"It was Chavic's," Ben was disappointed that he was involved in a police interview again. This was his fourth in the last twelve months.

"Chavic?"

"Yes. He said he was Roman's twin. He was convinced that Freddie would come to my house. He was waiting and things sort of got out of hand."

"So the man with the brush in his eye is Roman's twin brother?" The police officer was speaking slowly ensuring that all statements were clearly recorded. McNally was convinced she could conduct an interview better than this snail, but remained quiet, silently sulking.

"Look, are we finished here? I have to get my son back to his foster carers."

"Why is he in care?" asked the officer. Page's replacement was new to the area. Ben realises that whatever he said would sound terribly damning. My wife died and I became depressed and couldn't cope. I was in a brawl at a poker den. I was arrested at a dogging site. None of these statements would paint an accurate picture of past events.

"We have had a difficult time," Ben said quietly. It was the best he could come up with. "And the Police still have £4,032 that belongs to me," he added unnecessarily.

"You say the dog caused the paintbrush to be lodged in," he paused to check his paperwork before continuing, "Chavic's eye?"

"Yes. It was a freak accident. Everybody in the room was amazed." Suddenly everything became crystal clear to Ben. The girl at the poker room, the waitress, she had seemed shocked when she had the paintbrush in her hand. Page now admitted that she denied any intent; that it had just happened as if the brush had a life of it's own. That is exactly how it had appeared to Ben from his position on the floor. And today, here in my own house, another paintbrush had zeroed in on Chavic, like a sophisticated NATO heat seeking missile. It could have been a freak accident, but the way it had almost stopped in mid air before setting off across the room was rather spooky. Then there was the time Bobbie had stabbed him in the buttock while playing around with one of Mary's paintbrushes. Taken together as three linked incidents, it was too much of a coincidence. Ben realised that maybe the paintbrushes did have a life of their own. Maybe Mary was acting from beyond the grave; on a secret mission.

-.-

The kitchen had been set up as another interview room. Brie sat at the table, visibly upset by the day's events.

"As I have already stated, we were dog sitting for Ben; this man just turned up out of the blue. Simon was so brave."

"Why did he have a gun?" Barnes was enjoying taking the lead.

"How should I know?"

"You are married to him?"

"Simon didn't have a real gun. It is a replica; a toy. He is a bit obsessed with cowboys, always has been. Look, he was protecting me, can't you understand that? It was the mad man who had the real gun."

-.-

Back in the lounge Ben had been replaced by Ron as the police systematically took statements from all people present at the scene.

"Why are you here?" the new guy asked.

"I'm with the boy," Ron answered.

"Which boy?" he was being dogmatic.

"I don't remember his name, my memory is not what it used to be, but he is a good kid."

"What happened in there today?" he was determined to get a true picture of events.

"We all came back for my crutch and this gunman was in the house. He went crazy, threatening to kill everybody. He was hopping mad. That's all I can remember."

"Did he shoot anybody'" he asked in a monotone.

"The cowboy took one for the team; in the leg."

-.-

Chavic was refusing to talk. He was trying desperately to think of a way out of this mess. He thought that he needed medical treatment for his eye before it became infected. He had been given painkillers but was convinced that he would lose the eye. The police had taken the gun; it was only a matter of time before they traced it. He was in a real pickle and could see no way out. The two officers guarding him never took their eyes off him, and the handcuffs held him securely every time he tried to shake them free.

Brie had been escorted out of the kitchen, back to the holding area, and had been replaced by Joan; the Social Worker.

"They were scoring well until I walked into the front room. Food, sleeping accommodation, hygiene in the bathroom; all had scored highly. The father, Mr

274

Thomas, had already passed his personal interview; he had really turned things around in the last few months."

Barnes had waited patiently to get a word in. "What scene met your eyes when you entered the lounge?"

After everybody had been interviewed it became clear to the police that the evidence and statements corroborated each other.

"Seems that maybe they are all telling the truth sir," said McNally. A uniformed officer walked into the lounge holding a piece of paper. He read it to the group.

"Ballistics have traced the gun, sir. It is implicated with eight deaths. Various locations spread all over the country."

"It would seem that Chavic has far more important questions to answer." Barnes stated to the assembled group of officers.

-.-

Freddie was back in the graveyard considering his next move. The police were everywhere; the road had been cordoned off with tape. He was in no mood to move; he sat in the graveyard watching events unfold down the hill. He felt secure with his back on the headstone; he sat on the same grave as before. He was beginning to envy the life of 'Thomas Francis Williams'. Life must have been simpler in 1866; there was plenty of freedom. Food and shelter were your only concerns; OK health may have been an issue; what with raging plagues and no real cures for all sorts of common ailments. But life was simpler. Imagine a life without, electricity, cars, mobile phones, forensics, DNA testing, CCTV. A man could wander this wonderful country and remain anonymous, almost invisible if he so desired; Even as late as Victorian times 'Jack the Ripper' had remained undetected and un-named. What exactly did the police have to incriminate Freddie? He was being stitched up for the death in the poker room. He had panicked back in the courthouse; had attacked the guard but he was sure that he wasn't dead. He was certain of it. The worst he was facing was two counts of assault; and with the delightful Collette Singleton representing him he could look forward to a reasonable sentence. Eight years she had said; but that was before the guard was injured. Freddie had to think; think long and hard. He couldn't run for ever, things would only get worse.

"Are you Ok there?" asked a quiet voice. Freddie wasn't sure if he was hearing voices in his head. That option was removed when he turned to take in the presence of the local vicar. Reverend Martin Markland wore horn rimmed glasses and sported a trim beard. A bald head gave him the appearance of an upside down head. He spoke quietly again in a kind caring manner.

"Are you OK?"

Freddie was too surprised to run. The Reverend didn't appear dangerous; and the sudden movement and shouting in the graveyard might attract the attention of the police down the hill. He decided to remain seated and talk.

"I've done some terrible things Father." Freddie heard himself say.

"This is an Anglican Church my son, drop the Father stuff." Martin was visibly rattled by the Catholic reference.

"What do I call you?" Freddie knew he had pushed the right buttons.

"Reverend will do nicely."

"OK Father," Freddie just couldn't help himself. It just slipped out.

"We are not a Catholic Church, please call me Reverend Martin."

"Forgive me Father for I have sinned," Freddie was being contrite.

"Drop the Father thing. I said this is an Anglican church. We do not do confessionals; but I am willing to listen to a troubled soul, as a friend. Maybe I can give you some guidance."

"Surely we are all the same in God's eyes'" Freddie challenged.

"Quite. What things have you done that are so terrible, that you seek God's forgiveness? God will forgive you. You must learn to forgive yourself." Martin was back in control of his emotions.

Freddie could feel himself soften towards Ben and Tommy. He could see that it was nothing personal. He must try and see things from other people's perspective.

God will find a way. It hit him like a bolt of lightning; a road to Damascus moment. If he were to find God maybe the court would go easy on him. A repentant sinner was worth ten convicts that never saw the light. Freddie was warming to the theme. He began talking to Reverend Martin, pouring out all of his sordid past. He didn't mention the people he had killed, of course not. He only talked of the two latest assaults in a truly repentant mantra; rocking back and forth on the grave as the words spilled out. Martin only needed to hear enough to be a supportive religious sage. Freddie had found God, and it felt good.

"No matter how low you fall, there is always a way back if you take the Lord's hand. Do you want the Lord in your life?" Martin was using his most sanctimonious expression, the one he reserved for saved souls.

"I think I do," Freddie whispered into the cold night air; his breath causing a fog to form in front of his face.

"Are you ready to take his hand?" Martin reached out to touch Freddie lightly in the wrist. Freddie forced himself not to pull away, not to brush off the contact.

"I think I am," Freddie's eyes were burning with sincerity behind the fog.

"Give yourself up, son. Make a fresh start."

"I will Father," Freddie just couldn't resist. Freddie stood, breaking the contact, and stretched his limbs. "Will you vouch for me Reverend Martin?"

"Of course I will, my son. Come inside. Have a hot drink and maybe a bite to eat. We can pray together."

278

"That is very kind of you Father, but I really must be getting on." Freddie continued stretching.

And so it was that Freddie began the long walk down the hill towards the police officer standing next to the crime scene tape; towards redemption. Though he may walk in the valley of death he shall feel no evil. He was feeling cleansed already. He began humming an old favourite to himself, 'Has anyone here seen my old friend Martin?' I have found God, he whispered to himself. If he said it often enough he thought that he may just believe it himself. He pulled up the oversized collar on his white shirt to gain some protection from the wind as the police officer noticed him approaching the taped crime scene.

A police car drove off down the hill to the main road. An officer removed the tape that blocked access to the main road traffic. Inside the vehicle Stefan was handcuffed; he was to face serious charges involving numerous counts of murder once the hospital had seen to his eye. He had travelled a long way from his homeland. The Ukraine seemed a million miles away now. His parents and brother were dead. He had lived a life of violence since his childhood; had known no other life. He could see no way out of his situation. His best defence was to play on having a troubled childhood, seeing his parents killed in front of his own eyes; that can have a long lasting effect on a child. It sounded convincing, that was the way he would go, as soon as he was out of the hospital.

Back in the house Barnes was collecting all of the electronic recording devices and assuring everybody that the police had finished with their enquiries for the present time.

"We will be in touch regarding court appearances regarding the shooting." Barnes realised disappointedly that he had said 'regarding' twice in the same sentence. He walked out of the front door; all four officers followed him out to the waiting police car.

"I must be off myself. I need to write up my report," announce Joan as she tidied her files before tucking them under her arm. She too disappeared out of the open front door. It was beginning to be quite a procession.

"It's been a long tiring day," said Bobbie, "But we still need to get Ron to his daughter; and visit Simon once his leg has been treated."

"OK Tommy, get Ron's crutch and let's get on the road again." Ben could hear Willie Nelson in his head, but decided to leave it, especially as Simon was not there; he was already on the way to hospital.

"What about all of this mess," Bobbie asked as she spread her arms to take in the result of Spangle's burst nappy.

"Let it go dry and crusty," Ben suggested.

"We can't leave the house like this. I'll start cleaning. You get a new nappy on Spangle," Bobbie was already in the cupboard under the stairs where all the cleaning stuff was kept. Ben wandered off to get another nappy.

They were using 'Pampers' from Boots; extra large. The pet shop had laughed when they had asked for dog nappies. 'No such thing mate, try Boots.' So here he was in the study opening another packet. He stood for a second taking in the study. The police had taken all of Mary's paintbrushes as evidence. He would miss rubbing his fingers across them. He noticed that the canvas on the easel, the one he left on display had a floral painting in vivid greens and reds. What was happening? He now believed, after the events of today, that Mary was acting in some kind of guardian angel capacity. But what was this painting. He studied it closely. It was definitely her style. The last time he had gotten excited about this kind of thing, it had been Freddie playing around. But there in the bottom right hand corner was her signature – 'MT' in white paint.

It all made sense. She was protecting me, all of us. She was a guardian angel. Now the painting, it was beautiful. Ben took it as acceptance of his blossoming relationship with a florist, a sign. She was at peace. I was so stupid to ever doubt her. He was smiling broadly in the knowledge that she had been somehow involved in the avenging of her own death in the poker room, in the arrest of his evil twin brother Stefan, involved in his buttock stabbing. OK, maybe that was a bit weird, but it was in the early days of his relationship with Bobbie. Maybe Mary was jealous, and now the painting, of flowers, is acceptance of their relationship. His mind was racing with all kinds of crazy thoughts, but they were disturbed by the telephone ringing. He went to answer the hall phone but it wasn't the house phone. He checked his mobile in his pocket but no number was displayed on the screen. The sound of a classical office phone rang again. It sounded so familiar; he had the same ring tone on his mobile. He followed the ringing back into the study where he noticed Mary's phone vibrating on the table where he always kept it. The mystery phone he had found with the key; and now it was ringing. He snatched it up feverishly and checked the small screen. No caller display, of course not; even techno phobic Ben realised this was not possible without contacts in the memory. There was just a number. Ben pushed the green button to answer.

"Hello," said Ben; his face was motionless waiting for a response.

"Hello, who is this please," a male voice enquired.

"What can I help you with?" asked Ben far too abruptly.

"The rent on the room is due."

Chapter 20

They were back on the M62 after refuelling the Golf at Birch Service Station. The gloom hovering over Saddleworth Moor continued to hold its secrets as darkness slowly descended on The Pennines. Their headlights pierced the night. A light fog began to form on the higher ground as they slowly inched their way into Yorkshire territory. Tommy and Ron were dosing off, trying to sleep in the rear seats. Ben was sat in the passenger seat still buzzing with thoughts, not all of them positive.

"So this guy just rang out of the blue and gave me the address of this 'room.'" He did the finger quote mark mime for effect. "God knows what I will find there tomorrow. I am dreading it. I mean, just when I was feeling so elated about the painting, about it being a sign of her approval of our relationship. Just when I could really feel her presence, all the weird flying paintbrushes seemed to make some sort of sense. Now this room, full of god knows what sordid stuff, just turns up out of the blue; a cheap bed, tacky clothes in an MFI wardrobe. I hate the thought that she used to change into stuff like that. Sixty thousand pounds in a secret account; red stilettos, that's what started all of this."

"Ben, you've said all of this already, back on the M56. Don't you think you are beating yourself up too much going over it again? There might be a simple explanation for all of this. Why don't you wait until tomorrow to find out the truth?" Bobbie was being supportive but she, even with all her patience, was tiring of him going over old ground.

Tommy was asleep in the back seat. Ron was staring out of the window into the night. He wasn't really listening to the conversation drifting between the front seats. He was more interested in the view of the lights twinkling on the hills. They looked rather familiar. The turn off for Huddersfield was soon upon them and they started to pay more attention to the female voice on the Sat Nav.

"Ben, give Sally another ring. Tell her we will be there in ten minutes," Bobbie was very well organised when she was driving.

"Hi Sally, estimated time of arrival is ten minutes." He paused as he listened to her on the other end of the connection. "That is very kind of you but we need to get straight back to drop Tommy off." There was another pause. "No really we can grab a bite when we get home. It is going to be a long night."

"You have reached your destination," the Sat Nav soon announced triumphantly. Bobbie parked the car on the street outside of the house. They had been here once before with news of Ron's whereabouts. This time they were delivering him home. They woke Tommy and helped Ron out of the back. He was keen to walk himself down the drive; the returning hero; the prodigal father. The light came on in the hall just before the front door was opened by a smartly dressed woman. Ben was taken aback for a second. She seemed younger than Sally and was walking freely. Sally appeared behind her in the wheelchair which was being pushed by a young man.

"Come in. Come in." Sally couldn't wait to get them inside the house, out of the cold.

"Hello Dad," she said, fighting back tears.

"Hello Sally." He had been repeating her name over and over in his head as the landscape passed the car window. It seemed to work.

"This is Carole and Frank; your grandchildren. Do you remember them?" Ron smiled broadly, looking for any sign of recognition. He didn't see any, so carried on smiling. He thought it was the best thing to do.

"My children come around most days to check on me. I am quite independent in my own way. The chairlift is a great help, and the wet room with the seated shower comes in really handy. You will love it here Dad." Sally was talking too quickly in her excitement.

"We have made up the back bedroom for you. It is really nice Gramps," Carole said. "Do you mind if I call you Gramps? I always used to when I was younger."

"Gramps is fine." Ron was still smiling. They all waited until Sally had travelled slowly up to the landing on the stair lift before following her. Ron waited for the lift to be sent down so he could use it himself. Eventually they were all huddled in his room as Frank opened the wardrobe to display the vast amount of shelf space.

"You're father's luggage is still on the cruise ship. I will give them a ring and have it delivered. It can be my homecoming present." Ben was being magnanimous.

"Thank you young man," Ron was warming to his new surroundings. The room was very cosy with a single bed and small table. The table had a bedside light and a framed photograph. Ron was staring at it. A younger Ron stared back standing arm in arm with a woman.

"That's Mum." Sally was crying.

"Edna? Is that Edna?" Ron was leaning forward to get a closer look.

"Yes that is my Mum, Edna." Sally was still crying. It was difficult not to join in; such was the emotionally charged atmosphere in the bedroom.

"We really must be making a move. It is getting late," announced Ben to stop himself becoming tearful.

"You remembered your wife Edna without being told her name. How did you do that?" asked Tommy.

"I don't know son. It just jumped into my head." Ron was struggling to understand events. It seemed that light bulbs were being switched on in his brain at random moments. He kept smiling and waited for the next one.

"Let's all go downstairs again for a cup of tea and a biscuit," Carole suggested.

"We really do need to be getting along soon," Ben resisted.

"We insist," insisted Sally. Once downstairs they gravitated into the sitting room.

"Before I forget, I must empty my crutch. It really has been a godsend with its magical supply of money." Ron had brought the photograph with him.

"Did you really sell your house and disappear off the face of the earth; travelling on a cruise ship?" Bobbie asked sceptically.

"It seemed like a good idea at the time. I was feeling lonely and confused."

"But you had us Dad. You always had us." Sally was gently chastising him; but her overwhelming emotion was one of relief at having him home safely.

"I was getting a bit forgetful." He was waiting for inspiration from his inner light bulb, but none was forthcoming.

"It must have cost a fortune, cruises aren't that cheap," Frank said.

"I got a good deal. It was five hundred pounds a week for a frequent traveller block booking, including single supplement."

"How do you remember that?" asked Tommy.

"It is written down. Here in the crutch with my money." He removed the rubber cap off the base and began to unscrew the bottom section. It came apart to reveal rolls of paper. The first one was the contract Ron had mentioned. The rest were wads of twenty pound notes. Tommy, being a mathematician began counting.

"There is two thousand pounds here Ron."

"Two thousand, but your house must have been worth at least a hundred and fifty thousand, Dad."

"He has been away for five years. At five hundred a week that is.." Frank began calculating.

"One hundred and thirty thousand pounds," Tommy announced. The others seemed impressed by his mental agility.

"The important point is that you only had enough for four more cruises. What were you going to do in a month's time?" Ben was being the grim reaper. They all looked at each other but nobody had an answer.

"Something would have come along," said Ron positively.

"Something did come alone," Sally said nodding towards Tommy. "I think you owe Tommy a big thank you."

"Thanks son." Tommy was looking rather embarrassed, a sign that Ben picked up on.

"We really must be going. We have a long journey ahead of us."

"But the tea," Sally protested.

"We really must be on our way," Bobbie took charge.

"We'll keep in touch. You are always welcome here."

Freddie was sat at the desk in the police interview room. His hair had grown since the trial. His red roots were showing below the brown dye as his Afro took shape. He was listening to Colette as she ran through his case notes.

"It is to your credit that you gave yourself up; came in voluntarily. We do, however, have a problem with the prison guard who you attacked in the court house. The accumulative effect on your sentence could be substantial."

"What am I looking at?" asked Freddie as he stared blankly at the wall mirror.

"It could be ten years," Collette answered, eying Freddie for any reaction.

"I will accept whatever punishment is ruled by the court. It is God's will," he said flatly as he stared at the wall covered in safety notices. Collette had noticed the change in Freddie since she had arrived at the station. She had been surprised to get the call informing her that he had walked into the police station; and now talking to him, he seemed calmer than she had ever seen him. Then there was the religious thing; was he genuine?

"God's will?" she questioned.

"I know I have done wrong. I repent my sins. Reverend Martin has offered guidance; we will pray together every day." Freddie was really getting into the role.

"Reverend Martin?"

"Yes, at St Hilary's. He has kindly offered to act as my mentor; my spiritual guide. He is outside waiting in the corridor." Collette indicated to the officer sat in the corner that she would like to leave the room. He opened the door. She looked out to see a bald bearded dog collar smiling back at her. He nodded slightly in recognition.

"Does Freddie want to talk with me?" Martin was genuinely concerned.

"No, no. That will not be necessary." She closed the door and sat down again. She needed to think this through.

"I believe I may be able to get you out on bail, if you are prepared to live under Reverend Malcolm's wing."

"Martin. It is Reverend Martin."

"Would you be prepared to do that?" she continued, ignoring the correction.

"He is my mentor. He shows me the way. He is my spiritual guide, the man who can lead me back to righteousness." Freddie was getting carried away; he realised that he may be overdoing the religious vigour. "It is only two counts of assault. One was self defence, the other an act of blind panic," he added for balance.

"Let me talk to the legal people. I will be back."

It had been a tiring drive back over the Pennines for Bobbie. The Fletcher's driveway was lit up like an airport runway. It wasn't until they were walking Tommy to the door that they realised that the lights were coming from the eyes of the assembled gnomes that formed a guard of honour on each side. They were very unnerving. Ben remembered the talking gnome in the porch; he was determined not to be surprised by him. They rang the bell.

"Welcome to the Fletcher's," said the gnome.

"Fuck off," said Ben as he kicked out at the gnome causing it the wobble on its base. He grabbed at it to prevent it from falling onto the tiled floor. The wires became dislodged from the back of the gnome, sparks flashing wildly making the porch light up like a Christmas grotto. The door opened to display the Fletcher's silhouetted in the bright hallway.

"Welcome home Tommy, right on time." greeted the Fletchers in unison. They were standing inside the open front door, smiling at Ben as he danced with the gnome.

"Come in, come in. We still have time for a game of scrabble before bedtime."

Tommy stepped forward to be engulfed by the brightly lit hallway.

291

"See you at the weekend Dad," he said over his shoulder. "See you Bobbie."

Bobbie was pleased that he had acknowledged her. She happily followed Ben back to the car.

"The gnome really spooked you, didn't it?"

"No it didn't," Ben lied.

"Then why did you lash out at it?" Bobbie teased as she adjusted her seatbelt.

"Just drive, will you."

During the short drive back up the Wirral Ben returned to the topic that had dominated his thoughts all day.

"What do you think I will find in the room tomorrow?"

"I have no idea. Just wait and see."

"I am dreading it. The address he gave me is in a rough district. Seabank Road sounds so nautical, giving images of sand, fresh sea air, flocks of gulls. In reality it is one of the most run down derelict areas in Seacombe. Will you come with me? I am meeting him by the Town Hall."

"Ordinarily I would, but I really have stuff I have to do for the florist; restocking and such. It can't wait, I'm sorry."

"OK. I will go on my own." Ben sulked just a little.

-.-

"This is your room. I know it is not The Hilton but it is warm and cosy," Martin oozed saintly friendliness. Freddie examined the room. It was on the small side, a bed, no television or radio. Frugal furniture populated the far plain magnolia wall. The only entertainment on offer was the Bible on the bedside cabinet. Music vibrated through the floor as Sunday's service was practised by the organist. Freddie had been placed in the loft space above the pulpit.

"Do you like it?"

"I love it, I will get hours of comfort from the Holy Book," Freddie lied.

"Is this wardrobe big enough for your clothes? Where are they?" asked Martin.

Freddie thought for a second before saying "Not far, father. Not far at all. I will have to collect them." Freddie could almost see Tommy's house out of the small window; down the hill. He could call any time to recover his suitcase from the attic room; any time soon.

"Let me show you around the church. This is your home now. God's house is open to all."

Chapter 21

It was raining. Heavy raindrops were bouncing off the stone steps that cascaded down from the main entrance doors of the Town Hall. Ben sheltered in the doorway watching the rain. It reminded him of the night Mary had died; the only difference today was the daylight. He had come a long way since that tragic night; he had found the mystery driver; had witnessed him die; had subsequently been tracked down by his psychotic brother. Perhaps now he would discover why the whole chain of events had started in the first place. He needed an explanation for the secret money, for the room, for the red stilettos. He became aware of a man shuffling up the steps under the protection of an umbrella emblazoned with a company logo. Ben caught his eye. Was this him? The man brushed past him into the dry reception area without a flicker of recognition. Three more men entered the Town Hall without contact being made. The meeting had been arranged for eleven o'clock. It was now twenty past. Ben was beginning to wonder whether he had been stood up when a voice whispered from behind a pillar.

"Mr Thomas. Psst."

Ben hadn't seen him arrive. Had he been there all this time watching me watching the steps? Did he really expect to be taken seriously? The 'Psst' noise he used to attract Ben's attention was unbelievably clichéd; very 'B movie' spy genre. Ben turned to take in a thin rather timid looking man in his early thirties. He was wearing a trench coat to protect himself from the rain; He was obviously an admirer of the 'Sam Spade' image. Ben looked him in the eye which caused the budding spy to look away in embarrassment.

"Phillips?" demanded Ben.

"Yes. I don't want any trouble. I am just the rent man," he said without looking at Ben. He continued to talk while he studied the street. Apparently it was much more interesting and less threatening than Ben.

"The room is just around the corner," he informed a passing car. "It should only take us two minutes."

"After you," said Ben as he adjusted his collar to the cold and rain. They both crossed the street in a trot, keen to gain shelter from the shop awnings on the other side.

The row of shops was showing signs of wear and tear. There was a tattoo parlour, a pizza place, a pawn broker offering to buy gold at good rates. The cheap poster in the window said so. On the other side of two boarded up properties was a cheap weathered door. The green paint had faded and begun to peel. Number thirteen hadn't made a good start if it was trying to impress. Phillips opened it with a silver key and invited Ben in, stepping back to ensure there was no physical contact. He really was a mouse. The hallway smelt of garbage; cigarette stubs were littered in the corner. The thought of Mary using these premises jarred into his brain. He was struggling to come to terms with the whole concept. The stairs led up to a landing with stained walls; a small landing with three doors. Phillips stopped outside 13C. He inserted a brass coloured key off the same ring that he had used downstairs. Ben hated the very thought that Mary could have been bringing clients to this room, being groped as she was on the stairs. It didn't bare thinking about.

"This is it. You have an option on another twelve month if you want to continue the lease." He left the door open a few inches and stepped back. Ben was sweating, small beads forming on the side of his head. He was reluctant to enter; afraid of what he would find. God knows what Mary did in here. He expecting to find a cheap bed, a red light, maybe some clothes that she used to change into, cheap trashy clothes. He took a deep breath and stepped in. The room was quite a surprise for Ben. The dull light slanted in through the large window illuminating the whole room. There was painting stuff, lots of excellent work. There must have been at least eight canvasses stacked against the wall. In the middle of the room, getting the best light from the window; was an easel. It supported a rough charcoal sketch of Holly, awaiting the finishing touches that oil paint could bring. It was ready to come to colourful life. On the table was a file with a Gallery contact and a business card. On the floor, piled up behind the door, were unopened mail; junk mail mostly. Ben sat on the floor wondering how he had ever doubted her, and began reading them.

"We will not be taking up the option Mr Phillips. I will have the room empty by tomorrow." He turned to continue reading; not expecting a reply, it was more of a dismissal. One of the letters caught his attention; 'If you have any more, I'm sure we can do more business, your work is really popular – Gantt Gallery.' Ben's mind was racing. What did 'more' mean? Had she already sold work to the Gallery, maybe sixty grand's worth? Ben got his mobile out and began punching in the number that was on the letterhead. He looked back over his shoulder but Phillips had already left. The phone connected and was answered promptly.

"Gantt Gallery. Joseph Smythe speaking."

Ben asked lots of questions over the course of their conversation. He learnt that Mary had sold a number of pieces. That's what Joe called them, pieces. They were Mary's paintings; produced lovingly in secret but suddenly they were pieces. Joe was reluctant to reveal financial dealing at first, but when Ben explained what had happened; that Mary was dead; he softened, especially when he learnt that were more posthumous pieces sitting above a pawn shop. He confirmed that Mary had shifted enough pieces to explain the balance in her account. He didn't exactly use the work shifted, preferring 'attracted considerable attention,' but Ben knew what he meant. He may speak nicely but he was just another money-grabbing middle man.

"So can we arrange a viewing; see the new pieces," Joe asked.

"I will be clearing this place out tomorrow; I can bring them to your Gallery, Joe. The address is on your letter."

"It is Joseph; and that would be splendid. Tomorrow it is." The line went dead.

Ben had a busy day ahead organising transport but continued with the mail. He had to know everything. The next letter that was of any interest was from a Swiss clinic specialising in treating children with cancer. They were offering a place, at a price, to treat Holly. It wasn't cheap but Mary's secret stash would cover the treatment. It was probably her last chance, but had tragically come too late. Ben wiped his eye. Should he show the letter to Brie and Simon? Where was Mary when there was a difficult decision to be made? He put the letter in his back pocket; he was leaning towards showing them. They would definitely be getting the portrait.

-.-

Bobbie had spent all morning ordering stock. Valentine's Day would come around soon enough. She had to be prepared. Christmas was just around the corner. Holly and ivy may be a Christmas cliché but they were popular; were good sellers. She had been rushed off her feet most of the morning and needed the caffeine fix that a good Latte provided. She entered Starbucks and watched the rain from a window seat. So much had happened since she was last here, waiting for a blind date with that policeman. She had met Ben. Things were going great. He was wonderful in a roguish sort of way. He had pulled himself together; she really appreciated him helping out at the florist's. We just needed to get Tommy home and life would be pretty much perfect.

The glass door burst open and an umbrella, covered in a garish red and yellow company logo, was operated in violent repetition. It was opened and closed very quickly, causing a flapping sound similar to a flock of flamingos taking flight. She watched as the umbrella was hung up with the owner's coat. The man walked to the counter to order. Bobbie didn't really believe in coincidence, but it was rather bizarre that he had walked in at that exact moment. She couldn't really avoid him; he was literally standing next to her.

"Hello Peter," she offered. Page had seen her immediately; the second he entered the store. The exaggerated umbrella manoeuvre had been for her benefit; to attract her attention.

"Hello Bobbie. Ground hog Day."

"What are you talking about?"

"You know, the film with Bill Murray when he relives the same day over and over; sort of a déjà vu moment. We have been here before haven't we?" He realised that it was not a good start. He was nervously talking too much.

"Oh I see. Yes, we did meet here. It was raining that day too. How are things going?"

"You must have heard that I was suspended after the Fungus trial. 'Perverting the course of justice' was the official line. I was forced to resign. The pension is secure though, it could have been worse; not a complete disaster."

"I see you still have the snakeskin boots," Bobbie was trying to lighten the mood.

"They are my trademark."

"What were you thinking Peter. You were a good cop, why did you tamper with the evidence?"

Page felt that he could talk to Bobbie. He always thought that their first date could have led to something more. He opened up.

"I was really after Chavic; I had been for years. So when he was killed; it was job done. Result. I wasn't trying to stitch Fungus up, It was more a case of trying to protect the girl; the story of my life really. Now she has gone; disappeared into some godforsaken Third World central European cess pit."

Anybody passing Starbucks would have taken them for an established couple as they sat in the window seat; chatting away intimately.

"It's really nice talking to you Bobbie. Maybe if our first meeting had gone this well, things could have been different." Page had an earnest look on his face. He was speaking from the heart. Bobbie was flustered for a second; lost for words. It didn't last long.

"It was a coffee; we were both on the market, looking for love. Lots of people are out there doing the same thing. Yes I was looking, but amazingly it found me. What did you think? That you are a policeman and my name is Bobbie. Do you think that is enough for us to be together?"

He looked hurt, a trapped animal.

"I'm sorry, that was unkind, I'm sorry. It was uncalled for." She couldn't apologise enough. Page was wounded but kept his composure. "So what are you going to do now? What are your plans?"

"Technically I am no longer a policeman. I am retired. Well it was that or be discharged. All happened under a cloud. I was rather stupid. But I am in the process of starting up a security firm."

"Really, thought of a name yet?"

"No, I'm still working on it." He looked confused. Bobbie felt a sudden pang of sympathy for him; he had been through so much lately.

"Look, my best friend is having a charity bash. You can do the security, your first job, maybe get some recommendations." Bobbie was desperate to remain on friendly terms; it was her nature.

"Thanks. That would be great." She was so kind. He was still wondering about what might have been.

"You might meet someone there Peter."

"I'm still looking. You never know. There is someone out there for me. I just know it." He looked determined in the window reflection. He almost believed himself. He stood and walked to the coat stand, making sure his snake skins made that clicking sound on the floor. He had his coat back on; umbrella at the ready. He was back in character.

"It was nice to see you again Bobbie. I will be in touch about the Charity." He left, flipping his umbrella into position and disappearing amongst the mass of humanity bustling along the pavement.

-.-

"Do you want a coffee, honey," Simon asked. He had been doting on Brie ever since they received the good news. He had been delighted about the pregnancy, once he had had the results of the DNA test. The last couple of months had not been easy. Holly's passing had been devastating for them both. Brie's descent into alcohol dependency was now a thing of the past. She was determined to have a healthy baby, was taking no risks at all. The fling with the reporter was another matter. Like any man, Simon had struggled with the imagery that kept invading his mind. No matter how many times Brie had reassured him that it meant nothing; that it was a moment of weakness; of insanity, he still felt the pain of betrayal. He was starting to believe her, but it would take time. He had taken a bullet for her at what they now called 'The Siege.' In a strange way the experience had brought them closer together. Brie's confession about the ventilator and her wish to die had been a low point, but his chivalrous behaviour and wish to save her had pulled them closer. He still annoyed the hell out of her with his cowboy obsession and stupid 'song game', but they were taking things a step at a time.

"Yes please, that would be lovely," she replied as she continued to pour over charity paperwork at the table. As he walked into the kitchen to put the kettle on, there was a familiar knock on the front door; a secret code. He flipped the switch on the base of the kettle, checked that the small orange light came on, and then raced to open the front door.

"Come in Ben. What brings you here?"

"Is Brie in?"

"In the conservatory, come through." They both wandered into the dining room and further into the extended conservatory where Brie looked up from her papers.

"Don't get up," Simon was fussing over her condition.

"Ben. What a lovely surprise; what brings you here?" She was genuinely pleased to see him.

"I have had an amazing day. Do you remember the mystery phone that Mary left?" They both nodded in acknowledgement. "Well it rang yesterday. It is hard to believe, I know. So much has happened lately. We have taken Ron home to his daughter; Tommy is back with the gnomes. Anyway, the phone call led me to a room that Mary was renting. You know how crazy I was about the red shoes; the connection with Chavic; I didn't know what to expect."

Simon could tell from Ben's animated excited speech patterns and from the wide grin that had never left his face, that whatever Ben was trying to tell them was good news.

"Ben, get to the point will you. What was in the room?" Brie had a flair for straight talking.

"There were paintings; lots of them. I have brought them home. A dealer is coming round to view them. Mary had been working in secret and selling them apparently."

"Why would she do that?" Brie asked.

"Brie, do you remember when I asked you if you knew anything about what Mary was up to, when I was going crazy not knowing?" Ben didn't wait for an answer, but continued. "You said she had said that she was planning a surprise. I think I now know what that was." He produced the letter from the Swiss clinic that had been in his back pocket and handed it over. He watched as Simon and Brie read every word. He watched as realisation slowly dawned on their faces; as tears of joy intermingled with sadness to trickle down their faces and drip off their chins.

"Mary was prepared to do this? But it costs so much; how could she possibly afford.." Brie was cut short by Ben's raised hand.

"She sold a lot of paintings. The money in the secret bank account all came from her work."

"She would do that for us? Do it for Holly?" Brie was sobbing. They had not noticed the package under Ben's arm; such was the dramatic impact of the letter. He now held it in both hand and removed the cover.

"Mary would have also wanted you to have this," he whispered as he handed over the portrait. The sight of their daughter's face, smiling back at them healthily, was just too much for them both.

"We will treasure it." Ben wasn't sure who had answered him; such was the atmosphere in the room. He left them to it. They never looked up from the sketch as he left; both of them gently stroking the paper.

-.-

"What a day. I have never been so busy in my life. The Gallery Guy, Joe, rang. He insisted on collecting the painting from the house. He didn't trust me not to damage them. I can still hear his voice, 'There is an industry standard that needs to be met when transporting pieces'. He will be here soon. I went round to Simon's. Simon and Brie were very moved by the picture; they were delighted. How was your day," Ben was full of beans.

"I bumped into Detective Inspector Page today. He seemed a little down so I invited him to the charity do," she said while looking at Ben for approval.

"You did what? You know we don't see eye to eye."

"He is starting a security firm. I felt sorry for him. I sort of offered him the job at the bash; you know to

305

start him off." She pulled her best seductive, scatterbrained appealing face. The one Ben found irresistible. She knew she had acted out of turn. They were interrupted by the doorbell ringing before the conversation developed into their first argument.

"Come in Joe."

"It is Joseph." He was dressed in a herring bone suit and sported a monocle over his right eye, complete with gold chain. Ben wasn't surprised in the least; his appearance matched the impression Ben had formed during their phone conversations.

"Where are the pieces?"

"In the study. Follow me." Joseph followed, rubbing his hands together in expectation. He had been looking forward to this moment all day.

"These are very good," Joe enthused as he flicked through the portfolio, "Very good indeed. I particularly like this one." Joe was admiring the painting that Freddie had done when he was staying in the attic. The one Ben had mistaken for a sign from Mary.

"Are you serious? Do you think it would sell?" Ben hated the fact that Freddie's work was of any value; but money is money, right?

"Without doubt. It is one of her better pieces."

"Take them all. They are going to a good cause."

Ben escorted him back to the front door. He watched as Joe expertly packed the paintings into the specially designed holding bay in the back of the pick-up van.

Perhaps he had a point about transportation techniques. He watched him close the door carefully, happy in the thought that there were no more secrets between himself and Mary.

The van crunched into second gear as it pulled away from the kerb to reveal the figure of Freddie. His hair had grown back into the familiar Afro, red with brown highlights.

"Hello, Ben. I've come for my suitcase."

Chapter 22

"I won't lie to you Freddie; I am not pleased to see you. You are a wanted man; it has been all over the news." Ben was visibly agitated as he stood uninvitingly in the hallway.

"That is old news. I am out on bail under the mentorship of the wonderful Reverend Markland at St.Hilary's. I'm surprised you don't know him; after all you do reside in his parish. But then again, if you are not a God fearing Christian." Freddie left his statement lingering in the air; a subtle criticism of Ben's lifestyle.

"You make me sound like Attila the Hun when it is you who can't live in society as a normal human being." Ben was ready to fight his corner.

"I have no problem with you Ben; you did the right thing in court. No problem. I have now found God and will be happy to serve whatever sentence the court decides. I have a tag," he said as he pulled up his trousers to proudly display the blue plastic ankle bracelet. "I have a ten o'clock curfew, very generous in the circumstances. I just need the suitcase and I will be on my way."

"You know where the attic room is, help yourself." Ben was finding it difficult to be civil. Freddie disappeared silently up the stairs just before Bobbie arrives home laden with shopping.

"Help me put this stuff away will you honey." They fell into the well oiled routine that they had developed in the kitchen; the five plastic bags on the kitchen floor being methodically emptied.

"Do we really need tinned rhubarb?" asked Ben.

"You never know, it is always wise to have the cupboards stocked. Shit, I have forgotten Spangle's dog food. Would you be a sweetie and pop to the village and get some. Oh, and your suit needs collecting from the dry cleaners." Ben looked puzzled. Bobbie continued to speak.

"Don't tell me you have forgotten? Your College reunion is tonight, Simon and Brie are picking us up in a taxi at seven." Bobbie's words seemed to be a jumbled mix of noise to Ben but eventually he made sense of them.

"Hello Bobbie, nice to see you again," said Freddie as he reappeared with his suitcase.

"Hello Freddie," she was surprised to see him, but judging by Ben's reaction things were under control. Everything was cool. Freddie fiddled with his finger into the knife hole in the suit case. It seemed a lifetime since he had been on the ship with Tommy. That job is long gone. It was dawning on him that life after prison may be more difficult than he had first thought. A stand up with a criminal record would be a tough gig.

"How is Tommy?" Freddie asked. Ben realised that it was first time his name had been mentioned since Freddie turned up on the doorstep. It seemed odd considering Freddie had been almost obsessed with his son.

"He is still in care, I only see him at the weekend," Ben gave nothing away.

"A family should be together. It is god's wish." Freddie was overdoing the saintly act.

"I am just up the road at St Hilary's drop in any time. God be with you." And with that he left, plodding up the hill without a second glance.

The interior of the church was very impressive; high sweeping arches dominated the ceiling. The main building was of solid granite construction; completed by skilled stone masons centuries ago. It must have taken years to finish. The large stained glass window that dominated the east wall was magnificent, a swirling mass of religious humanity. Freddie was truly impressed. OK, it could not compete with St Paul's Cathedral, or Notre Dame, or even St Patrick's on Fifth Avenue; but in sleepy Wallasey it was impressive. What was not so impressive was the room Freddie was sleeping in. The noise coming through the floor during Evensong and the preceding practise was annoying, but that paled into insignificance when compared to the noise the bell tower made every fifteen minutes.

Freddie had not slept at all last night, and was not looking forward to this evening's campanological offerings. The bells were incredibly loud, mind numbingly so. They had to be set on a timer, surely the bell ringers didn't stay up all night. He would have to look for it before bedtime.

"Welcome home Freddie," Martin smiled. He was dressed in his formal regalia, ready for the imminent service.

"Hi Reverend," Freddie was keen to stay in his good books; they needed to be tight. "Do you find it easy doing the service; public speaking cannot be easy, even for you."

"It helps to practise my child; and believing what you preach helps a lot. Belief is a wonderful thing."

"I'm pretty good at speaking to a crowd. Do you think there is any chance that I could perform, speak from the pulpit? God's word needs to be heard."

Martin was still smiling. He practised that as well. As he stood there thinking hard, he just couldn't come up with any reason to reject Freddie. His manic green eyes were burning into Martin's head, freezing any logical thought process.

"We will see my son. We will see."

-.-

It was one of Ben's worst nightmares. The pet shop was full of smells and noises that were totally alien to his world. There were rabbit cages that smelt of wet straw. The never ending chirping of budgerigars filled the air. One wall was full of shelves stocking anything from squeaky dog toys to rat poison. Ben approached the counter and asked for six tins of dog food.

"Which brand do you want?" demanded the teenage girl dressed in jeans and a blue shirt displaying the shop logo on the breast pocket. 'Pet U Like' in white lettering. Ben was thinking more of petulant such was her brusque manner. Ben studied the shelves behind her which were populated by at least eight different types of dog food. He considered ringing Bobbie to confirm which one Spangle preferred, but then had a recollection of a green tin being opened in the kitchen yesterday; the fowl smelling contents being lovingly scooped into his bowl.

"The green one please," Ben answered, not caring if it was Spangle's little favourite. He didn't give a shit. Ben took the bag, paid and got out of the repugnant shop as quickly as possible. He rushed home, deliberately forgetting to call in at the dry cleaners. He never wanted to go to the re-union in the first place.

The taxi was awash with conversation. All four occupants had varying opinions on the night that lay ahead.

"I'm not very keen on this. There will be too many memories of Mary. Apart from that, you will feel uncomfortable Bobbie. You will not fit in," Ben said from the front seat; his head half turned so as to be heard between the front seats. He was riding shotgun, expecting to pay the fare when they arrived.

"Nonsense; I will be fine," replied a visibly apprehensive Bobbie.

"I'm really looking forward to it. I have been for weeks. I wonder if the old gang will all be there. It will be amazing," Simon was almost jumping out of his seat with excitement.

"Twenty years is long time. Perhaps you will not recognise any of them. They may have changed," reasoned Brie from the middle seat.

"Come and change the world, changes," Simon was into the Bowie classic immediately.
      "Do shut up darling." Brie was beginning to regret coming already. The taxi pulled to a halt outside the Student Union building. Ben paid the driver and jointed the group showing invitations to the doorman.

The building had been decorated especially for the occasion. Colourful ribbons and balloons adorned the room; they hung around all four walls .The room was dominated by the banner 'Class of 92' screaming out in bold red letters above the entrance doors. The room had not changed in twenty years, the drinks machine was still in the far left corner, an eating area was segregated on the right. The furniture had been obviously updated, but the lay out was exactly the same. Ben's thoughts wandered back in time, to a young carefree couple sharing a coffee; their whole life ahead of them. He knew it was a bad idea to come to the re-union; knew that it would be impossible not to think of Mary and the way they were. A large area had been cordoned off as a temporary dance floor in front of a raised stage. The hired musicians were busy setting up their equipment. Brie was studying the photographs on the wall from their Yearbook.

"I'd forgotten how pretty Mary was," she whispered to Simon.

"Pretty woman walking down the street." Simon just couldn't help breaking into song.

"Not tonight Simon, please." Brie was visibly annoyed; she had had enough of the stupid game.

"You didn't look so bad yourself back then," he replied.

"Are you suggesting that I no longer do?" She was fishing for compliments.

"You haven't changed a bit. You are gorgeous."

Ben was close to Bobbie's side; he appreciated her supporting him at the re-union and was determined that she would not be left alone in room full of strangers. He was struggling with the whole re-union issue; wasn't sure that it was a good idea. There was Mary's picture in the Yearbook, frozen in time. It brought back memories of their student days again; of their first meeting. They had all been so young, ambitious and fun loving. Mary always had paint on her clothes, on her face and hair. He now knew that she did it on purpose; a kind of image thing.

314

Miles Southern wandered over dressed in a white suit. As he got closer it became obvious that the suit was expensive silk. He hadn't changed since University. Physically he had put on a few pounds, but not many. His facial features were very tight; he either spent hours in the gym or he had been under the surgeon's knife. He looked disapprovingly at Ben's jumper before speaking.

"Benny boy, how are you? Nice to see you have made an effort." He wasn't interested in the slightest; he couldn't wait to talk about himself. Ben remembered him as the most pompous, self-centred, egotistical, bombastic prick he ever had the misfortune to encounter during his student years. He particularly disliked his propensity for calling him Benny; hated it. He had almost forgotten those years, but they all came flooding back at the sound of his voice.

"Hello Miles; delighted to see you. You haven't changed a bit," said Ben. It wasn't a compliment. Miles studied the group. He nodded a greeting to Simon and Brie before studying Bobbie intently.

"A new squeeze I see Benny. I knew you and Mary wouldn't last. She was far too good for you. She had that arty, paint on the blouse look that she pulled off so effortlessly; so very sexy."

Ben was too shocked to reply. He felt his eyebrows with his right hand as he involuntarily bowed his head. How could he not know what had happened? Or did he know and was just being a crass idiot? Miles continued to speak, hardly taking breath; he had managed to turn

315

the conversation around to his favourite subject – Miles Southern.

"I'm a headmaster now, great school, great A Level results this year, the OFSTED report puts us in the top quartile for the region. Things are looking good. Here's the family." He reached into the inside pocket of his white suite to produce a six by four photograph of himself and his wife standing behind two smiling children. It was very 'Stepford Wives.'

"That is my gorgeous wife Maria and these are the delightful Louisa and Samantha," Miles was pointing out each member of the perfect family unit.

"They are lovely," said Brie with as much enthusiasm as she could muster.

"How are your children?" asked Miles. Brie's face turned to stone. It was frozen in shock, as if she had overdosed on Botox.

"We only had one. She died this year," Simon cut in, his face betraying his dislike for Miles. He was not a violent man, and was still suffering with his leg wound; but he would gladly punch Miles in the face repeatedly until it was liquid. Miles appeared untouched by the revelation and continued to dominate the conversation.

"Good God, is that Tim Walters over there? Has he let himself go or what? Where is his hair? And that waistline, he must be carrying an extra forty pounds at least since we last saw him. And there is Margaret Wilson. I've heard, from a reliable source, that she now runs a brothel specialising in BDSM."

"What's that?" Bobbie couldn't resist asking.

"Bondage and domination, it is all the rage these days," Miles was eying up the women in the circle for signs of interest.

"And the SM?" Bobbie was still curious.

"Sadomasochism," Simon cut in.

"How do you know that?" demanded Brie.

"Simon always was a sly old dog," Miles continued to stir things up.

"What a lovely suit. You really stand out in a crowd. It is the only white suite here," Bobbie was trying to lighten the mood; to change the subject.

"I am ready for the disco later. Maria and I have been practising for weeks. We hired a dance coach, which cost a fortune by the way, and have perfected a Saturday Night Fever routine. It should bring the house down." A couple walked past smiling, happy to be amongst old friends. They appeared to nudge Bobbie slightly causing her glass of wine to empty all over Miles. His jacket had a growing red stain across the breast pocket. The red wine had also splattered his groin area leaving it resembling a raspberry ripple ice cream.

"Oh my God, I am so sorry," Bobbie apologised. "This type of thing is always happening to me."

"You stupid woman. My suit is ruined," Miles was furious as he walked away towards the toilets to wash it down.

317

"You did that on purpose didn't you?" Ben asked through a huge grin.

"Was it that obvious?"

"I think we all enjoyed that." Simon joined in.

"He hasn't changed since we were students. He is still a complete tosser. He is a pompous preening arsehole. If you hadn't done that I swear I would have swung for him, but I'm in enough trouble as it is, I don't need any more. But, God, he is such a prick." Ben took a deep breath. "I feel better with that off my mind."

"Shall we mingle?" Simon was determined to enjoy the evening. They wandered over to the 'English' stand where a woman was holding a clipboard. Half the names on it were ticked. Why would you bother with a register thought Ben? We are supposed to be enjoying ourselves.

"Ben is that you?" clipboard woman asked.

"Melissa?" replied Ben as recognition dawned on his face.

"You are all here," she enthused as she noticed Simon and Brie. She quickly ticked them off the list.

"Do you remember the time we had to write a story for an assignment, and we decided to fantasize about a secret world in the attic?" she was almost jumping up and down clapping with excitement.

"It's a shame C.S Lewis beat us to it," said Brie. She had never liked Melissa.

"Just beat it," The last word was more of a wheeze as Simon was stopped in his tracks by an elbow in the ribs from Brie. The evening continued in a party atmosphere. Everyone was having a great time as the years rolled back. Brie wasn't drinking which was a good sign. She insisted that Bobbie had a dance with her, grabbing her hand and dragging her away toward the packed dance floor. The band was doing cover versions of hits from 1992.

"I bet that has never been done before at a re-union; How very original." Ben wasn't really in the party mood.

"Come on Ben, enjoy yourself. Live a little," Simon chastised.

The band had finished "Jump Around' by House of Pain which had whipped the crowd into frenzy. They followed up with 'Rhythm is a Dancer' by Snap. The place was bouncing.

"So back at my house when you were shot. You mentioned Brie was pregnant. Was that a ploy to throw Chavic or is it true?" Ben shouted above the music.

"True."

"Congratulations," said Ben mentally challenging Simon to take on a Cliff Richards classic. He remained silent. There were limits.

"I hate to ask under present circumstances, but can you be sure that the baby is yours?" Ben scrunched up his face in embarrassment as he leaned into Simon's ear so he could be heard above the music.

"Yes, the DNA test results were positive," Simon shouted.

"You had a DNA test?"

"Yes. I thought it was for the best."

"How very Jeremy Kyle," Ben teased. Simon smiled along with the joke, trying desperately to think of any song with Kyle in it.

The girls returned from the dance floor just as the band started into Night Fever.

"I thought this was a 1992 night," challenged Ben; "This song is 1977, that's not even close."

"Didn't Miles say that he had made a special request?" Brie asked.

"This should be good. I do hope that he falls flat on his pompous face."

Simon and Ben took the opportunity to join in with the song; their right arms doing the pointing motion that has become associated with the song all over the world. The people on the dance floor began to move backwards towards the walls to create a clear central area. A spotlight was illuminated by the technical team. A single beam highlighted the figure of Miles in silhouette. He was in the classical Travolta pose. He stayed motionless for far longer than was necessary until Maria joined him in a swirl of red satin. The spotlight followed them across the dance floor as they were off into their routine, two people moving as one in perfect rhythm. Maria's red dress was swaying seductively as she moved, the colour being complimented by the subtle pink suite Miles was wearing. He had spent ten minutes scrubbing it with paper towels in the men's room; carefully drying it under the hand drier until the red wine had been spread evenly. He wasn't happy with the result but it would have to do. He resembled a no frills pizza base with minimal tomato sauce topping. People in the crowd were beginning to notice; a ripple of laughter began to spread through the gathering.

"We know how to do it," Ben and Simon were still singing along with the music, arms pointing together like synchronised swimmers. Miles hated being laughed at; it was his worst nightmare. He stormed off muttering about 'Benny's bitch'. Maria continued to dance on her own. She was a bigger exhibitionist than her husband and they had after all, spent a fortune on lessons. She was in no mood to stop her well crafted routine; the perfect family unit.

The buffet had opened resulting in a stampede for the hot plates. Maria was left alone on the dance floor oblivious to the emptying room.

"The quiche is marvellous," Bobbie enthused, aware that Ben had become rather quiet and subdued. They were huddled in a small circle with china plates in their hands. Ben and Simon were passing time by reading name tags on other guests and trying to remember them; but if they were not in the English Faculty it was proving rather difficult.

"Hello boys." It was Margaret Wilson. Brie was lost for things to say to her, she thought it must be a psychological thing associated with the news that she was running a brothel. Brie could not imagine such a thing. She remembered Margaret as a hard working rather serious student; she had changed a lot, a complete metamorphosis. Brie was struggling to make conversation.

"You must come to our charity bash," she heard herself say as she handed Margaret a business card with 'Bright eyes Trust' emblazoned across the top.

"Wouldn't miss it for the world," whispered Margaret in a seductive tone.

Simon became detached from the group as he began talking to a couple of men who had retained their feather cuts from their student days; their gently greying bouffants contrasting sharply with Simon's neatly cropped head.

"I haven't played in public since leaving, but I practice regularly in the garage," said one of the silver foxes, "but, yes it would be great to have one last hurrah."

"That is a deal. I will see you there," said Simon as he handed them one of Brie's business cards.

Chapter 23

The clientele at Gantt Gallery's were high end. There was serious money in the room. Caterers were wandering around discretely in the background with silver service buffet food and fluted glasses of champagne. Joseph was in his element; pontificating about up and coming artists that he planned to nurture. He was tinkling his glass with a teaspoon to attract the attention of the gathered collectors. He didn't start until the chattering in the room had fallen silent.

"Ladies and gentlemen, Philippe le Grande has spent the last two years in Montmartre, Paris where he has been inspired by the white dome of 'Sacre Coeur.' His pieces show a deep understanding of light and colour that has not been seen since Manet was making a big impression at the height of his brilliance." Joseph may have been overdoing the hyperbole but there were pieces to be sold. His arm was outstretched to the right indicating a wall display full of the Frenchman's work.

"If, however, you are looking for an investment; nothing can compare with a posthumous artist. Some of you have already purchased the work of Mary Thomas last year. I can now reveal.."

He paused for effect. Scanning the room to ensure he had the full attention of the assembled art lovers. Ben was observing events from a quiet corner. He was shocked to hear Mary's name spoken in public. It seemed strange, kind of disrespectful.

"..that some new pieces have recently come to light."

Joseph continued to compliment Mary's work. He declared the afternoon officially open and soon little coloured stickers were being attached to the corner of Mary's work. Ben asked one of Joseph's little helpers what the stickers were.

"They indicate a sale, sir."

Ben was thinking that maybe he could attach more stickers on her work to make them appear more popular, but then he realised that nobody would buy them; assuming they were sold. He was not very good at thinking things through and so left it to the experts. He decided to attack the buffet with gusto; have one or two glasses of champagne. He began to mingle and overheard a number of conversations. They were all too high brow for him. 'Inner light' and 'chiaroscuro,' what did it all mean? Ben decided to have another drink and stay in the background. He must have fallen asleep in the chair, what else could explain him being shaken awake by Joseph.

"Mr. Thomas. Great news we have sold all the pieces." Ben scanned the wall to take in all the coloured stickers, including his own of the 'flowers' picture that he so wanted to keep.

"How much have we pulled in?" Joseph scrunched up his face in disgust at Ben's expression.

"The total generated, after my fee is deduced, is twenty two thousand pounds." Joseph was rubbing his hand again. Ben smiled broadly. With the sixty grand in the bank; that was a total of eighty two grand, not bad for a few paintings.

"That is fantastic. Can you make an electronic transfer to this account," Ben handed over a piece of paper that he had taken from his wallet. "And can you deliver my painting please? You have the expertise in the transportation field after all." Ben was pleased with his comment. Joseph smiled back as he shook Ben's hand vigorously. The day had gone extremely well; it had been a record take. He would be more than happy to repeat the event in a couple of month's time. Time for Philippe to replenish his stock, unfortunately there would be no more pieces from the hand of Mary Thomas, but today had been a great success.

"It will be my pleasure sir. No problem."

-.-.-.-.-.-.-.-.-.-.-.-.-.-.-.-.-.-.-.-

We have our first job, at a charity function. Mainly crowd control; stopping gate crashers, watching for under-age drinking, that sort of thing. There is nothing too heavy involved. Do you understand?" Page was instructing two young men who were barely listening. He had arranged lunch with them at 'Brigettes' to brief them about the job. He had selected them from a large number of applicants. They were tall, broad and on minimum wage. They were perfect for the job.

"Yes boss," they replied in unison. They were quick learners.

Page hadn't been entirely truthful with Bobbie at their chance meeting. When he said that he had started a security firm, it would have been more accurate and truthful to say that he was 'thinking' of starting a security firm. He had hit the ground running; now things were moving fast; he had recruited his staff; all he had to do was to think of a name for the company and get the uniforms made.

"What size chest are you both?" They both looked back at him vacantly. This was going to be more difficult than he thought. Page tried again.

"Have you ever worn a jacket?" There was still no response.

"Let's order some food and think about it, shall we?"

"Yes boss," they both understood food.

-.-

"Eighty two thousand pounds; that his fantastic honey," Bobbie said as she put the kettle on.

"It was brilliant; lots of really knowledgeable art critics, all of Mary's work was sold. It couldn't possibly have gone any better. I actually bought one myself." Ben was beaming.

"Do you want a coffee," she asked as the kettle boiled.

"I'd love one; I just need to make a phone call." He checked his watch; calls from the land line were expensive before seven. He selected a number from the contacts of his mobile and listened to it ring.

"Hello Joan, yes it's Ben Thomas; Tommy's father. No, everything is fine. I was just wondering if you could reconsider your ruling. Things may have seemed out of control the other week when you called, but things sort of got out of hand; ran away from us somewhat. If I didn't have visitors it would have turned out quite differently I can assure you."

Joan was listening on speaker phone. She enjoyed wandering around the house naked after a long day at the office.

"I thought I said to only use my home number in an emergency."

"This is a sort of emergency," Ben voice echoed around Joan's lounge.

"I need my son at home. He needs to be at home. Things are fine now, you said so yourself."

Joan was feeling a degree of sympathy for Ben. He had been so close to passing the assessment. If only things hadn't got out of hand.

"I will be calling on the Fletcher's soon for a follow up assessment. If anything rings any alarms bells things may change," she offered. Ben seized on any crumb of comfort.

"So there is a chance that Tommy could be home for Christmas."

"I'm not making any promises Mr Thomas."

"Thank you for even considering the possibility," said Ben as he pushed the red button on his mobile to disconnect. Joan replaced the phone back into the docking station before drawing the curtains with as much dignity as she could muster. The assembled teenagers, outside on their bikes, were most disappointed.

Ben's doorbell rang. "I'll get that, you finish your coffee," said Bobbie. She scurried down the hall to open it. The blurred shape of two intriguing figures showing through the opaque glass.

"Come in please. Ben, it is the police again," she shouted down the hall.

"What is it? Has something happened to Tommy?"

"There is no cause for concern sir. It is more of a follow up call; tying up loose ends," said McNally. She had three stripes on her lapel; she had finally been rewarded for all her diligent policing.

"This is officer Giles, he is new," she said as she gave her new partner a cursory nod. He looked so young; really young, fourth former young. Ben was mildly shocked at his pubescent appearance.

"What can I do for you PC McNally?" She tapped her shoulder to indicate that the conversation would not continue without recognition of her status.

"Sergeant McNally," Ben understood the charade that was being played out.

"There are a number of issues that need clarification. Firstly I wish to apologise for the distress and discomfort caused to your dog. A settlement of two thousand pound has been awarded. You will be receiving a letter of confirmation and a cheque in the post," McNally was talking through clenched teeth.

"Did you hear that Spangle; the nasty policemen are buying you a present." Bobbie fluffed up his fur around his neck as his tail wagged uncontrollably. He looked so much happier since his nappy and neck brace had been removed; almost back to normal.

"You said there were a number of issues?" Ben was beginning to enjoy himself.

"Yes I did."

"How many exactly?"

"Four. The second issue is Stefan Chavic. He is to be charged with eight counts of murder. We thought you should know."

"Thank you." It certainly was a weight off their minds knowing that Stefan was to be off the streets for a long time.

"Thirdly, His brother Roman had a memory stick. We have finally cracked the encryption code. Some very important local people have been incriminated in a huge money laundering scam. No names; I can't give you any details but we thought you should know."

Ben realised that he was being told because Roman had killed Mary and never been charged. It seemed so long ago now; but Ben was more relieved that he had learned the truth regarding Mary's red shoes and her secrets rather than learning of the deeds of her killer.

"And the fourth?" asked Ben.

McNally reached into her bag to produce a brown manila envelop. She handed it over.

"Here is four thousand and thirty two pounds. Your money has been released from the compound."

Ben counted it in front of both officers. He had taken one hell of a beating for this money during the poker game; he was making sure none of it had mysteriously disappeared while in police custody. He finished counting.

"All present and correct. Will that be all?"

"Yes we are finished," said McNally.

"Good day Sergeant," said Ben as he held the door open. She walked past him onto the drive. PC Giles followed obediently behind.

"Good day officer Giles," said Ben. There was no reply; Giles was too shy. Ben was disappointed; he had been looking forward to hearing his voice to check whether it had broken.

Chapter 24

The snow had started to fall lightly; covering the streets with a white dusting, leaving the roads resembling the icing on a Victoria sponge cake. Vale Park had been decorated with fairy lights; all colours of the rainbow. Brie had defended the decision to have the Charity event in the winter; reasoning that people were more likely to buy things as Christmas presents. There was nothing like a car boot sale to bring out the punters. She welcomed the snow; she thought it gave the occasion a magical touch. The main bandstand stage was being prepared for the first act and stall holders were busy displaying their wares ready for the opening. All around the fenced area in front of the bandstand food and drink stalls were steaming with hot produce ready for the ensuing crowds. Above the front of the stage, a large blue banner with yellow lettering stretched the full width; it read 'Bright Eyes.' Vale Park was ready to rock.

Page was at the gate talking to his two man team. They were both dressed in vivid purple outfits, trousers too short and jackets too tight; they resembled two schoolboys who had outgrown their uniforms. The green logo, prominent on both the breast pocket of their jackets and on the peaked caps, read 'Page Boys'. Page was also wearing the same uniform; his was immaculately tailored. However, his dapper appearance was spoiled by his trousers being tucked inside the snakeskin boots.

"I want you two to mingle with the crowds; watch out for pickpockets and petty theft. I don't think any real trouble will start until they sell some of that drink," Page nodded towards the beer tent.

"OK go, go. Spread out you two, just wander, I will do the entrance gate," he was fussing nervously. Some youngsters had arrived early; waiting patiently at the gate.

"Are you going to let us in, or what? My brother is in the band," a girl demanded. She was dressed for summer; thin leggings and a thinner transparent blouse. She was in for a long cold night unless she stayed under the sheltered areas. Page opened the gates. He looked more like a zookeeper than security in his garish purple outfit.

"Tickets please," he requested as the gathering crowd began a steady advance. Everyone was getting the back of their hand stamped in exchange for their ticket. Page worked diligently, as if you had been at the Post Office all of his life. He was concentrating so much that he didn't notice Bobbie's party approach. He took her hand automatically.

"'Page Boys'; nice name, very catchy," she teased.

"Oh hello Bobbie, do come in."

Ben and Tommy were waiting in line, sniggering at the uniform.

"I don't want that ink on my hand; it will never come off. I've had it before at nightclubs," said Ben. He had never liked Page, ever since Mary died. He had always behaved like an absolute idiot where Ben was concerned.

"Rules are rules. It makes it easier to check people later on," Page almost felt like he was back in the police force; just for a moment.

"What if we decide to wear gloves; it is snowing you know," Tommy had decided to join in the debate. They both realised, from his facial expression, that Page wasn't changing his mind; so reluctantly agreed to the ritual branding.

"Did you see the uniform? How corny. 'Page Boys'; How very original," Ben was still bitching.

"Look Dad, there are two more over there by the stage; and their uniforms don't even fit properly. Page could call himself 'Page One' and those two could be 'Page Two and Three.'" They were all laughing at Tommy's joke.

"Wouldn't you want a girl as 'Page Three', Bobbie joined in. She was proud of that one.

Margaret Wilson arrived dressed very seductively. The tight belt on her coat highlighted her curvaceous body which tapered to her waist before exploding into life under her top buttons. She had splendid breasts. Page couldn't take his eyes off of them; he tried out of

333

politeness, but he just couldn't do it. He was mesmerised.

"You are a very naughty boy," Margaret said in her husky tone.

"Sorry, I didn't mean any harm."

"No harm done. I like your boots; very Bohemian. I like a man who tries something different." She was flirting with him; twirling her blonde hair between her fingers; seeing if he would react.

"Aren't you going to stamp my hand?" She was holding it in front of her as if she was at the Versailles Palace; very regal. He played along; taking it in his hand as if to kiss it.

"My lady; if I may be so bold." Where had that come from? He had surprised himself.

He stamped her hand very gently; holding on for too long, before he realised the queue was backing up behind her.

"Enjoy your evening," he said as he looked past her shoulder toward the next person in the queue.

"Margaret; my name is Margaret," she stated.

"Peter, Peter Page."

"I am delighted. I'm sure we'll meet again before the night is out," she said before disappearing sedately into the crowd gathered round a jewellery stall.

Brie was on the stage tapping at the microphone; checking that it was live. She closed her eyes for a second, considering all the hard work that had gone into the organising of the event. Finally she was ready.

"Ladies and gentlemen; my husband and I would like to thank you all for attending this charity event on such a night. 'Bright Eyes' was formed this year in tribute to our daughter Holly. It has gone from strength to strength and now is listed as a Registered Charity. It is events like this that keep us going. People working tirelessly, making donations, to ensure that the work of the Hospice can continue to fight children's illness. Today we have an up and coming contemporary band; 'Spiral'. Later we have a guest appearance. The grounds are decked out with all manner of stalls; if you can't buy it here then it just doesn't exit. There is food and drink available over there, and the toilets are here." She pointed down to her left at a row of hired chemical toilets. "So thanks for coming and enjoy yourselves."

'Spiral' struck up into the opening chords of a well know 'Killers' song. They were young; lithe and energetic on stage. The crowd were enjoying their performance. Brie had joined Simon at the side of the stage.

"My husband and I? You have been listening to too many of the Queen's speeches," Simon teased.

"I get really nervous on stage, this is a big crowd."

"I know honey, I'm only teasing. I love you just the way you are." It was Brie that broke into the Billy Joel hook line. She thought it would annoy him if she beat him to it.

The younger guests were starting to dance in a frenzied manner; heads popping all over the places as they hopped hypnotically on both feet; 'Page Two' and 'Three' were concerned that things were getting out of control. The snow was beginning to compact beneath the dancer's pounding feet; could possibly turn to ice. They didn't want the dance floor to turn into an ice rink; a death trap. Some dancers were already beginning to slip around. They had to stop people doing The Pogo; why can't they just dance nicely?

"Stop the dancing; it could be dangerous. Stop the dancing." 'Page Two' confronted them from the left while his partner was doing the same on the other side of the ice rink. The drink fuelled dancers dragged the purple pair into the centre of the seething mass, where they had no choice; that had to join in to keep their footing. As the snow continued to fall, coloured fairy lights reflecting in every flake; they merged into the crowd, bouncing in time to the incessant bass guitar. Two boys from prep school crashing the party.

Page had been watching from the main gate. He wasn't impressed with their performance. He would have to deal with everything. He strode off to intervene, taking care not to slip in the snow. He was snaking his way through the crowds, slowly making his way to the front, when his arm was gently pulled. He turned to confront his assailant.

"We meet again Peter," smiled Margaret, holding a glass of wine in a plastic cup.

"So nice to see you again," he replied; desperately trying to remember her name as he noticed that her blond hair looked even more attractive with small snow flakes melting into the roots.

"You must come and see me some time," Margaret had turned up the heat, really giving him the full treatment.

"Perhaps we could have a drink one night?" Page was surpassing himself on the smooth meter.

"You must come to mine; let me entertain you." Margaret had a knowing smile on her face, as if she was toying with him. Brie and Simon had rejoined Ben and Bobbie under cover in the beer tent.

"Great speech Brie; very moving," Bobbie was tapping her forearm in a comforting manner.

"Good God. Is that Page over there talking to Margaret? She will eat him alive," Ben was astounded.

"I'd forgotten that I had invited her; but I must have, at the reunion last week," said Brie.

"Do you think we should tell him that she runs a brothel?" asked Ben, but he already knew the answer.

"Those things are best found out first hand, don't you think?" Simon responded while Alanis Morissette echoed around his head.

"Look at the crowd; they are having a great time. I love the way the security are joining in with the fun," said Bobbie. They all turned to watch the heaving mass of humanity bounce relentlessly to the music. It was hypnotic.

"Look, Tommy is joining in. That's not like him," added Brie in a surprised, excited manner. They all watched as Tommy bounced up and down in time with the music. His fist punched the air as he reached greater heights than the rest of the crowd. He was performing this manoeuvre repeatedly as he got nearer and nearer, leaving the ice rink far behind. He was shouting something which they couldn't decipher above the music. Once he was nearer it became clear.

"Dad, Dad," Tommy repeated as he came to a halt by their side.

"What is it son? What's wrong?

"Nothing is wrong. Kade, you know; the girl from the ship. She has e-mailed me. Her mother is fine. She lost a bit of money, but she is fine. Kade is coming back to work in February. She would like to see me; to thank me for all my help. I didn't do much really; just suggested some ideas, but she wants to thank me. She wants to see me." He was jumping up and down again.

"That is great son, really good news. Be careful on the snow."

"I must reply to her."

"It would be cheaper if you waited until you were home and used the computer. Your phone bill will be through the roof, son."

"You can't expect him to wait; not after all this time. Can't you see he is beside himself with excitement?" Bobbie was being motherly. Tommy had already begun typing as he walked away for some privacy.

"Loves young dream, how lovely," said Brie.

"Sometimes that is all it takes; a little bit of kindness," said Bobbie.

"I knew he felt a connection; you know, really felt it. He was hurting; life can be cruel sometimes, but she got in touch" Ben was being fatherly.

"I know. Sometimes you love someone but they do not feel the same way," said Brie.

"Sometimes people are lucky enough to find love more than once," said Ben. They all went quiet as they realised that he was talking about Bobbie. She snuggled into his side to talk about the florists, but he shushed her.

"I mean it."

Ben was watched the snow fall onto the dancing crowd. So much had happened lately. Sometimes you have to let go and trust that, although the past will never be forgotten, you must allow people to move on. He watched his son typing into his phone; the picture of happiness. He could see his mother in him. The kind, loving, giving person that he loved; stilled missed. He was a calmer person these days. He knew the truth about the mysteries that had been driving him crazy. He was happy with Bobbie; falling for her, but it was appropriate to remember the past; remember and smile.

339

"What are you smiling about?"

"Nothing Simon; nothing at all."

"Your night hasn't finished yet; not by a long way."

"What are you talking about?" Simon nodded to the stage where the young group, 'Spiral', were packing up their equipment, to be replaced by another group. They were older; in their forties. The drummer from 'Spiral' remained at the skins while the new band plugged in their equipment. Ben recognised them as 'Walrus', minus the drummer. Simon was smiling; he was pleased with his little surprise. The band started playing the introduction to a Bon Jovi song. The sound of drums and bass guitar filled the night air. The crowd were clapping along, arms raised. Everyone was waiting for the vocals to start. Ben was pushed forward through the crowd. He made a token effort to resist, but knew there was no escape; he had to do it, it was his party piece at University. He was now on stage reaching out for the mike. He stood waiting for the introduction to end its eight bar repetition before starting on cue. His beautiful tenor voice, which had moved so many people at Holly's funeral, now informed the crowd that Tommy used to work on the docks, that the union had been on strike and that he was down on his luck. He told them that it was tough; so tough. At the end of the song Ben took the applause and ignored the calls for more. Walrus could only ever play one song, even back in the day. Brie was back on the stage taking the mike.

"Thank you; thank you all for braving this cold night. I would like to thank you from the bottom of my heart. All gate money; proceeds from the stalls and refreshments will go to the charity. I really do mean all of the money; we are non profit making. If you could find it in your hearts to dig deep one more time, there are buckets at the exits where you can make cash donations. There is no obligation; anything you can spare. Thank you again; and before I go I would like to thank all the hard work done by the stall holders and especially our entertainment; 'Spiral' and 'Walrus.'" She raised her hand to the right but the stage was already empty. She accepted their applause and left.

Simon was busy collecting the buckets as the cleaners began their attempt to clear the park of rubbish. Quite a bit in here, he thought as he shook the bucket to assess the total accumulation of coins. The odd five pound note was trapped amongst the silver.

"Seems like a fair old bundle" said Ben, who had appeared by his side.

"It is surprising how much will be in there. It all adds up. Ever little helps," Simon seemed pleased with the total. Ben took the rucksack off his shoulder and handed it to Brie.

"There is £43,016 in there. It is yours; for the charity."

"We can't possible take.."

"Take it," Ben insisted.

"Where did it all come from?" Simon was incredulous.

"I told you there was sixty grand from the safety deposit box, then there was twenty two grand from the gallery sale. That makes a total of eighty six thousand and thirty two pounds."

"That is eighty two grand if you count correctly," said Simon.

"I have thrown in my poker money the police released from their evidence suite. I am giving up the game; bad for my health. I'm keeping half of the money to put Tommy through University. You take the other half for the Charity."

"Are you sure Ben? What about you?" Simon was reluctant to accept such a large donation.

"I have the money from Mary's life insurance and my pension. I will be fine, and I am working again after all."

"You don't get paid at the Bobbie's florist, you told me. It is more of a hobby, remember?"

"Take it," pushing the bag into Simon's hands.

"I will run out of time before I run out of money." There were at least three songs with the word money in the title running through Simon's head. It was impossible to choose between 'Abba', 'Dire Straits' or 'The Beatles?' He couldn't decide which one to sing, so did nothing.

"You are incredibly generous. Brie will be delighted," he said as he finally took the rucksack from his good friend.

"It's what Mary would have wanted."

Chapter 25

Ben, Bobbie and Tommy were making the short walk up the hill to the church. It really was a foreboding building; a dark dormant monster on top of the hill, its golden clock fingers adding a touch of glamour to the weathered stone.

"I still don't think this is a very good idea, Tommy," Ben was apprehensive about any contact with Freddie.

"You will change your mind once you have seen him. He was really funny on the ship, Dad." Tommy was full of youthful enthusiasm, a feeling that had been heightened by recent electronic messages.

"He is delivering a church sermon; he is not supposed to be funny, son."

"Everyone deserves a second chance Ben. You got one," Bobbie hit the nail on the head. Ben continued walking, remembering how low he had fallen when Mary died. He had been in a bad place, had nearly stayed there. Now he had Bobbie; saw Tommy on a regular basis. He nodded acceptance of her point and continued walking.

Simon and Brie were waiting at the main door. They were keen to sit as a group, to enjoy the service together. They walked in slowly, careful not to trample on the people in front, slowly making their way down the aisle. Word had spread that the service at St Hilary's had improved incredibly; they were becoming very popular. They found an empty pew near the front behind Page and Margaret; they seemed happy, although the bite marks on Page's neck seemed rather inappropriate for somebody of his age.

The organ started a slow groan as an elderly woman began pressing peddles. As it warmed up she transposed into a well know popular hymn. Everyone stood as Martin strode towards the pulpit. There was not an empty seat to be seen anywhere inside the church. The place was bulging at the seams.

"Welcome everybody. Please sit."

The arches that swept so majestically into the roof space resonated with the sound of shoes scraping on the floor and clothes being rearranged as the congregation duly sat down. One row of pews forgot to remove the hymn book off the seats. They sat on them uncomfortably, causing them to stand again, like a Mexican wave, to remove it. After an enthusiastic rendition of 'Now thank we all our God' the congregation sat down in an expectant mood. Some had already seen Freddie and were back for more. Most had arrived for the first time, attracted by recommendations. Wallasey is a small community; nothing remained a secret for long.

Freddie appeared at the pulpit; his red and brown afro a striking contrast to the white robe that draped to his ankles. His piercing green eyes combined to give him a most bizarre presence. He would not have looked out of place on 'The Simpsons.'

"Thank you. Thank you." Freddie's hands were raised in thanks. His mind was racing. He was thinking 'thanks to God' and 'thanks for the great welcome you are a great crowd.' He checked out the audience; looking for any empty seats. There were none to be seen. He continued his prepared set.

"Today I am here to talk to you about the evils of music. I don't include all music." His hands were mesmerising, raised high above his head then suddenly out in front of him clasped together as if he was asking for more in a remake of Oliver. "Some classical pieces can soothe the soul, and jazz, well I just love it. No! The problem is modern music. It is sinful misguided rubbish; pounding out an incessant sexual beat. I ask you; is it right that Caribbean boys, fuelled on drugs, encourage young girls to shake their booty? I ask you brothers and sisters; should gang bangers glorify guns and underage sex?"

He thought he had overdone it with the 'brothers and sister' quote. Way too Negro Baptist; the older dudes in the crowd may be having flashbacks to The Kenny Everett Show.

"It is easy to criticise these people but they are not really to blame; they have been influenced; brainwashed by the older generation of songwriter. The music industry of today may be a cess pit of sexual

346

inappropriateness, but it all began years ago, back in a world that seemed much more innocent and gullible."

Freddie paused for dramatic effect; looking from pew to pew for any sign of agreement with his argument. The church was silent; every person hanging on his every word. Even the bells had fallen silent; Freddie had made sure of that.

"There have always been paedophiles and sexual predators in the music industry. There are the obvious ones. Gary Glitter, Jonathan King, but it is the songs themselves that can cause just as much harm as any individual. Some lyrics back then, in the early days, were near the knuckle regarding young girls. 'Gary Puckett and the Union Gap' had a less than healthy attitude with these lines. He produced a card and began reading as if at a poetry recital. His voice was gently soothing.

'Young girl get out of my mind,

my love for you is way out of line,

better run girl, you're much too young girl.

Get out of here before I have the time

to change my mind,

because I afraid we'll go too far....

Freddie was speaking the words quietly for effect. He was using a hand motion with two fingers pointing like a gun barrel, indicating some kind of fingering abuse. At the end of the reading he looked up to challenge the audience; his voice changed, became more irate and demonstrative.

"Are these the lyrics of a balanced human mind? Are they?" He flipped onto the second card in his hand, as if he was shuffling a pack of cards. "Then there was 'Mungo Jerry', that happy, smiling band of brothers." He was back into his gentle poetry recital role. "They sang..

'If her daddy's rich take her out for a meal

If her daddy's poor just do what you feel.'"

Simon and Ben were beginning to enjoy the service. They were itching to sing along; the temptation was almost too much to bear. Freddie was doing the finger gun pose again, just in case anybody hadn't understood the theme of his sermon.

"These lyrics are clearly encouraging abduction and rape; just do what you feel."

Another card was flipped to the top of the pile in Freddie's hands. He tapped it with the back of his free hand for emphasis.

"I give you Neil Sedaka. His all American clean cut image hides a few things." Freddie was reading from the card again.

'Tonight's the night I've waited for,

because you're not a baby anymore.

You've turned into the prettiest

girl I've ever seen.

Happy birthday sweet sixteen.'

"OK, I accept that he understands that underage sex is illegal and is willing to wait…" Freddie paused for effect. "Wait until the day of her sixteenth birthday. Does that not imply that he may have had designs on her before she was sixteen? What a guy." Freddie was now on a roll, sensing that some people had begun to titter in the back of the church. Simon was desperate to sing but realised that although Freddie was speaking, reading in poetic prose, the words were already a song; so it didn't fit into there little game. Brie was watching him; willing him to behave himself.

"The Bee Gees, god bless them, even they got involved in the whole sorry mess surrounding this issue.

'Run to me whenever you're lonely,

run to me when you need a shoulder.

Now and then you need someone older…'

Freddie was doing the finger gun pose again, moving it from right to left in a probing motion; a knowing smirk on his face. People at the back were beginning to snigger, quietly laughing. It was becoming contagious, spreading slowly forward. He knew when he had a crowd in the palm of his hand.

"Sir Cliff Richard," he shouted, trying to be heard above the merriment, "He wasn't without blame," Freddie didn't need a card for this one; he knew the words off by heart. Everybody did.

""And some day

when the years have flown

Darling we may have some

young ones of our own'

Now he may not have meant to actually 'have' them, as in abuse them, but even young ones having young ones is surely perpetuating the cycle of teenage pregnancy that is part of the problem. We live in a world were generation after generation learn appalling parenting skills from an ignorant gene pool." He was aware that the majority in the crowd were Cliff Richards sympathisers, had actually started singing the song, so moved quickly on.

"It is not only men that are on the prowl for young meat. Mrs Robinson was perhaps the first 'Cougar' to appear on screen in the film 'The Graduate' when she seduced a young Dustin Hoffman. This trend has always been in song." He reverted back to his cards to read poetically.

'It was a hot afternoon the last day of June

And the sun was a swelter.

The sweat trickled down the front of her gown

And I thought it would melt her.

She was 31 and I was 17

I knew nothing about love

She knew everything'

OK, I accept that in this case Bobby Goldsboro is in fact boasting of being sexually abused by an older woman, but at the end of the day it is still abuse. So when you remember how far we have fallen; when you accept where we are today in the music industry; with all these present day music videos with their incessant sexually explicit imagery, just remember where it all started. I rest my case."

Freddie had enjoyed the gig, the congregation were on their feet applauding. It was almost like doing stand up. It was stand up, the similarities were amazing. He had to finish with a joke.

"An acquaintance of mind, he is only young; He has an eighteen year old Pilipino girlfriend. What's all that about? Most guys wait until they are sixty, and then buy one."

For the first time in its long and glorious past St Hilary's church rung out with the sound of laughter. Rolls of mirth cascaded down from the back pews and spread forward, like the applause in St Paul Cathedral during Lady Diana's funeral, until the whole congregation were on their feet cheering.

"Thank you Wallasey," shouted Freddie as he assumed the classical rock star pose; one clenched fist raised above his bowed head. He imagined that he was on a nationwide arena tour. T-shirts and DVD's available at the main door. Tommy didn't laugh along with everybody else. He knew that Kade was from Indonesia not The Philippines, but he still didn't like Freddie using his life for material. It was too personal.

351

Freddie and Martin stood at the main door as the congregation left the church. The masses were snaking slowly out of the church in single file, patiently waiting to have a word. Freddie thanked everyone for their attendance with a hearty handshake and a warm smile.

"What will be the subject of next week's sermon?" asked a young smartly dressed man, arm in arm with his partner.

"I haven't decided yet. You will have to check my blog," Freddie loved the attention. Martin was beginning to wonder when he would have the opportunity to return to the pulpit himself. He realised that Freddie was very popular, especially with the younger members of the parish; the collection plate clearly indicated that. It was just, maybe, getting a bit out of control. The sooner Freddie's court case came up the better it would be for all concerned.

Chapter 26

Mary had been watching Ben for two minutes. She thought that he was going to be fine. He had finally moved out of the dark. She had been worried about him for so long. It was nearly time to go. Her time was over. She had used her reprieve wisely; she had tried to solve all of life's little problems. There just wasn't enough time; she really did have to go. She was being called. She now realised that some people can sink to the depths of despair over the loss of a loved one. They can risk losing everything in their grief. But sometimes they can rebuild their lives, look to a brighter future without forgetting the past.

Ben was hammering a nail into the wall above the fireplace. He was determined to get it right; he never really had been proficient at household chores, but this time he wanted to excel with his handiwork.

"You should really get a proper picture hanger, you know, with two prongs to spread the load," Bobbie was fussing as she checked her order book on the table.

"A nail will be fine," replied Ben as he struggled to balance the string on the back of the picture. He wanted it to hang straight from the nail in the centre. He stepped back to assess his handiwork. It was perfectly straight. He was pleased with the result; Mary's last piece, the flowers that she had produced as a sign of her acceptance hung vibrantly above the fire. Bobbie was cool with the picture being on display. It was important to Ben; she understood perfectly. Mary also thought that it looked rather splendid.

A key turned in the front door. It opened to reveal Tommy glued to his I phone.

"I'm home."

"How was school?" asked Ben as he continued to admire Mary's work hanging on the wall.

"Boring as usual." Tommy was still consumed with his screen.

"I'm doing lasagne for tea; will you be joining us?" asked Bobbie.

"I wouldn't miss it for the world," replied Tommy as he hung his school blazer under the stairs and placed his Physics books on the phone table next to the paintbrush. He slumped into the comforting folds of the settee to continue texting Kade. He was happy to be home, but often wondered how the electricity on the garden gnomes at the Fletcher's had short circuited just at the exact moment the social worker was making a surprise visit.

What were the chances that she would be electrocuted as she rang the door bell; only a mild one, but enough to straighten her hair. The council had declared the whole house 'a death trap', 'an accident waiting to happen.' After that, Dad's recovery was looked on in a much more sympathetic light.

Mary had been very busy lately. She smiled as she watched her son. She hoped that he would be happy; hoped that he would have a good life. Young people have to experience love and find their own way in the world, make their own mistakes. She wasn't for one second suggesting that Kade was a mistake, it was just normal for the young to find their own way. Her only regret was that she would not be there to guide and comfort him along the way for ever.

She looked to her left to watch Ron approach the counter at the local store in Huddersfield. She smiled as he got his wallet out. Sometimes people find a way of adapting to their circumstances. They find a way to hold on to what they have, to what is important in their lives.

"That will be five pounds twenty two," announced the girl behind the counter.

"Oh, I nearly forgot, I'll have the Daily Express as well," Ron smiled, happy to be out in the community, out in his community. Ron paid the assistant and unscrewed his crutch to remove a hand drawn map of the local area. The route back to Sally's was clearly marked. He stepped out into the street, raised his face to the pale sunshine, and began the short walk home in a confident gait. He had always liked Huddersfield, he grew up here. Every morning, as he walked the streets, he remembered little things from his childhood. It was strange that he could not remember important things but things from his childhood, from years ago, were popping into his mind. I used to climb that tree with Billy Busby he thought as he turned into Sally's road. I wonder if Mrs Walters still lives in the corner house. The grandchildren are coming round this afternoon. He enjoyed being called Gramps.

Yes, Mary was pleased with here handiwork. She understood that sometimes people lose their way at times. Love can become damaged and strained; but as long as it is strong it can be re-ignited from the embers and grow even stronger. She turned to her right to observe her oldest friends.

"The website looks amazing honey, really tasteful," said Simon as he placed a cup of tea on the table.

"'Bright Eyes' has come a long way since last year. We are now a Registered Charity, but we couldn't have done it without Ben's generous donation. It really kick started the whole thing. It was so generous of him," Brie was almost crying again. Holly's beaming smile watched them both from the charcoal sketch mounted on the wall above the conservatory desk.

"He said he felt it was the right thing to do; felt Mary's presence willing him on to be a better person.

Like the film 'Ghost.'" Simon smiled as he took a deep breath ready to sing.

"I've hungered for you touch."

"A long lonely time," Brie was joining in, smiling. They both prepared for the high note, Simon holding her from behind, his hands caressing her visible bump as her head leaned back into his shoulder.

"I need your love," they sang together, a bit flat and pitchy. Where was Ben when you needed a high note? They seemed really happy. Mary hadn't seen them this close since their student days. How she wished she could turn back the clock and have those times again, but she couldn't. They were calling her again.

Then again, Mary realised that some people spend all their lives searching for love. They may try too hard sometimes and lose whatever relationships appear along life's journey, but eventually they find somebody they deserve, somebody that understands them. She was happy for Peter Page.

The leather straps on Page's wrists were tighter than he had expected. The more he struggled with them the more they chaffed into his skin causing red wields. If he didn't stop trying to fight he was sure they would draw blood. His shoulders were beginning to ache as he was held by the straps in a vulnerable crucifixion pose, hands stretched out in front of his head. He had to balance on his knees, cramping his stomach muscles, to prevent himself from falling forward. His feet were being protected by his snakeskin boots; they were the only thing she had allowed him to keep. He felt exposed in his nakedness; waiting for whatever punishment Margaret deemed fitting. If it all got too much, if he wanted to stop at any times; all he had to do was say the 'safe' word and she would stop. They were the rules. Page was beginning to have serious doubts as to whether he would be able to say the 'safe' word. It was nothing to do with his memory; he knew the word; he had been whispering it under is breath for the last ten minutes. The problem was the orange wedged firmly in his mouth which made any sound unintelligible. Any utterances he made were being interpreted as enthusiastic encouragement.

"You like that don't you? Margaret whispered into his ear. She was dressed in a leather bodice with her breasts exposed and uplifted. Her outfit was completed by a pair of red stilettos, shining in the dull light. He could feel her nipples gently rubbing along the length of his back as she straddled him from behind. He muffled that he did in fact like it. He liked it a lot.

Margaret pulled a small chain. Page followed the chain with his eyes until his neck was straining backwards. It was attached to two small claws that were suspended from the ceiling. They slowly descended from their position; the dim red lighting reflected off their polished chrome. She fitted the claw clamps to Page's buttocks, making him flinch as they bit into his skin. Another chain caused the claws to rise. She could have been at home adjusting the window blinds; such was her mastery of the controls. Page's buttock were slowly spread until the skin was stretched exposing his inner self.

"You like that don't you?" she was straddling him again thrusting her pelvis up against his buttocks, ensuring her nipples caressed his back. Page snorted a reply through his nose. It could have meant anything. She wandered over to a bucket in the corner, confident with her body; knowing Page was watching every move she made. The bucket contained a number of strap-ons submerged in disinfectant. The last time Page had seen anything like it was in music class back in Primary school, when the recorders were stored in a similar fashion. Margaret selected a large black number and began fastening the waist buckle. She wandered back; disinfectant still dripping from the end of her rubber extension. Page was convinced that she was going to titillate him; perform some role play. He became considerably more nervous as she remounted him; her nipples seemed harder on his back as she rubbed against him again. He could feel the rubber end of the strap-on playing around his cheeks; could feel its large bulbous tip playing around the edges of his entrance. She couldn't possibly push now?

"You like this don't you; you naughty boy?" their heads were close together as she whispered into his ear and bit his neck. He didn't answer; his rapidly growing penis did all the talking for him. She grabbed between his legs and gently stroked it before attaching a metal ring that enabled her to tug it gently with a leather strap. The strap-on slipped in slowly at first, Page writhing around like a bucking bronco. Margaret pulled on the

359

leather strap attached to the ring with one hand, as if they were the reins on a horse. She leaned back and balanced herself with her other hand raised in the air; like a bronco rider at the Calgary Stampede. She pushed harder and harder, her lithe body thrusting the full length of her strap-on deep into Page's body. She rode him hard, adjusting to the movement of his body which continued to thrash around in captive pleasure. She was good; she could have broken any time trial on one of those mechanical bulls that are used at fun fairs. Her strong thighs gripped hard as she continued to thrust in time with the rhythm of her arched back. She only stopped when she noticed a flashing light on the wall.

"I have another visitor. I will be back soon. You have been a good boy. A very good boy," Margaret whispered as she gave one last thrust into his quivering body before withdrawing her weapon and replacing it in the disinfectant bucket. She left through the door, but Page knew she would return.

Yes there was always somebody waiting just around the corner to fill a void in somebody else's world. Mary took one last look over her shoulder as she was gently ushered away. Oh please; just one last look. She was thinking that although people can change and repent their sins, a leopard never really changes his spots.

Freddie was concentrating as he placed the prayer books neatly in the pews. He had to get the exact number in each row. Today's service was important, a Diocese Dignitary was coming; the church had to be perfect. When he had finished he stood at the pulpit thinking about his next gig. The church would be full; they would be hanging on his every word. Congregations had never been larger, Martin was really pleased. Freddie could still hear the Reverend's words resonating around the high arches.

"I did have my doubts at first Freddie, but you really changed my mind; your sermons are very popular, they really bring the crowds in."

Freddie was getting carried away. He imagined himself being ordained, becoming an inspirational spiritual leader; maybe moving to America and becoming a preacher on the Southern Circuit, a modern day Billy Graham. He could make a fortune. Even better, he could take the Edinburgh Fringe by storm. 'The Preaching Prankster', he could just see it. He could re-ignite his career on the comedy circuit; get back in the groove, make it to the top. Maybe he needed a novelty religious name; but John Bishop has already done that. What about Father Fred? Too late again.

He must enjoy this while it lasts. He would be back in prison soon enough. He must pay his debt to society; he knew that. He looked forward to wiping his slate clean. He now realised that he would be alright as long as people laughed at his act; loved him. He hadn't felt the red mist for a while, but he looked forward to meeting Winston James again in prison. He remembered his dyed blond hair, his fingers on Freddie's head, soft and rhythmical. There would be no trouble getting a shank in prison. It was the only thought that keep Freddie going; the only thought that kept him sane.

Coming soon from the pen of Ken Jones;-

Gap Year - A 60 year old Vet decides to take a belated Gap Year, but events take a turn for the worse just when he is getting down and dirty with the kids in Thailand. Just who are these people?

Ken Jones lives in Wallasey with his beautiful wife Joan. When he occasionally breaks his unhealthy relationship with his laptop, he can be found playing chess or watching sport. He has three beautiful children; and two amazing step sons.

Lightning Source UK Ltd.
Milton Keynes UK
UKOW040915260912

199638UK00001B/14/P